WELCOME TO
YOUR UNIVERSE!

...Where religions hold a prominent place in providing societal cohesion, especially when the indigenous populations are making the transition from nomadic hunter-gatherers to more static lifestyles; and where the old faiths can also instigate major societal fragmentation....

On Antheer-D, religious fermentation suddenly comes to a boil, when diehard male-chauvanist zealots attempt to overthrow the growing power of the transmogrified one-time humanoid female, Ayra Organa, who is obviously hell-bent on clandestinely supplanting every male god in every planet's pantheon. Will the schism fracture human society? Or will calmer, more reasoned minds prevail? A thrilling science-fiction adventure, the first of the Gods & Frauds Series.

Borgo Press Books by WILLIAM MALTESE

SCHISM ON ANTHEER-D

GODS & FRAUDS, BOOK 1: A SCIENCE FICTION NOVEL

WILLIAM MALTESE

THE BORGO PRESS

MMXI

SCHISM ON ANTHEER-D

DEDICATION

For all of those who still believe...
despite everything.

CONTENTS

FROM THE FORBIDDEN TEXT OF THE HERETIC GIATH

"No god or goddess has created one creature, but creatures have created gods and goddesses. Lo, they have created them by the score. For creatures are somehow unable to admit to the reality that they are simply freaks of the elements and not some intricate parts of a divine plan."

WHAT, THEN, OF AYRA ORGANA?

PROLOGUE

1.

"The Book of Kyrie," Chapter Z, FALSE PROPHETS OF GORMET, filed in data banks, Brothers of Timile Monastery, Sector 900SZZ, recall 5:

"You are a fool, Kyrie," Dyrynum did whisper in Kyrie's ear, "for I have offered you food and drink. I have offered you riches beyond compare. And by refusing them, you have gained nothing."

"I am not deceived!" Kyrie told The Abomination.

Kyrie canted the Five Prayers of the Dinul, so that Dyrynum would retreat and give him respite.

But Dyrynum resisted with a power that Kyrie had not foreseen; and The Beast did call Kyrie a fool.

"You are but a pretender to the throne you seek," Dyrynum said. "I have seen many of your ilk, and I have learned to recognize them as I recognize you now. What a fool that you did not take the boluta, the malavu, the gelnoidu! For what will you have in the end but the jeers of those miserable swine who thought you were more than you were and will not appreciate having seen you as higher born than you really are?"

And the wilderness was suddenly dissolved, and Kyrie did find himself seated on a rock bench on the edge of a small circular amphitheater in which was spread-eagled on purple sand the likes of his naked sister.

And Kyrie did seek to turn his head from the girl's nakedness, but The Beast, positioned beside him, did somehow find a way that Kyrie should look.

"Lo, your sister," Dyrynum said. "See how enticingly her legs are splayed in obscene invitation?"

"It is but an illusion!" Kyrie insisted, and he did cant the Bandoc verses to make the apparition dissolve.

"Lo, the mates for your kin," The Beast proclaimed, pointing; as if by tele-transifguration, the naked Morg, the naked Cordox, the naked Klanz appeared. "They and more yet shall have her to a screaming death unless you kneel before me and do homage as I have bid."

And Kyrie, seeing that the Bandoc did not dispel the illusion, was fooled into thinking The Beast conjured not mists but real flesh and blood.

And Kyrie did kneel and touch his lips to the hem of The Beast's garment, tasting the foul flavors of excrement that was the robe.

2.

Excerpt from Leiobc 4, "Peter of Tsenic," translated from THE BOOK OF MYLOT PRETENDERS, Archives 10624 Blue/Red/Green, Star Stack 6, Quad 2B6, ref BB3:

On the eighth day of the debauchery, Peter, having passed through the seven levels of the Whore House of The Beast, was confronted by his host on the rooftop.

"See," Daniel did say, a sweep of his arm showing Peter many magnificent skyscrapers which had not been there minutes before. "You thought you had seen all pleasures, experienced all enjoyment, but you were deceived. For you see before you edifices of pleasure which have levels of ecstasy of which you could never have dreamed possible. Room after room offer experiences more intensive and gratifying than its predecessor!"

"Is it possible?" Peter asked, accepting the wine which Daniel did offer, sampling a mixture of flavors which was eight times better than what he had sampled on the floor below.

"Do you doubt it?" Daniel asked. "Has not all I have told you before been just as I have said it would be? The question is only whether or not you want dominion over this world, or over a few niggardly planets that can offer you nothing but subjects who give little more than simple prayers and an occasional burnt offering of diseased helaniae."

"I can have all of this?" Peter asked.

Daniel smiled, for he knew the past eight days had not been wasted.

"All you need do is kneel and kiss the hem of my robe," Daniel said, his flippant tone insinuating the price a paltry one for the rewards offered in return.

When Peter hesitated, Daniel pointed to a window of the nearest building.

"See what wonders are waiting!" Daniel proclaimed.

A giglot had appeared in the window, naked: chest muscled, arms folded, the traditional whip wrapped once around his bull-like neck. His korlean eyes locked on Peter's pale pupils, holding them, telepha-transmitting to Peter the legions of ecstasies to be known on just that one level of that one house, among the endless city of houses now stretching into the horizon.

The giglot smiled; his tongue was an obscene snake that wetted his lips in offering of pleasures beyond imagination.

Peter turned to Daniel, who was The Beast, and he dropped to his knees and did kiss the hem of Daniel's robe.

And the tastes and smells of The Beast's garment were a powerful aphrodisiac, and sent Peter's senses into even further swirls of madness.

Daniel raised his new disciple to his feet, much pleased.

"Go forth and enjoy!" Daniel told him.

And Peter passed over to the giglot on the banded rhine which was materialized for him to navigate the open space between the two buildings.

And the giglot did bow low before Peter, calling him master. For lo, The Beast had, indeed, made Peter master of this place.

And the giglot did offer up his whip and his body to Peter, as he had promised in those previous moments of telepha-transmission.

And, the day was nine.

3.

A possible fragment of THE HIERARCHY OF TYNBOTHIAN SANCTO-STRUCTURE (?), ARCHEO-SPEC on Jyrolisck IV, 240.76 D.D. Metallic substance: Gerallium alloy. Method of inscription: laterillic beam. Dialect: Tynbo, pre-Junanic:

And, The Beast was a woman....

CHAPTER ONE

Folk myth from the planet Delcan Prime, sub-sort IX, Sector Coordinates 6-2.4.46; recorded on telecom-tape by Dr. Philip Coupse, Ph.D. Ms.F., 1062.22 D.D.; see ref.64-9:

"But I am a biologist," he said. "What need have I of these pleasures of the body of which you speak? What need have I of these fortunes you heap like mountains at my feet?"

And, there followed that he tricked Him into giving him what he had wanted all along: that thing for which he had risked trodding such dangerous roads to begin with.

SHE WAS SEARCHING for him, flinging her mental sensors over spaces unfathomable to those simple folk housed on this planet of Antheer-D. These beings didn't even know she existed—not in a body evolved long ago from real flesh and blood like their own. In fact, they worshipped her as Dielum: The Child Eater; as countless people—on countless planets, in countless solar systems, in countless galaxies—called her by other names, saw her in other forms: Txn, The Dead One; Boxer, The Draxl; Porun, The Taker of Men Child; Hexca, The Mother; on and on and on.

But to Galun Rellix, she was Ayra Organa, The Beast.

And she was out to kill him!

Her sensors, invisible telebeams, spiraled across the vast reaches of space, scanning, searching, and probing.

One, a beta-2—a scan so weak that it was but a mutant throb

of the beta-1, born of some inexplicable split during travel through Sensaspace—veered from its projection. Its deviation left a minute footprint in Sensaspace, a pathway which would later be picked up and analyzed in greater detail by the computer linked to Ayra Organa's brain.

Galun was sleeping—deep sleep, dream sleep. A mistake, of course. He had done his best to guard against it. He had programmed the MEDICANT-IV to interrupt his regular sleep sequence, to re-schedule him through the other levels of less dangerous rest.

But the MEDICANT-IV often overrode such programming if its delay components somehow computed that an override was necessary for the well-being of a patient's health.

MEDICANT-IV was a medical-adaptor unit, monitoring the life impulses of its patients and playing doctor and nurse, diagnosing, and prescribing treatment.

MEDICANT-IV had diagnosed fatigue—it had prescribed rest. Galun had resisted. MEDICANT-IV had computed to take the matter into override.

Galun should have known better. If he hadn't been so fatigued, he would have taken more precautionary measures. But, then, he hadn't thought he was going to doze off. Certainly, he hadn't expected to progress so swiftly through all intermediate phases of Dream Sleep without first waking.

Mental sensor beta-2 veered again, leaving yet another check mark in Sensaspace, the short end of the slash denoting its new direction.

Galun's eyes jerked beneath his closed lids. The recording needles on MEDICANT-IV weaved and traced jagged lines, even while overriding all attempts to submit program information insisting that the patient should be revived immediately.

"Galun Rellix?" a voice asked.

And, the dream Galun had been having—something about wading in the taxl-green mossil pond on his home planet Delcan Prime—faded into opaque grays and whites.

"Galun Rellix?" the voice repeated warily.

The fog of his dream swirled, forming new substances that materialized to a new picture.

He was still on Delcan Prime, but he was no longer preparing to wade in the taxl-green mossil pond with Wendy. He was younger, now, sitting beside the large tondrume tree that grew off to one side of the house.

"Galun Rellix, where are you?"

His mother was standing on the landing, searching the area for him. She couldn't see him, because he was hidden by the tree. She looked worried. After all, she had been against the move to the country. So many strange sights and sounds! So many strange animals, like the huge woolunk bear which had turned up in the shadel room the day before.

"Perfectly harmless, Bessa," her husband, Galun's father, had told her. He had been amused by his wife's terrible fright upon seeing the large, ungainly animal. "They actually make wonderful pets."

But Bessa Rellix couldn't imagine the woolunk as a pet. As a girl, the only pets she had known had been flinikies, small winged creatures that one could keep in small cages off the dining room. They sang sweet songs to help with meal-digestion, which made them welcome pets—certainly not like woolunks, which tipped over banacles and looked bigger than the living cubicle the family had owned in the safety of the city.

"Galun Rellix?"

Yes, his mother was worried. She was always worried that he was going to be picked up by some wild thing and carted away.

"Don't be silly, darling," her husband was forever telling her, whenever she got up enough nerve to voice such fears. "There are no dangerous wild things remaining in the area. This vector is being surveyed for development. Anything even resembling a wild thing has been shipped off to Deep Forest regions down south. Before long, even the woolunks will have taken flight from the sights and sounds of invading development."

Bessa had not been convinced. She was city-born, city-bred. She had agreed to live in the obscure outer region only because she loved her husband, and his progression upward in his field of Eco-Living made time spent in the field a necessity.

"Galun Rellix, where are you?"

"Here," he answered. He was occupied with the xyl his father had recently bought him. It was a hedrographical sutu that, when squeezed, could be manipulated into countless shapes and sizes.

"Where exactly is *here?*" his mother asked.

"Here," Galun repeated, suddenly tired of the xyl. He tossed it to one side, watching it convert to a ball and roll down the hill. He wondered if he should oblige his mother by making an appearance, or risk her anger by staying hidden.

"Galun Rellix?" I want you to tell me specifically where you are. Specifically. Do you hear me?"

"Behind the tree."

"Where is the tree?"

"Here."

"What planet, Galun Rellix?"

"Delcan Prime."

"Not Delcan Prime, Galun Rellix. I know you're not on Delcan Prime. You haven't been there in many tireum."

What was she talking about? Of course, he was on Delcan Prime! Wasn't he? He recognized the house. He recognized the yard.

Yet, he was no longer a child, was he? Time had passed. The picture he was seeing, the picture of which he had, somehow, become a part, wasn't quite real…something from his past.

Why did that thought disturb him?

"You're not on Delcan Prime, Galun Rellix," his mother said. Or was it his mother? "I do know that much. But, you won't escape me forever. You know that, don't you? I will find you. I will find what you have taken with you. So, why don't you make it so much easier for the both of us by just telling me, now, where you are?"

"Delcan Prime," he repeated. "Outer-area four. The near-settlement district."

"That was a long time ago, Galun Rellix," his mother said,

standing on the projection, shaking her head in evident disappointment. "Just think how long ago it was. You've been to Rysox since then. You've taken the Quass root. You've tripped to the High Cascade. You've spoken in tongues. Gathered disciples. Gone into the wilderness. Talked with Zurl. Played games and thought you had won. Done what other kind of mischief in your laboratory? Gotten off to where with your petty secrets? And why are you hiding, after all? Why have you left your laboratory when you risked so much to acquire it in the first place?"

"Laboratory?"

How could a youngster of five have a laboratory? His mother wouldn't even let him have the beginner's chemistry packet his father had brought home from Fundies.

But, then, he wasn't five, was he? He was more like three-hundred-and-five. He had been to Rysox since Delcan Prime. He had sampled the Quass root. He had tripped to the High Cascade, where few had survived before him. He had seen things, heard things, been told things. He had gathered disciples, followers, crowds of people who had come to hear him mouth words put on his tongue by The Dzi Scholar.

There was something about a plan, a dangerous plan. And Galun had been a vital part of that plan. Paldon, The Dzi Scholar, had chosen him from all the others.

"You show an aptitude for biology," The Dzi Scholar had told him. "Until our minds have evolved to the state of our enemy, we must supplement our progression in the laboratory. You shall get us that laboratory!"

Who was the enemy? Why had Galun been selected? Where was The Dzi Scholar?"

"Come now, Galun Rellix," his mother was insisting, still standing on the projection. I'm going to give you one more chance. Where are you, now, Galun Rellix? Where are you right at this very moment? Tell me, because I want to find you. I want to talk to you. I want you to explain why you have disappeared. There are so many questions to which I want answers. There are so many answers you can give. Galun Rellix? Galun Rellix…

Galun Rellix…Galun Rellix?"

"I fled the laboratory," he said.

"Yes, I know that, Galun Rellix. But fled to where? Fled why? Where are you Galun Rellix…Galun Rellix…Galun Rellix?"

Why was he taunting his mother? He had promised her he would never do it again, not after the time he hid within the gylincopia hedge, hearing her frantic cries when the crack from the tarrum-quake might have had him.

His mother only ever called him Galun, even when she was angry at him. Never…ever…did she include his last name.

"Where are you Galun Rellix? Tell me where you are!"

His mother *never* called him Galun Rellix!

"Galun Rellix…Galun Rellix…Galun Rellix?"

Mentally, he dissolved the picture, converted it, with much difficulty, into an ocean-spray of grays through which he desperately sought to swim to the surface.

"Galun Rellix…Galun Rellix?"

It wasn't his mother asking that question! His mother was dead—cremated. Filed in the subsection of the Kylic crypt: R24D-3. He had muttered the Bilo script, kissed her death urn, committed her soul….

"Galun Rellix?"

Suddenly, he knew who it was who was trying so desperately to reach him.

"Noooooooooo!" he screamed, suddenly breaking to the surface of consciousness.

He came awake in a room dark except for the softly diffused light emanating from the dials on the MEDICANT-IV. He was sweating. His pale blue skin was drenched with moisture. His eyes were stinging from lemic acid. His inner circulatory system was frantic as it pumped cyro throughout his body.

He had been asleep!

He adjusted his recline bench to a sitting position. He reached for the switch that put MEDICANT-IV on audio.

"I was in Deep-10!" he accused.

"You have merely had a nightmare," a low, monotone voice

answered. "Nightmares are to be expected during any return to Deep-10 after forcible abstention over a prolonged period. Tensions needing to be released have been allowed to compound and—"

"I have programmed you to interrupt all Deep-10!"

"—unhealthy buildups often result in nightmare occurrences," the computer finished, not having stopped to comment on Galun's accusation.

"You were programmed not to allow Deep-10!" Galun repeated. And, to emphasize his point, he typed that exact message on the computer's keyboard.

There were several seconds of pause as the machine digested the input of information.

"In any case, where a patient's life-forces have been endangered by such programming, I have been instructed by my maker to override accordingly. Patient's insistence to avoid Deep-10 on a seemingly permanent basis has shown indications of unbalancing body chemo-makeup and increasing fatigue potential to levels that are unacceptable."

"You may well have killed me!"

"We are not allowed to perform functions detrimental to the well-being of our patients," the computer insisted.

Galun realized that it was quite useless to argue with MEDICANT-IV. He should have known, all along, this was going to happen—in fact, he had *known* it would. He should have made doubly sure that he had protected against it. After the fact, the only thing he could do was try to find some way of keeping it from happening again—if it hadn't already screwed things up beyond repair!

Had he told The Beast his location?

A chill passed through him from the tip of his fur-covered head to the soles of his seven-toed feet.

If she knew where he was, she could even now be preparing to milk his brain of the secrets he had sworn to keep from her.

"You will replay the nightmare," Galun instructed the computer. "I want audio and visual in its entirety."

He swiveled toward the small screen to his left and waited, watching the computer work to comply with his request. A digital clock back-tracked quickly to the time when Deep-10 had first begun, stopped, and, then, began to play forward, at a slower pace.

He heard a voice—her voice—calling to him over the void of time and space that presently separated them from each other.

"Galun Rellix?"

The question was weak, possibly delivered by only a mere beta-2. He would have to make sure, though. For her to find him, now, would ruin everything and abort centuries of careful planning.

A scene appeared suddenly on the screen, a scene wherein he was young, back on Delcan Prime. He was about to go wading in the taxl-green mossil pond with Wendy.

Wendy was the first girl with whom he had wanted to explore langillu. It was well that she had refused him. Anyone who had performed langillu, and, then, sampled Quass root didn't survive tripping into the High Cascade.

On the screen, the children and the green-mossil pond blurred to gray.

"Galun Rellix?" came the all-too-familiar insistent voice.

Galun wipe the lemic acid from his forehead with the back of one seven-fingered hand.

CHAPTER TWO

"Ayra Organa: Before the Fall" from THE HIERARCHY OF TYNBOTHIAN SANCTO-STRUCTURE:

Zanocoba appeared, as he had been bidden, swathed head to foot in the merlian which was his only protection when summoned by the Cantacle of Rajh.

"Your request?" he did ask The Suicide, for his summoner had, by mere participation, forfeited his life.

"To see your image before original transmogrification," The Suicide requested.

And it was done, Zanocoba smiling at such curiosity that would kill the cat.

"Not as you imagined, I should suspect, huh?" Zanocoba did query. "Certainly, not a sight for which too many would sell their souls."

The Suicide dead, Zanocoba did probe quickly to retrieve the vision given in payment. But, the vision was missing, having been simultaneously transmitted, and, therefore, lost to The Beast forever.

It was in those days that The Beast did begin to suspect there was a conspiracy afoot against it.

IT HAD ONLY BEEN A BETA-2. Galun erased it, using the pro-trance to retrace through Sensaspace to its source.

The experience left him completely drained, trembling with the fear of having had his wave-planes so close to those of Organa that—had she but suspected his audacity—Organa could well have had him for the taking.

Galun had risked it all to cover his mistake. Even with that one risk now past, he could not be assured that he had erased all trace, because erasures were never one-hundred percent in the realm of Sensaspace. Even the inconsequential beta-2 would have its ghost left in evidence, much as a pyrnostoscope could show the faint imprint once writing had seemingly been completely retrieved from any surface.

But, detection of a ghost-imprint took much time and energy, perhaps more time and energy than Organa was willing to spare. For, she had other things to occupy her time, besides one missing scientist. Nor could she really yet know for certain how much of a threat that one scientist was. Had she known, she would have possibly gone to even greater lengths to find him.

"Is it done?" George One asked, obviously concerned. He couldn't know what was done, his small mind quite unable to comprehend for even a moment the complexities behind Sensaspace and a beta-2.

George One was a creature of the primitive world to which Galun had once again returned. George One had been programmed to function as a vassal, by the implantation of a myron cube within the lower right cortex of his primitive brain. The procedure, while simple, was also condemned by Lantytic Law as genetic interference. Galun, though, had no qualms whatsoever about having inserted the myron cube into George One. At this point of the journey, Galun figured such genetic tampering was merely child's play, taking into account the interferences already introduced.

"As much is done as can be," Galun informed. "You remember your instructions regarding the machine?"

"A pressing of button three when the window shows blue."

"And if the blue remains?"

"Manual disconnection. I am to bring you back to consciousness without aid of the machine."

"On no account should I remain asleep after the window

registers blue. You completely understand the importance of that?"

"I understand."

"And any incoming messages on the tele-communicator will warrant an awakening, also. Understand?"

Contact from Quan was long overdue, but Galun couldn't afford to wait any longer before getting some sleep. If his line of exhaustion was allowed to increase, it would be apt to contribute to complete chemo-imbalance, making Galun useless to anyone.

"I understand."

Galun positioned himself on recline and shut his eyes. He heard the resulting buzz which warned that his system's stability was dangerously near imbalance. Left on its own, MEDICANT-IV would have insisted on letting Galun dream himself to destruction.

Still, even with George One in attendance, it took Galun a long time to surrender to the threat he feared every time he slipped off into unconsciousness—mainly because he knew how vulnerable he was in such unguarded moments. And Organa would have her sensors out, searching everywhere for the scientist.

Three times, George One shook Galun back to consciousness. Twice, it was because of the failure of the blue to disappear from the computer window, indicating that MEDICANT-IV was quite prepared to allow the onset of Deep-10. Lastly, it was to inform that there was a message beaming into the tele-communicator.

Galun revived, feeling only somewhat recovered.

"Patient has not sufficiently rested," MEDICANT-IV announced in dull monotone, its attempts to allow Deep-10 having been constantly thwarted by the watchfulness and interference of George One.

Galun unhooked and went to the tele-communicator.

The signal, audio but not visual, was a seemingly a random intercept from deep space: a broadcast from the Star System Meta-K. It was a purely undecipherable signal, but, then, it was meant to be. The inherent message could not be found, literally, within the haphazard jumble of space static, and, thus, was not available to anyone, even the users of mid-macrotoloters. It was merely the fact that the sounds arrived, in their predetermined jumbled order, which signaled that Quan was on his way. There was no way for Quan to relay *why* he had been delayed. Such mysteries would have to be cleared up, face-to-face, upon his arrival. To trust such information to any coded broadcast over the tele-wave system, no matter what the stellar frequency, would have been to court disaster. Ayra Organa's mind was hooked into every corner of the galaxy.

Soon enough, Organa would know that there were things happening on Antheer-D. Whether or not she would associate those happenings with a missing scientist, and the suspicion of conspiracy, was something else again. There were, after all, pretenders arising all of the time on one or more of the planets that Organa's spirit force controlled. Antheer-D had a history that held echoes of Organa's own origins, but that would still not give her any indication that the happenings, there, warranted closer watch. After all, Antheer-D was a long step downward on the evolutionary ladder from Organa's origin, the Great Planet Atla, which had perished in the vortex of Cataclys IX.

Antheer-D's link to Atla, though valid, was tentative, attributed to the crash-landing of the Spacecraft M42B in the days when Atla was just beginning to break through those scientific barriers that would soon thrust it into its fabled greatness. At the time of M42B's crash, however, there had been no Gorda Banks to stimulate dormant brain cells in humanoids and stuff minds to full capacity.

Captain Stone Hanlic had been a Cowlee, a class on Atla supplanted in importance by the Powr class after the invention of the Gorda Banks made intellect supreme. The ship-wrecked captain's matings with indigenous Antheerineans took even the Atlans over two-hundred tireum to discover, and, finally, to accept that Hanlic's Antheerinean descendants did, indeed, have many of those very same genetic markers present in the

Atlan pilots who had guided the giant Bisoluitic spacecrafts of Atla to supremacy within the galaxy.

That Antheer-D had remained basically undisturbed prior to the Great Atlan Conflux—except for an occasional sample plucked from the local population for purely scientific study—was because the Atlans had thousands of slaves from which to pick who were physically and mentally superior to Antheerineans. Even as pets, or work animals, the Antheerineans had been considered substandard.

Hanlic's injection of superior seed, and resulting evolution, hadn't much improved the stock. After more than a quantiuminium having passed since Atla had been siphoned into the vortex and ejected as space dust into the void beyond the veil, the Antheerineans were still hardly impressive in either their physical or intellectual makeup.

They were primitives in the most literal sense. Even with the assist of the myron cube, they could be trained to do only the simplest tasks.

Nor was the Antheerinean girl, Mave—even with the generations of selective breeding which had gone into her being—anything of great exception.

But, then, Galun had never found the humanoid form, or its brain, to be worth any special note—which had provided the main source of his surprise when he'd learned from The Dzi Scholar that Ayra Organa had evolved from such unlikely beginnings.

"You judge humanoids purely by what you have of them to be seen around you today," The Dzi Scholar had chided. "These examples, though, have all evolved out of their original matrix. We see today's Terarlians, the Antheerineans, the Etharians, and we make value judgments based upon that. But, our fault is not grasping that these were never the epitome of what their humanoid form once had to offer. During the Great Atlan Conflux, your and my ancestors were as backward to the Atlans as the Antheerineans are to us today."

"You're sure Organa was a humanoid before the first transmogrification?" Galun had persisted. It was still hard for him to believe there had ever been a race of humanoids progressed to a point where they could be considered by The Dzi Scholar as anything but the most primitive creatures.

Maybe, it was so hard for Galun to believe, because he had seen Ayra Organa in the form of Zurl—and Zurl wasn't humanoid. But, then, neither was Ayra Organa—any more!

"We have the image of her original form," The Dzi Scholar had told Galun, "snatched from the mind that registered it seconds before it died. An image purchased at a very high price, I might add. One Barothian dead, one soul lost forever to damnation, and The Beast made suspicious, all so that we could, perhaps, glean the one fatal chink in The Abomination's armor."

"And if we fail?" Galun had asked. "After so many generations, so many tireum, isn't it conceivable she has surrendered all those original hungers inherent within her humanoid form?"

"Then, all is lost," The Dzi Scholar had answered. "And all that we so labor to achieve will come to naught."

CHAPTER THREE

From the forbidden TEXT OF THE HERETIC GIATH:

"No god or goddess has created one creature, but creatures have created gods and goddesses. Lo, they have created them by the score. For creatures are somehow unable to admit to the reality that they are simply freaks of the elements and not some intricate parts of a divine plan."

MAVE STILTER HAD A BROTHER who had been a kylinx—a kylinx being a grotesque creature that came from the womb to give witness that the bearer had copulated with a demon.

Kylinxes were suffocated at birth, stuffed in burlap bags, and buried in the dead of night, for it was thought that they would, if allowed to survive, bring only catastrophe to the community in which they were born.

Mave's brother hadn't been the only kylinx the Stilter family had brought into the world, either. Over the years, there had been a whole line of the wretched creatures, at least one each generation, as far back as even old Granny Maxil could remember, and Granny was going on a century now.

"Danielle and Walter begat a kylinx, as well as Sandy and Torn; Sandy and Torn begat Mary and Henry, as well as a kylinx; Mary and Henry begat a kylinx, as well as Joseph...," intoned the old woman, sitting on the porch, rocking in her chair, detailing the flawed Stilter genealogy to anyone who wanted to take the time to stop and give a listen.

It was doubtful the Stilter family would have avoided ostracism, at the very least, expulsion, at the worst, if not for so many of its women being god-seers. Everyone in Wetspur had come to know, very well, the value of a bona-fide god-seer in residence; none of the town's inhabitants would have moved elsewhere for love or money. Ordinances had been established specifically to keep the crowds from moving in. A police force had been formed specifically to keep strangers moving through.

Everyone in Wetspur was positive Mave was the next Stilter-family god-seer, likely to have her official Visitation any day, and, thereby, assure that good times would continue.

No one could remember when, or even if, a Visitation had ever occurred to anyone *but* a Stilter woman—except, of course, for the Great Visitation when everyone had, for however long, briefly been god-seers en masse. The resulting fires and the thunderous noises of the Great Visitation were still mimicked each year at the Celebration of the Descent, held at the Little Chapel of the Missile in the Woods.

Damn, but it would have been something to have seen the Great Visitation, actually to have reached out and touched He-Who-Emerged-From-The-Flames! But those had been simpler times. After that—some blasphemers, long since stoned, had said, *because* of it—much innocence had been lost, despite the benefits of suddenly having fire, as well as possession of those shiny pieces of metal which still proclaim a family as one having been witness to the spectacle. It was said that the Stilter family had four broadswords, all made of the sacred metal, and buried in the basement of their house. Was it any wonder that people looked the other way when a Stilter birthed a kylinx but stoned to death any other woman even suspected of having done the same?

Danielle Stilter was said to have witnessed the first Visitation *after* the High Visitation, although there had been people, at the time, who said the girl was merely conjuring a tall tale to satisfy her lust for her cousin, Walter.

Actually, truth be known, the whole of Wetspur had been shocked to its core by Danielle's announcement that she had been "instructed by god" to marry her cousin. Walter upset, seemingly uninterested in his cousin, sexually or otherwise, because he had already been promised pretty Cissy Rhine...as any of the present Rhine family would still be most pleased to tell you.

"You think I *want* to marry him?" Danielle was said to have screamed. Maybe she'd suddenly remembered the rumor that the quickest way to get a demon in your bed, and a kylinx in your belly, was to marry one of your own kin? "But if I don't marry him, if he doesn't marry me, the Barrybinks will send ghosts to dance our streets!"

Well, Kylic Moss, Wetspur's mayor at the time, would stand for none of Danielle's incestuous nonsense. It had been up to him to give the go-ahead for any couple to tie the knot, and he said, flat-out, there was simply no way he would wed Danielle to her own cousin. He didn't much care that pervert Barrybinks might be turned loose on downtown streets.

Well, all hell broke loose. Winds blew, and dust came so hard and so fast that no one could tell if it was night or day. Animals took to dying all over the place, found with trails of their steamy innards scattered all over the countryside, as if something had opened them up, upended them, and, then, carried them for miles with their guts dropping out.

People were damned upset, especially since the heretofore Great Visitation had been accompanied by such good times. In fact, it wasn't too long before even the old die-hards began to whisper that maybe Danielle and Walter *should* get married. Damned spooky it was, not knowing when it was daylight or dark, banshees howling, animals dropping dead...

And about then, the mischievous Barrybinks, themselves, began to be spotted. Pale blue, they were, with bumpy heads covered with a thick blue fur, and with big splayed toes on their feet. Each of their hands had an extra two digits and their eyes were the color of spoiled egg yolks.

Nothing like them had come during the Great Visitation! The Great Visitation had brought forth only He-Who-Emerged-From-The-Flame, a handsome devil whose picture still hung in the church. Human he was; the Barrybinks obviously anything but. Some thought the Barrybinks demons out to lie down with all the women of the town to sire whole litters of kylinxes with which to fertilize the countryside, but Danielle insisted all would return to good-time normal if only she married her cousin, Walter.

"They say only good things will come from Walter and me tying the knot," she kept saying, sitting on the floor, her bony knees drawn up to her chin, while she rocked back and forth.

Kylic Moss turned up dead, no obvious reason why, except, as most thought, because the silly bastard wouldn't get the message after being hit over the head with it.

The town folk quickly voted Danielle's father their new mayor. The first thing he did was marry his daughter to her cousin Walter.

Cissy Rhine put up a hell of a fuss, but, by then, even Walter was among those persuaded to accept the hand fate had dealt him.

I-do's were no sooner said than the Barrybinks pulled out of sight, the wind stopped, the dust settled, good times came and didn't end even when Danielle and Walter's first born was a kylinx.

After the Kylinx, there was little Gretal. Cute little thing she was, too. And when she walked in from the fields one day, proclaiming that *she* had had a Visitation, and seen god who had instructed that she marry her brother, well....

"Honey, you don't even have a brother," Danielle reminded.

"Sure do," the little thing said, stepping right on up and patting her mother's belly which, at the time, was as flat as a pancake.

Danielle missed her period the very next week, and little Tad was born eight months later.

Tad and Gretal married, and there were good times. They

begat Mary and Michael, who married, and begat Josepyh and Tammy who married, and….

Until…there was only Mave. No brother, no sister, and—with her mother and father dead—no chance of her ever having siblings. So, the people of Wetspur wondered which of her cousins Mave would wed. The question was much discussed, and there arose the disturbing rumor that Mave may well have been the last of the god-seers.

Who started the last-of rumor, no one could say, but it persisted, spread, and began to make a lot of people extremely nervous. There had been such good times in Wetspur since Danielle Stilter had first married Walter that Wetspur had become by far the most prosperous village on Antheer-D.

Finally, the rumor went in an entirely new direction as a result of the sermon delivered by the Astronaut Craig from the console of the Little Chapel of the Missile in the Woods. Astronaut Craig said that books brought through the fire of the Great Visitation, by none other than He-Who-Emerged-From-The-Flame, and handed down from one astronaut to another, predicted just such times as they were all in and hinted that salvation would be achieved by looking "to the likeness of the first Astronaut Hanlic." For there would "come one who looked like Stone Hanlic, without being him, but being someone destined to be even greater." That had everyone guessing, until Astronaut Craig wondered aloud if Mave Stilter didn't, after all, have a certain resemblance to the portrait of Astronaut Stone Hanlic that hung the church's back wall.

It was an idea that might have been taken as blasphemy, except that Astronaut Stone Hanlic had never professed himself a god, even if the villagers had made him one.

Suddenly, Astronaut Craig's small chapel was filled to capacity every Wednesday to the extent that he had to install a PA system in the chapel's nosecone, so that his one-theme sermons could be broadcasted to the overflow-onto-launchpad crowds that came to hear it.

Astronaut Craig's sudden popularity was something new to

him, in that he had never before been much of a draw. His initial arrival in Wetspur, after the death of Astronaut Kilner, four years before, had been so much of a yawn that several members of the existing congregation had quietly slipped back into the old ways of offering up animal sacrifices to Dielum in the oak grove on the south slope of Cranbrook Mountain.

"Good times will not desert Wetspur!" Astronaut Craig proclaimed, and he had people believing him, because they so desperately wanted and needed to believe.

Clarence Farley stopped his animal sacrifices to Dielum in the oak grove, and returned to Astronaut Craig's Wednesday services.

Astronaut Craig didn't disappoint Mr. Farley, or the people who continued to pack the module and spill out onto the chapel as far as the picnic tables in the trees.

Of all the people drawn to Astronaut Craig's preaching, Mave wasn't one of them. She had never liked Astronaut Craig. What he was saying, now, didn't ingratiate her to him, either. Who did he think he was, after all, except someone appeared out of the blue to proclaim himself successor to Astronaut Kilner? Why did he insist upon playing prophet and making Mave into something he had to know she wasn't?

Mave: god-seer? Ha! What god had she ever seen? Not even a Barrybinks, let alone a god, had ever appeared to her in any forest or glen, to insist she marry her cousin Len, or her cousin Rob. There had been no threats from on high, no promises of ghosts on the streets, if she and Len (or Bill) didn't hurry up and tie the knot.

Astronaut Craig was a charlatan, for sure, manipulating the superstitious and ignorant peasants, in order to obtain their silver and gold fuel pellets by way of offerings placed in the nosecone-tip he passed around each Wednesday.

Well, Astronaut Craig and his foolish congregation were going to be in for one big disappointment, or so Mave thought as she strolled through the dinglum trees, to be confronted, suddenly, by none other than the apparition Captain Stone

Hanlic, Astronaut (she'd recognize him, anywhere, from his church portrait), who told her of the many fantastic things to come.

For, Mave was descended from men and women who had once ridden the skies in whole ships made of the same metal now found on Antheer-D only in the blades of ceremonial broadswords, like those buried in the Stilter basement.

And Mave would, one day, ride in one of those ships.

What's more, Mave believed her vision of First Astronaut Stone Hanlic where she hadn't believed anything said by charlatan Astronaut Craig, because Astronaut Hanlic's eyes drew her in, body and soul, to show her the universal scheme of things and just what part Mave, god-seer, played in it.

Finally, released from the throes of her epiphany, Mave headed directly to the Little Chapel of the Missile in the Woods and experienced the crowd opening for her as she crossed through them, on the launch pad, and entered the chapel, where, at the console, she literally forced Astronaut Craig to one side and promised, via the new PA system, that all of the people of Wetspur were, indeed, in for continued good times...BUT... only...IF...they, one and all...bowed down to her, Mave Stilter, and offered up their worship.

Astronaut Craig was the first to drop to his knees, and, as was prophesied in the books saved from the flames of the Great Visitation, did proclaim, "Our Savior, She is come!"

CHAPTER FOUR

"Ayra Organa: Before the Fall" (section 12—The Martyrdom of Saintal Ann) from THE HIERARCHY OF TYNBOTHIAN SANCO-STRUCTURE.

And, in the eight direme of the tenth filor, The Beast did produce THE GRIMORIE OF TORKBA and did say to Saintal Ann:

"Know you this work?"

And Saintal Ann did tremble, saying she did not.

"A pity," said The Beast, "for there are three copies. One in the Abbey of Lowit, had you but known to make the search amongst those particular ruins."

And The Beast, having revealed the viability of its source, was then free to open THE GRIMIORIE and cant the Formulae of Bridg, which did allow it access to the Saintal's circle.

"You knew you would lose, did you not?" The Beast did ask, preparing to take its vengeance for successfully having breached the defenses the Saintal had stacked against it.

"Yes, I did so suspect it would happen," Saintal Ann confessed.

"Then, why?" The Beast would know.

For Saintal Ann was much beloved by the people and would be sorely missed within the damnation fire into which The Beast's victory did give it full leave to consign her.

"So others, come after me, will have knowledge of THE GRIMORIE OF TORKBA, and, having that knowledge, may count it amongst their defenses when the final march is made against you, worlds needing to be saved."

And The Beast, in a snit, did commit the martyred Saintal's soul forever to the fire and the brimstone.

THE ASTRONAUT CRAIG, OF COURSE, had to be terminated, because Organa would have known, the minute she was in his presence, of the myron cube inserted in the lower right cortex of his brain. In knowing, she would have suspected complicity and would have called for the initiation of investigative procedures, in that myron cubes had been designated genetic interference, and were against Lantytic Law.

Galun had no desire to align himself against the Lantytic Counsel *and* Ayra Organa. Therefore, it was imperative that he cover his ass, as he went along, terminating Astronaut Craig, now, knowing that it was highly unlikely that Organa would bother with a termic-probe of a man long dead before, even after, she was pressed to appear on the scene. And, by the time of her arrival, the Astronaut's replacement would be swept along in the wake of the snowball effect set firmly into motion by his controlled-by-Galun Astronaut predecessor.

Galun's main concern, at the moment, was Quan Znoba, form-changer, now in the guise of Astronaut Captain Stone Hanlic, with Mave Stilter, in the grove of dinglum trees.

Galun had them on his view screen, carefully watching the visuals, monitoring the audios, and checking the digital readouts. For Quan Znoba was not, like Ayra Organa, one who could come and go at will, whatever the shape of things, whatever the size, whatever the sex. For Quan, there were rules and regulations to be strictly adhered to and followed. Even then, his transformations were energy draining, for he was already near life-end, especially since the humanoid format required the absorption of so many of his arms, legs, and antennae, as well a whole reassignment of internal organs within a confining humanoid physique that had its skeleton on the inside, rather than, so-much-more conveniently, on the out.

Galun adjusted the volume, checking the regulator dials that compared the forcefulness of Stone Hanlic's voice, now, with what it had been moments before. The measurements indicated a lessening, for Quan was growing weaker. Would there be strength enough remaining in him for him to carry this last form-change through to completion before final dissolve?

The task would have been difficult enough as originally conceived. How much more difficult it had become, though, with the advent of complications that had become evident within moments of Galun having opened the transporter pod and having stepped back in alarm, having been confronted by the Bild.

"There have been complications!" the reco-voice had said immediately. And Galun had stopped short of blasting the Bild away, his lazo-mar aimed at the alien creature's bulbous, vein-ridden and mouthless head.

What if Galun had pulled the trigger? What if he had destroyed that form which Quan had chosen to aid him in his escape from the asteroid belt around Mzorki? Galun could still shudder at that thought. After all, Quan had been late in arriving, and Galun had expected foul play. Then, to have met the pod, opened it, and found the Bild, had the whole plan tethered in tenuous balance. With one release of the lock guard on Galun's lazo-mar, the ray would have dissolved the Bild into jelly-blob.

The Bild had sat there, unmoving, unseeing, unhearing, not even knowing where it was, except that it sensed combustible flesh and was hungry to ignite and consume it. And the reco-voice, triggered for continual play, upon the lifting of the pod lid, repeated, once again, its pre-recorded message which could have meant many things to many people:

"There have been complications!"

What intuition had persuaded Galun to bide his time, to wait, to assume that the reco-voice, although not one he recognized, was one programmed especially for his benefit? What had told him that the Bild hadn't been prepared to drown Galun suddenly in hellish flames?

For the Bild were conniving and vindictive creatures. Their nourishment was derived from the disintegration of burning flesh. Rumor was that they had been conceived by Ayra Organa in the belly of hell to give a preview of what awaited unbelievers once beyond the veil.

So deceptively innocent in appearance: the bulbous head (for there were no limbs, no eyes, no ears, no mouth, and no sexual organs). Rope-like veins swam constantly within the milky-soup cupped within the stretched and taut egg of transparent membrane.

On Telsor X, they had consumed the populations of whole cities, ingesting the stench of crackling flesh for days on end. As a result of that grotesque feasting of gluttonous genocide, there had come together life-long enemies to form bands of alliance in an effort to stop the Bilds' progression through the universe.

And Mina-Por, Jahur 5, and Ramol/Crier were all consumed in the confrontations that followed. The strength of the Bilds increased as whole solar systems were sparked and melted of their inhabitants. Nations disappeared into greedily consumed mists of hellish steam—until the Bilds *were,* finally, stopped on Ketra-Tor, a three-planet system whose life-forces became sacrificial lambs when sprinkled with Lineariac-2, like meals seasoned with salt.

For Lineariac-2 (a compound found on Welanium, initially assumed of no apparent worth) was, identified by Computa-Morax-Quile (that bastard mutant brain combined hastily from the data banks of Bild-threatened worlds), as a "spice" that would corrode the soup aswim within Bild membranal walls, and would dissolve the veins and containing shells.

So, a billion Bilds come to feast on Ketra-Tor, and—like too-full balloons—did burst and dump their runny lives in quantities so great that whatever little on the planet had escaped the flames was soon dead of suffocation by goo.

The Bilds had, since that defeat, fallen on hard times, and they were thought by some authorities to be close to extinction. There had even been talk of adding them to the Endangered

Life-form Register, except that too many worlds in that panel's membership still had memories of the damage the Bilds had done. More than a few, some very highly placed, would have welcomed the Bilds' hastened extinction.

On Telsor X, there was still a bounty of 20,000 Ruhr paid for any recent tele-recorder of a Bild termination. Such a reward was no small amount, especially when newly discovered Z5 deposits on that planet had sent the value of the Ruhr spiraling on galaxy monetary exchanges.

It hadn't been any vision of reward which had seen Galun paused and wondering whether the Bild found in the pod on Antheer-D should be terminated on the spot lest, Galun, suddenly in flames, would be detrimental to the grand plan that put Galun on Antheer-D to begin with. Rather, it had been coincidences which had made Galun hesitate: the coincidence of expecting a pod and finding one landed in the right coordinates; the coincidence of there being a reco-voice triggered by the opening of the pod lid. Why, after all, would a Bild have gone to the bother of using a recording, since the Bilds communicated only to each other, and, then, not by sound but by chemo-waves? So, for whom had the recording been made—if not for Galun? The final coincidence was how the Bild, who must surely have sensed a meal at hand, hadn't reacted to it. It could have toasted Galun in the blink of an eye, certainly faster than it had taken for Galun to consider, and reject, releasing the lock on his lazo-mar.

Quan had, thus, survived the disguise which could have had him killed.

"I was followed," he had told Galun, transformation to Quan's original form still in process, at the time, and distorting his voice.

Galun hadn't asked by whom Quan had been followed. There was a whole list from which to pick and choose, none friendly.

"They were using tyro-scans," Quan had continued. "There had to have been at least three ships, all locked in on mine, because I couldn't shake them until the interference of the asteroid belt around Mzorki. Once in the belt, I had no chance of coming out without again being spotted. They were just out there, waiting for me. My qualis kept picking up traces of their scanner probes, but I couldn't get any definite fixes because they were using some kind of sophisticated veiling devices I haven't come across before. They could have held me in there until the fires on Kylon-XII froze over."

"You exited as a Bild?"

"I counted upon their not expecting me to offer them a prey so enticing. Would someone trying to escape them emerge suddenly with a 20,000 Ruhr bounty tag strung around his neck? In the end, they rightly decided, yes, but, by then, I had swung around Mzorki and entered the solar draft from Psyras Blue."

"Do you think they know?"

"Of course, they know! They've known since Zanocoba found Drawler had transmitted the vision of The Beast's origin as a woman. It's only the 'how we plan to do it' that has them guessing."

"You do know that I almost killed you in your form of Bild?"

"You do know that I almost killed you in my form of Bild? One doesn't transform on merely the physical plane, you know, if one hopes to be convincing in a ruse? In my efforts to fool the enemy, I almost went too far. I might still have gone too far. I'm down to life-end, you know? Can we accomplish what we have to in the time in which we have to do it? I know what we had scheduled, but we are dealing with primitive humanoids, are we not?"

He had paused. It was obvious, from the heavy breathing of organs taking form beneath the still-changing sheath of flesh, that the ordeal had nearly drained the shape-shifter's resources. And he had soon been expected to assume the form of First Astronaut Captain Stone Hanlic.

"You don't suppose The Beast anticipated Drawler's question, do you?" Quan had asked, the fading of his voice indicating that volume grls had been channeled elsewhere in the seething mass of converting tissue.

"Would its anticipation have mattered? The conjuration formulae were strictly adhered to. The life was forfeited in the end," Galun had reminded.

"*We* followed the rules, you mean? Yes, we did do that, didn't we? But have you ever stopped to wonder just who wrote the rules, and if anyone ever gets powerful enough to bend them just a little? Or, worse, if there is anyone powerful enough to rewrite the rules altogether?

The volume had faded completely. Galun was left feeling uneasy and with a need for delving deeper into that particular line of thought, because, yes, he had asked himself all those questions. And it made him uneasy every time he even suspected there was no way any of them would ever overcome the woman—who was no longer a woman—whose intellect certainly wasn't standing dormant, in wait for them to catch up to her.

Quan, had transformed into the humanoid form of First Astronaut Stone Hanlic, and was, now, seated in the grove of dinglum trees with Mave Stilter. And Mave was fooled into believing she was actually conversing with a god. After all, what did Mave Stilter know of gods, when she could so easily be duped into believing a simple form-changer was a deity? She was such a simpleton! And, to think that so much depended upon this humanoid, bred back to a state that was as close as any humanoid could ever come to the gene pool of the real Stone Hanlic upon his crash-landing on Antheer-D. No amount of skillful inbreeding, no matter how many centuries were available, would be able to revert genes to that of the original, because Stone Hanlic had mated with Antheerineans, forever diluting his contribution in the process.

What made any of them think they could win, using this wretched tool? No matter what was said, Galun couldn't believe Ayra Organa had ever—even in her most primitive state—come from stock anywhere near the simplicity of Mave Stilter. Granted, Organa had had the advantage of the Gorda Banks, but still…

And there was the legend that Organa still had access to one or more of the Gorda Banks which hadn't been siphoned into the vortex with Planet Atla and been ejected as space dust into the void beyond the veil. If that were true, then all of this was really a useless exercise!

The alarm sounded, bringing Galun's attention back to the view screen. He turned up the volume.

He punched off the alarm—it immediately reactivated, which meant that Quan's life-force was ebbing dangerously low.

Galun felt tremendously guilty, realizing that Quan had come prepared to be yet another martyr to the cause, as others had done before him. He was prepared to give his life, and was doing so, now, without a qualm. To look at him, there in the form of First Astronaut Stone Hanlic, it was hard to know he was suffering at all. But he *was* suffering. The swinging of the dials told Galun all he needed to know about the turmoil at work beneath the calm façade facing Mave Stilter.

Galun was getting old. He had somewhere lost his urge to become a martyr. Where was the young biologist who had once faced Ayra Organa, one-on-one, and tricked her into giving him his laboratory in which he had computed the inbreeding steps necessary to purify the genetic Stilter strain?

Or had he tricked her? Had she known all along why he had wanted the laboratory from her?

The alarm buzzer sounded louder. The rhythm-dial swung all of the way to the right and stopped there, soon joined by others.

"So you understand what you must do?" First Astronaut Stone Hanlic was asking. His voice was calm, cool, evenly modulated. But the form-changer behind the voice was definitely in the last throes of dying.

What if Quan died without finishing what he had to do? What would poor, simple, and helplessly stupid Mave Stilter do, seeing First Astronaut Stone Hanlic dissolve before her eyes into the death chrysalis of a form-changer?

"*Do* you understand what you are required to do, Mave?" First Astronaut Stone Hanlic repeated. "What you must do to assure your people will survive and thrive? For without you, they will quickly go back to worshipping Dielum in the grove. And Dielum is little concerned with any of you, and will never be, unless you give him…."

Galun saw Quan's pain lines. Did Mave see them? How could the stupid humanoid bitch miss seeing them?

Mave saw nothing. Such was the level of spiritual bliss into which she had ascended that she was lucky even to be hearing. And, in the end, things did depend upon her hearing, and upon her being able to act upon what she heard.

It was so…so hopeless! Didn't Quan, sacrificing his life at that very moment, see how hopeless it really was?

How could any of them expect Mave Stilter to stand up to the scrutiny of Ayra Organa and survive the ordeal, when so many of those on a far higher intellectual plane had perished in the process? Madness! Utter madness!

"Understand?" First Astronaut Stone Hanlic managed finally.

The alarm still buzzed. All dials were swung to the far right, seemingly stuck there.

Quan, the form-changer…hovered on the brink of death!

"Understand, Mave?" First Astronaut Stone Hanlic again repeated his question for the young girl seated on the ground at his feet.

"She is too far gone, Quan," Galun whispered in reply, each of his hands clenching six fingers around a seventh. "She doesn't understand. She hasn't heard a thing!"

"Tell me, my daughter," First Astronaut Stone Hanlic insisted. His face was etched with deep pain lines. Texture breakdown was in full mode, especially around his eyes, around his mouth. Was the girl's mind registering those changes for future play-back? "Tell me you understand!"

"She doesn't understand!" Galun insisted.

"I understand," Mave said.

"Liar!" Galun accused, shaking his head.

"I want you to go over it, again, for me, Mave," First Astronaut Stone Hanlic said.

"There's no time!" Galun screamed. If there had been no walls around him, no earth piled around those walls, anyone could have heard his vented frustration to the center of Wetspur. "Don't be a fool! Get the bitch humanoid up and send her out of there. Now! If she sees your conversion to death chrysalis, she will have the imprint of that on her brain, and Organa will have at it for sure."

Mave began speaking…slowly. Was there ever a humanoid who spoke so slowly?

She spoke, and First Astronaut Stone Hanlic sat, dissolving slowly before her.

The non-stop alarm buzzed incessantly in Galun's audio vents. He slammed his fists into the machine, trying to make the warning stop, but the buzzing wouldn't stop. The dials had stopped and held as far right as possible.

"For Dielum is a cruel god," First Astronaut Stone Hanlic said. "He will ask for human sacrifices as in the old days before the Great Visitation, Mave. I tell you, your people will be made to suffer much if you do not intercede on their behalf."

"I will intercede," she told him.

"You must be strong in that resolve, Mave. You will be tempted into faltering."

"I will not falter."

"Promise me you will be strong in your resolve!"

"Yes."

She took his hand in hers. Did she feel how the molecules were shifting, rearranging, changing? She kissed his palm.

Her eyes glazed. What were they seeing…if anything? Quan, the form-changer, transmogrifying into his death chrysalis? Stone Hanlic, First Astronaut Captain, who had emerged from the flames of his M42B to impregnate Antheerinean females, one of whom had been Mave Stilter's ancestor?

More importantly, what was the mind's-eye seeing and recording for playback by Ayra Organa?

For, the time would come when The Beast would dissect this humanoid form, like a bug dismembered beneath a scathe-telenscope. There would be no secrets hidden from the magnifying lens. The Beast would have them all: the success or failure of centuries of planning, hanging in the balance!

You must go now, Mave," Firsts Astronaut Stone Hanlic said.

For a moment, Galun thought the woman wasn't going to turn loose. He had sudden macabre visions of her fingers becoming hopelessly caught within the emerging silk strands, like a fly within the exuded web of some spider.

"Turn him loose, you stupid little fool! Galun commanded, his intake of breath a loud hiss when she finally did let go.

"Forward, Mave," First Astronaut Stone Hanlic said. "From this moment onward, there is only that one way for you to go. And you must go now to tell your people what you must do for them. And you must never, ever, look back."

"Yes," she said.

She stood.

"You…must…never…ever…look…back!" First Astronaut Stone Hanlic commanded. "Never. Ever. Promise?"

"Yes."

"Go, then!"

"Yes."

She turned away from him.

Galun watched, horror-struck to witness every pore of First Astronaut Stone Hanlic's body ooze more strands of silky fiber, some so light that the air around them caused them to flutter and seem alive. Strands caught in strands, mingling with each other in a uniting dance of death.

The chrysalis was forming, and all Mave Stilter had to do to see it was to turn around. And seeing, she couldn't fail to know that something was amiss. Even in her induced state of religious ecstasy, she would surely be shocked into the awareness that a real god did not sprout silky hair like a dandelion puff.

And she was going to turn! Yes, she was!

But, no, she had just stumbled slightly. She kept on going,

down the path to Wetspur, down the road to meet with a more powerful god, not knowing that the one with which she had just conversed wasn't a god at all but a form-changer who, finally, wrapped securely in his cocoon, was....

The alarm buzzer stopped.

...dead!

CHAPTER FIVE

Terarlian folk tale of Germanics tribal origins:

And the King, riding forth to give battle with the rebels who had deigned to align against him, did capture the town of Tal-burg, pressing many of its survivors into his service.

And there was a blacksmith, one townsman named von Corbet, who continued to be sympathetic to the enemies of the King, only pretending to be turned against them.

The blacksmith, of lowly status, was hardly considered a key player in forwarding his comrades' cause. Yet, he did, one Friday, as a token gesture, leave out one nail when shoeing the King's charger.

On morning next, the King rode forth into another battle, and his horse did throw its ill-attached shoe and stumbled to break an equine leg. The horse down, the King, its rider, was on foot, more easily set upon by his enemy, and killed. The King, once dead, his men did soon withdraw from the field, many of them dying in the retreat.

For loss of a nail, the shoe was lost. For loss of a shoe, the horse was lost. For loss of the horse, the King was lost. For loss of the King, the battle was lost. For loss of the battle, the war was lost. For loss of the war, the kingdom was lost.

Yet, how could the lowly blacksmith have ever fathomed any of that?

THE POD, WHEN JETTISONED from Antheer-D, would

leave an imprint on the atmosphere. But, imprints were not something unique or strange, even for Antheer-D's atmosphere. Ships had come for years to this, and to other worlds, if just to observe—usually from complete concealment—the ways of the primitives.

Over the ages, there had been much curiosity regarding the Antheerineans. Humanoid forms were rare as parks' teeth in the cosmos. Terar, Ethar, and Antheer-D, in fact, were the only three known planets who showed evidence of survivors from Cataclys IX. The irony was that, had those inhabitants not been at such primitive levels of development at the time, they too would have rode Atla into the vortex which squeezed it to space dust.

It was said that madness reigned in those days of Cataclys IX, especially on Terar, Ethar, and Antheer-D, where human-oids, called upon by a certain "something" inherent within their genes, did try to heed their lemming call by flapping arms and attempting to take flight from buildings and from mountain-tops. Without the technical skills required to build crafts that could fly them to their deaths on far-off Atla, they died by splat-tering themselves on local jagged rocks and on smooth paving stones. At the time, as now, nothing much flew on these planets, except winged creatures even more primitive in ancestry than the ground-hugging humanoids.

Antheer-D had it the worst of the three surviving planets. After all, it had residents whose genealogical soup was most closely linked with Atla through the crash-landed astronaut Stone Hanlic. Most of its residents did try to fly, and ended up broken and bloodied in heaps so high that more climbed atop those heaps of corpses in order to attempt taking wing. Legend said that most of those generations who did survive on Antheer-D were made crippled in the lemming rush, and were mad as hatters for as long as they existed within the aftermath.

Ethar and Terar had early on, in their history, known the spermal spurts of Altans (countless tireum prior to the likes of Stone Hanlic setting sail through stella-space), so, by the time of the fatal lemming call, their soup was much diluted.

Thousands died in the mad rush to reach the crematorium of their kind, but all planet-locked humanoids eventually had a cool-down that allowed them to face the inevitable fact that they were without means to reach the place that so strongly and so tenaciously called out to them.

What time clock in the humanoid gene had suddenly run its course to send so many of them rushing to destruction? After all, at the time, Atlans were capable of great intelligence, or so The Dzi Scholar insisted. They had had the Gorda Banks to swell their minds to states beyond the imagination of bygone days. They had conquered galaxies around about them, so that none could stand against them.

But, in the end, it was a something within themselves that had sent them to destruction. Where once they had spiraled out, into the universe, by way of colonization, that was suddenly reversed, all affected by the suction that drew them back to Atla, even more quickly than they'd left—like countless drops of water caught within the vortex of an unplugged drain.

Get back to what? To a world possessed of a madness, all its own, to the point where many said Atla wasn't of rock or stone—or if it was, it was of a kind unseen, until then, or since? For the monster planet left its orbit, on its own, and spiraled to a point in space that vacuumed it up—and all it brought with it— into oblivion, leaving no evidence of what had passed except for the faulty memories of those humanoids who had survived, in states of questionable sanity, on other worlds.

It was that last recorded cataclys, so great in its multiple of its predecessors, that it was called IV *AND* V, the combination being IX. Anyone who spoke of IX made reference to a nightmare so indelible in its horror that all disasters, before and after, were dwarfed in comparison.

Cataclys IX plunged whole galaxies into intellectual darkness, leaving cities and machines with no one knowing how to run either. What secrets lost! What few miracles ended up being left, in the aftermath, to puzzle and amuse the pitiful remnants of that lemming rush.

Now, on a world peopled by genetic pieces that had—through no fault of their own—survived that long-ago catastrophe, Galun shivered in response to the passage of a beta-1 not too far away—a beta-1 sent out on its search by the one true-blood Atlan rumored to have survived Cataclys IX.

What had kept Ayra Organa from perishing in the holocaust? Had she been a mutant with a faulty genetic time-clock? Had she merely possessed such inner willpower that she had successfully waged battle against those inherently programmed commands that would have destroyed her?

Or, was the vision imprinted on The Suicide's mind a false one? A decoy, a ruse, to throw them off the track, to make them waste centuries in forming battle lines against an Atlan survivor, a human, a woman, who didn't actually exist?

Zurl, whom Galun had confronted on Delcan Prime, had been anything but human, seemingly anything but a female! And, yet, The Dzi Scholar insisted that Zurl and the Atlan woman, the latter registered on The Suicide's brain, were one and the same. Galun doubted it. Galun had always doubted it.

Yet, if he doubted, why was he here? Why had he committed to come this far?

He had been tricked, hadn't he? He had been manipulated, molded, fooled, much as the Antheerinean god-seer, Mave Stilter, was being manipulated, molded, and fooled. It wasn't hard to sculpt malleable minds if one was smarter than the acquired gray matter—as Galun was smarter than Mave Stilter, as The Dzi Scholar was smarter than Galun.

Galun was merely a piece on some gigantic game board, a piece that could just as easily be sacrificed as had been Quan, the form-changer; or, Drawler, The Suicide; or Ann, the Saintal.

In fact, Galun was being sacrificed right now, wasn't he? Because he was going mad! No Delcan Primenian retained sanity for long without journeying into Deep-10. Ask MEDICANT-IV. It knew. It was programmed for preserving life. It would have overridden every time Galun rested if there hadn't been George

One standing by to prevent that override from happening.

Who was it, on high, running the show? Who sat the other side of the game board? Ayra Organa? Or did The Beast sit on *both* sides of the board, compelled to play with himself/herself/itself, since there was no one remaining in the universes capable of offering up a challenge?

Not that it really mattered. Galun, while resenting that his destiny had somehow been taken out of his hands (if it had ever been there to begin with), knew he had no viable alternative but to go on. After all, what purpose was there in living if one didn't have goals—whether those goals were self-originating or programmed by another? Galun's goals had been programmed for him a long, long time ago. Those goals re-enforced each step along the way: On Rysox, by The Dzi Scholar, through the Quass Root that had tripped him into the High Cascade, and into confrontation with Zurl.

He was merely getting too old for the game. His mind and his body were giving out on him. Gone were the days when he was made alive by the mere playing. Were he to face Zurl today, he wouldn't have had the courage necessary to bargain for the laboratory—maybe because age had brought him a closer peek at what he was up against, out there, where his youth had kept his enemy slightly blurred and out of perfect perspective. Once, he thought he could accomplish the impossible, and thinking it was half the battle. In old age, the reality of his disintegrating body and mind brought painfully home the realization that most creatures in the universe were not self-perpetuating. The few who were had the ultimate advantage of never having to pass on data from one generation to the next, from one mind to another.

Galun no longer believed that the battle against Organa could, or would, be won. That didn't mean he would give up in the attempt, for so much of his existence, to this point, had been devoted to the attempt that he couldn't stop now. He was a programmed piece on the game board. Therefore, he would continue to function until forces completely beyond his control decided to remove him—in one way or another—from play.

He terminated George One and stuffed him into the pod with the death chrysalis of the form-changer, and with the body of Astronaut Craig. He did so, knowing his days were now more numbered than before. With no one left to assure that he didn't progress into Deep-10, there could be no sleep at all. Yet, George One had to be jettisoned, just as Astronaut Craig had to go. Upon Organa's arrival on Antheer-D, she could be allowed no possibility of finding evidence of myron cubes. The Beast would scan for them, immediately, always suspecting their use in cases of Transcendence.

Galun programmed the pod for a flight path that would utilize gravitational pulls, solar drafts, and even time warps to disguise and jumble, as much as possible, anyone's attempts at retracing it to point of origin. Destination was the iono-storm off Forrsim-B—hardly a spot to draw undue attention, since its dissolving winds had for years been the sacred dumping grounds for the death chrysalises of form-changers.

He jettisoned the pod, standing back to watch its rise and fade into the atmosphere. The swiftness of the jettison left it doubtful it was witnessed by an Antheerinean. Even if it had, at this point, such a register would have been distorted by minds now geared to witnessing those wondrous things expected at the Transcendence of god-seer Mave Stilter.

He re-formed the shielding barrier, momentarily breached by the jettisoning, and returned to the view screen.

Mave was sitting in a small boat on the edge of a large lake to the west of Wetspur. All around her was a multitude of people, formed into a fan along the shoreline. Heads bobbed each time the young girl spoke.

Mave's handmaidens—there were now only three, but there would soon be more as crowds grew larger—were busy dispensing fish and loaves of bread. There was hardly enough to feed everybody, but who would know in the end? Those who had brought food would share in their surge of religious brotherhood. Those who hadn't brought food, and never would get any, would simply *imagine* they had eaten. It was the type of occurrence from which miracles were inferred. Miracles were necessary accompaniments to any Transcendence.

"I will intercede!" Mave Stilter proclaimed. "For, I have seen First Astronaut Stone Hanlic and have spoken with him on your behalf."

"Praise be to the god-seer!" the crowd rumbled in unison.

"The First Astronaut Captain has foreseen the re-ascendance of Dielum, and has outlined the way for your well-being and salvation."

"Praise be to the First Astronaut Captain!" came the uproarious reply.

In truth, though, no matter what words were said, many Antheerineans looked forward to the prospect of a re-ascendency of Dielum, The Child Eater. Already, The Shamal of that god was on the move, whispered human sacrifices in the offing.

Old talismans were being retrieved from secret caches.

Mave Stilter's father had dug up one of the four sacred broadswords from the basement and sent it to The Shamal Gorf to be baptized in the blood of first Baby-slaying.

"We have been promised good times!" Mave proclaimed; her breasts were bared as had been the custom in the long-ago. "For, I am made to look favorable in the eyes of Dielum. Or, so the First Astronaut Captain has assured me."

"Praise be to Mave Stilter! God-seer! Intercedent!"

"Verily, I say unto you, be not afraid!"

The multitude did rejoice in their promised salvation.

CHAPTER SIX

Wise-statements of the Great Astronaut Captain:

Do not kill.
Do not lie down with your neighbor's husband or wife.
Do not steal.
Do not tell false tales concerning your brethren.

BETTY MAE, THE WHORE of City Pegal, Antheer-D, was sure that she had died. Also, she was sure she'd gone to Hell, for she certainly couldn't imagine this as Haven Max, wherein all good Antheerineans went upon having done a life-time of good deeds, having followed the laws, and having done whatever else had been asked of them while existing within their fleshy humanoid forms.

She knew why she was in Hell, too. And, knowing what she now knew, she would have certainly liked a chance to re-live her life on Antheer-D, because she would definitely have mended her ways. No joys of sinning on Antheer-D could possibly be worth what she was going through now.

Not that she was all that sure just what *was* happening to her, for sometimes she couldn't see at all. Sometimes, she saw only vague shapes through a soupy gray blur. Usually, she couldn't hear, or, if she could, she couldn't understand any of what she was hearing.

Usually, what she smelled were "medicinals" that brought her close to nausea. There were stinks, too, that invariably accompanied the release of her bowel and/or bladder.

She could feel, although she wished she couldn't—because she seemed to be in constant pain. Not just on the outside, where someone or something was continually prodding, pinching, scrubbing with wire brushes, washing with irritants, and slapping on great swaths of tape, then ripping them off, but there was pain on the inside—pain in her private places; pain that spread like fire upward into her guts. At times, she thought there were giant pinchers reaching in, taking hold of her entrails, and yanking to plop them hot and steamy onto the floor.

She screamed often. Anyway, she thought she screamed. She couldn't hear her sounds, except as they managed to echo inside of her poor, aching head. But, she opened her mouth wide enough, and she went through all the motions.

She had heard somewhere—probably in childhood tales—that there had once been an early Antheerinean who was chained to two big rocks by some offended deity, probably Dielum. This early Antheerinean was sentenced to have his liver eaten forever by giant harplings. That's how Betty Mae felt most of the time; as if her innards were being eaten by giant harplings.

She wondered—when the pain allowed her to think of anything except the pain—whether or not Billy Bob was chained out elsewhere, going through the same hellish torment. She suspected that he would have to be, if there was any justice at all. Not that she would have wished this torment on him for anything, but it would have been infinitely unfair for Betty Mae to have had to shoulder the complete guilt for the both of them.

She should never have run away with Billy Bob to the Willate Forest. Oh, yes, she could see that now. She would have even gotten down on her knees, and admitted as much, if someone would just show up on the scene to ask her to confess her past sins and do penance for them. But, if there was actually substance to any of those shadows existing within her limited line of vision, it never materialized, never came forward to explain how many centuries Betty Mae would have to endure before there was relief—if there ever would be relief.

She had to void body waste—again. That was one of the most horrible torments she was constantly put through. She had always been embarrassed by certain body functions, under normal circumstances, mainly because her mother had taught her to be that way. She had never let even Billy Bob see her during those kinds of private moments. And, now, here she was, unable to move, locked down like a patient in some great and stinking hospital ward, pissing and shitting, possibly, in front of each and every fellow resident of Hell.

"Pleeeeease, noooo!" she protested, sure it would have been heard as a squeal if she could only have made it heard, even by her.

She felt "them" again, touching her, dragging sandpaper over her skin. Hurting her...hurting her—why were they hurting her? What had she ever done to them?

Then, again, she knew what she had done. Oh, yes, she knew. She had run off with Billy Bob. Was that so bad, though? She and Billy Bob had wanted just to get away. Wrong? Oh, yes, certainly wrong, in that her parents had been against the shacking-up of their daughter with Billy Bob Carl. They said he was a bum, a no-gooder, a creep, a dip, a snag. He was certainly no one with whom they wanted to see their daughter.

Honor your father and mother was one of the wise-statements of the First Astronaut Captain, made during those first days after his emergence from the flames. And by disobeying her parents, Betty Mae had ceased to honor them. She had gone against the wise-statement of the First Astronaut Captain, for which she had been consigned to never-ending damnation.

"Oooooeeeeeiiiiii!" the attending nurse-balor exclaimed in appalled dismay. "The wretched humanoid female has soiled herself—again! Wretched creature! Wretched species! Foul... utterly...utterly...foul"

"I've explained," Murlock of Rysox said, turning to The Dzi Scholar beside him, "that the condition is correctable when the humanoid is conscious and unrestrained. The nurse-balor, however, continues not to believe me. It's quite the turmoil, around here, believe me; although, I am happy to report that our experiments are quite on schedule."

"If the nurse-balor continues to be concerned, find someone to improvise a linkup to take care of the humanoid's body waste. We should have anticipated this dismal turn anyway. The species is really such a disgustingly primitive one, isn't it?"

"Mmmmm," Murlok answered noncommittally. "Does all of this make you think The Suicide's image was incorrect?"

"Do you know just how often I've asked myself that question?" The Dzi Scholar replied, leading the way out of the hospit-cubicle, through the eyelo-scans that automatically bombarded them with disinfectant to destroy any contamination they might have picked up from exposure to the humanoid creature.

"The Suicide followed the rules to the letter," Murlock assured. "I was in on his briefing. A brain scan was made to assure the formulae were perfectly imprinted. It seemed safe to assume there was no deviation."

"It's never been The Suicide's adherence to formulae which has worried me," The Dzi Scholar replied. He stopped and turned to Murlock. "Don't tell me that it hasn't crossed your mind that Organa is playing by a different set of rules than we are, possibly even playing by a rule book of her own making."

"If and when I do think such things, I immediately try to suppress them, for my own well-being," Murlock admitted.

"We must simply assume that Organa is confined by some containment, mustn't we?" The Dzi Scholar said, taking up the walk again.

They were headed through a walkway carved by lasers into the mountainside. The passage—as were all the parenthe-sizing rooms—was lined with cilysal; the whole underground complex was shot-through with thriene, all in an attempt to keep this small pocket in the universe secure from penetration. Whether the precautions were successful, or not, really couldn't be known for certain, since the factions responsible for Tilox—as the place was called—weren't really completely certain as to the scope of power had by their chief adversary. There were doubts that cilysal and thriene were sufficient in themselves. Pocket 12 and Pocket 120 (the former shielded just with cilysal, the later just with thriene) had both been penetrated. It still remained to be seen whether a combination of the two offered suitable shielding. Of course, there was always the possibility that a completely impenetrable forcefield was the last thing to be desired. It had been suggested by some that Organa's inability to scan certain areas of the universe with even her most sophisticated beams was enough, in and of itself, to set off alarm bells in her computer linkups, for who would erect such barriers if they didn't have something to hide from her?

It seemed to be the old adage that you couldn't win for losing, except that there were life-forms—like The Dzi Scholar and Murlock—who refused to believe that even Ayra Organa wasn't bound by some constraints.

"It is a bit inconceivable to imagine our adversary having evolved from a creature like that one attended now by the nurse-balor, isn't it?" Murlock ventured. They still hadn't come to the end of the passageway.

"More than a bit inconceivable," The Dzi Scholar agreed. "More like totally inconceivable. But, what we have in there is a product of water-downed genes. Ayra Organa evolved from humanoids existent before Cataclys IX. If only there had been another true-blood Atlan survivor."

"A male, you mean?" Murlock asked, a sardonic smile playing within the sound of his voice.

"Of course, a male," The Dzi Scholar answered. "Isn't that what all of this is all about?"

CHAPTER SEVEN

Pg. 2, KILNOR'S COMPLETE GUIDE TO VINOLIUM AND ITS THREE MOONS, edited by Darmul Fon, published by Vinolium Press, LTD:

Aglit *(aglitunus spinalitus)*—a microorganism found dispersed through the entire Vinolium Ocean Systems. Aglits contain small non-barb stingers that detach upon contact. Individual stings received by swimmers go invariably unnoticed and offer no medical complications. However, aglits, for some reason not yet determined, at times congregate in extensive "plorts" as much as three-blocks long and two blocks wide. Submersion in such, with resultant multiple stings, has been known to produce immediate paralysis and eventual death to a swimmer. Due to the difficulty of predicting or detecting such congregations, "Swim at Your Own Risk!" signs are required by law on all public and private beaches.

THE FORTRESS ON BNTH had physical boundaries that stretched from the Black Glass Sea of Torne to the Drandee Drop of Escarpment II. Its corridors and rooms honeycombed the mountain in which it sat, forming a labyrinth to which no one—but one—held the secrets or the keys.

The place was peopled with the sycophants of The Beast—those servants a collection of life-forms of which some were easily definable (i.e. Clintorians, Myronians, Dyonarians), and others not. All but The Beast had substance. All but the Beast had mass that could be touched, or at least detected, and tortured. They could all be made to bleed life liquid when they were cut or punctured. Even the form-changers—and there were several in residence (like other life-forms, held indentured for reasons known only to them and to The Beast)—were confined within certain limits that, while possibly allowing the reorganization of their molecular structure, did not allow the apparent disintegration of it. Granted, there were artificial means of inducing invisibility. There was, also, the tele-mind-bend, used exclusively by the Zylonic Clones. But, the rhynboidal cloe, and the tele-mind-bend were purely illusion-producing. Beneath the illusion existed, at all times, substances to be detected.

However, there was no detector which could have pinpointed the life-form presently within the Emeru-Room, that central room within The Fortress maze. The Beast had long ago shed physical substance, surrendered all sexual confinements, except—of course—when such were necessitated. The Beast ruled supreme on many worlds, and it needed substance, on occasion, in order to deal with its worshipers. In particular, primitive life-forms were usually more impressed by substance than by purely vacant space inhabited by undetectable intellect and emotion.

The fortress had not been constructed to house any materialization of The Beast, for The Beast seldom used such forms beyond the planes in which its worshipers existed. The fortress had been constructed for the protection of certain accumulated items that were, although tangible, necessary for the well-being of their owner. The fortress, then, was more of a vault than a home, and, the fact that The Beast could be found there, when not occupied elsewhere, could be accounted to the presence of those objects locked inside.

The Beast did have enemies who could have benefited had they had access to those few possessions of substance still considered necessary by The Beast.

Not that The Beast was usually overly concerned about its enemies. They were usually able to offer no more bother than a gnat to a Borlean horsecat. However, there had been certain evidence, over the tireum, that there was a growing, organized effort to challenge its power. Apparently, the organization spanned more than one world, more than one system, more than one galaxy. Such an organization was a novelty. Usually, the pockets of rebellion were isolated areas of the universe, one paltry creature, here or there, assuming it could, somehow, rise up and triumph over The Beast, but failing to know just how powerful the adversary was, and, in the end, easily enough tripped up and squashed.

Organization was always unique. The Beast could remember (and its memory banks, linked as they were by mega-metats to the computer, were extensive), a challenge-by-organization only twice before: the Druidic cults in the Xix System and, of course, the Cone Triad in the Solic System. The latter had actually managed to extend its influence to twenty-five planets and ninety-six moons before The Beast had decided that things had moved too far, and had stepped in to close it down.

But, even the Cone Triad hadn't displayed the ingenuity of this present movement. The Beast had uncovered nests of this insurrection that had been shielded by cilysal and thriene. Now, that, as primitive as it was, had called for a bit of imagination that The Beast couldn't recall having encountered before. In fact, had such happened back in the times when The Beast hadn't yet withdrawn and assimilated information from Section X of the Gorda Bank, it might have actually been truly concerned by this challenge.

Now, however, The Beast was only amused. It enjoyed little games, even though there could be only one outcome to them, this latest one included.

There had been only two possible sources capable of offering a real challenge to its supreme power, one having perished in Cataclys IX. The other The Beast still truly feared—as it lurked possibly within it. Although The Beast had discarded most, if not all, of its original molecular structure, how could it know if it had phased out that one ticking time-bomb which had sent its ancestors running in their mad lemming race toward destruction? In its humanoid form of Ayra Organa, at the time, The Beast had somehow been saved, but how? What had there been in that form's genetic makeup that had saved Organa, while all around her had raced willingly into the vortex to be ejected as space dust beyond the void? Had Ayra Organa been an anomaly who, by having slightly mutated, missed the call to join the lemming race? Or, had the clock, programming her entrance into the race, been somehow stopped, eventually to be jarred back into activity? Was the time mechanism merely faulty, ticking off in tireum what had been but seconds within the time clocks of others? Would The Beast one day feel the stirrings of inner uncontrollable need, which would send it off into outer space toward a new hole timed to open for its late arrival?

Thought patterns shifted. After all, there was little point in dwelling on aspects still completely beyond even its control. The conspirators were another matter. The Beast had only to decide when and how to stop them. *When* would, of course, depend upon how long they continued to amuse it. *How* would depend upon how well they had played the game while the game lasted. So far, they had put up a pretty good showing.

The Beast called up the known and possible clues they had already provided:

There was the disappearance of the biologist, Galun Rellix, from his laboratory on Delcan Prime, plus the fact that Galun Rellix was somehow eluding Deep-10, despite the threat doing so offered to his sanity. What, but conspiracy against his benefactor, would have pried Galun Rellix loose from the laboratory he had risked his very life to obtain? And what had he taken with him from the laboratory memory banks? The Beast had located those blanks, although there had been extensively complex procedures initiated to cover up their exit. And, if Galun Rellix was involved, now, it was logical to assume that he had been involved from the very beginning, back to a time before he had even confronted The Beast in its guise of Zurl on Delcan Prime. How interesting a prospect that added!

There was The Suicide who had confronted The Beast's guise of Zanocoba. Of everything for which The Suicide might have asked, he had asked to see The Beast as Ayra Organa. And The Beast had obliged, learning too late that the image had been transmitted by The Suicide. But, transmitted to whom, where?

There was Saintal Ann who had martyred herself, but for what reason? As far as The Beast could determine, she had done so merely to discover what weapons The Beast held in reserve. What had she said, just before dying? "So others, come after me, would have knowledge of THE GRIMORIE OF TORKBA, and having that knowledge amongst their defenses, when the final march is made against you, see that worlds are saved."

There was the form-changer, Quan Knoba, who had converted to a Bild within the asteroid belt around Mzorki and made his escape from the tailers The Beast had assigned to him.

There was the pod containing the death chrysalis of a form-changer that had been routinely scanned on the brink of the iono-storm off Forrsim-B; hardly strange in that the dissolving winds of the iono-storm had for years been the chief garbage disposal for dead form-changers—except that this particular pod had contained not only a chrysalis, but two humanoids. Of course, by the time The Beast had received the computer readouts, the pod and its contents were beyond recovery, even beyond further, more intensive, scanning. What if the death chrysalis cocooned Quan Knoba? Tracing the point of the pod's origin had been impossible, the pod having apparently made it a mysterious aspect of its flight plan to maneuver through every gravitational pull, every solar draft, every warp, within stella-miles, the result being a jumbled propulsion trail.

What of the humanoids on board?

The Beast found the purported presence of the humanoids of special interest, especially because of the current activity on Antheer-D. Antheer-D was a planet whose creatures had evolved into decidedly humanoid forms after the genetic contri-butions of a marooned Atlan, Stone Hanlic.

Was it a coincidence that The Suicide had seen The Beast

as Ayra Organa, an Atlan, and that Stone Hanlic had been an Atlan, too? If not a coincidence, then what was the meaning behind it—if any?

Was it a coincidence that Mave Stilter, of Antheer-D, had chosen this particular moment in time to receive a Visitation from Stone Hanlic, an Atlan long dead before Mave Stilter had been sprung from her mother's womb? It certainly warranted some looking into—certainly the use of a termic-probe, or two, to check for myron-cube implants, or any other possibilities of genetic interference on the planet.

The Beast would soon go to Antheer-D. There, in its guise of Dielum, The Child Eater, it would see what the Stilter woman was up to—if anything.

Possibly, The Beast should have gone to Antheer-D a long time ago, but the humanoids were of so little consequence that it was quite willing to let a cult of them form around its past ancestor, Astronaut Captain Stone Hanlic. The Beast and Astronaut Captain Hanlic could, after all, have conceivably been related. It was rumored that all Atlans were related since the Great Stella Flood, when the travels of a Blue Star caused the tides to swell and swallow all of Atla but a few isolated mountaintops. Of course, Captain Hanlic had been pre-Gorda Banks, even of the Cowlee class, but who knew to what heights he might have aspired if he hadn't crash-landed on Antheer-D?

The Beast would have possibly held off going, even now, except for the possibility that the events on Antheer-D were somehow connected to the conspiracy. If that were the case, The Beast's adversaries would undoubtedly be expecting it to arrive. The Beast, a willing game player, would certainly have hated to disappoint them.

Besides, it was time The Beast aborted this new cult arising around the Stilter woman. If The Beast could be magnanimous about Captain Hanlic's memory gleaning a few insignificant worshipers on a primitive planet, it wouldn't be quite so generous as far as Mave Stilter was concerned. Whatever genefragment of the Atlan, Captain Hanlic, existed in Mave Stilter's body, it was hardly enough to warrant The Beast willingly surrendering souls to her keeping—even the souls of primitive humanoid low-lifes.

Souls, after all, were the primary measure of The Beast's power.

CHAPER EIGHT

Pg. 502 quote attributed to Dr. Harold Roose, M.D., Ph.D in CAN YOU BELIEVE THESE BLOOPERS? Edited for Watoot Publishers by William Jenxz:

"It is quite inconceivable that any of the various methods of tele-hypnosis or aversion therapy could ever be used to persuade any life-form to commit an act which would, while the subject is conscious, go against his or her moral grain."

THE VOICE CAME to Billy Bob out of the darkness in which he was immersed.

At first, he believed that the voice wasn't even a voice. He had been so long in silence that he felt that the sound, when heard, was nothing but an audio mirage conjured within his sound-deprived brain—if he still possessed a brain.

"You have sinned, Billy Bob," the voice said. "You have sinned mightily, and have been sent here to do penance."

Where was *here?* That was what Billy Bob wanted to know, although he certainly had his suspicions.

"You must suffer to do penance," the voice continued. "Pain is the necessary catharsis. Do you understand?"

Billy Bob wanted no more punishment. Billy Bob was ready to repent his sins on Antheer-D. Surely, he wouldn't be put thorough more of this, would he? He tried to remember if Hell went on indefinitely. Was there no hope for lost souls?

He should have paid more attention to the religious teachings of Astronaut Craig. He should have offered up sacrifices to Dielum, The Child Eater. At the very least, he should have gone to more of the sermons given by the Astronauts in the Little Chapel of the Missle in the Woods. But who would have believed Billy Bob would die at age twenty-five, in the prime of his life?

Had he died when he was supposed to die…say, at forty or—if an oldie—nearer fifty…he would have had time to repent on Antheer-D. Shit, wasn't that the way it was supposed to go: sin in youth, repent in old age? It was simply not bloody fair that he hadn't been allowed days—once his juices had cooled—wherein he could have prepared for death at leisure.

Died—he had died. That was what had happened, wasn't it? It was so hard to remember.

He'd been in bed with Betty Mae, in the bedroom of the cabin he had built for them in the Willate Forest. They should have been safe there. They had walked for days into the wilderness, away from where the townies went hunting, away even from where The Shamal penetrated, on occasional forages, to gather sacred horic boughs for secret ceremonies. Billy Bob and Betty Mae should have been safe!

So, what happened? How had a man and his woman managed to die in their bed? It wasn't as if they were oldies who could have expected to drop off in their sleep. They had both been young-uns, both vibrant, both made healthier by their exposure to the wilderness.

Had Betty Mae died with him?

Had they, in fact, died in bed? Now that he thought of it, they had gotten out of bed, hadn't they?

"It was so difficult to remember!

"You and the Whore of City Pegal sinned!" the voice said, penetrating Billy Bob's brain like a knife penetrating warm butter.

Billy Bob and Betty Mae *had* gotten out of bed.

"Don't!" Betty Mae had warned, reaching to touch his muscled arm. "It's only an animal, Billy Bob. It'll go away."

"That ain't no animal I ever heard!" Billy Bob had answered, beginning to pull his rawhide pants over his naked thighs.

Betty Mae had trembled. He remembered her trembling. She had only come with him into the Forest because he had assured her they would be safe there. Like all townies, Betty Mae had a certain fear about the Willate Forest. She knew that there had been times, in the past, when men were supposed to have actually passed regularly through the tall trees, but those times had long ago gone. Few but The Shamal made trips through the trees any more, except like when word leaked out of Mave Stilter of Wetspur, god-seer, having been blessed with a Visitation. Even then, though, any exodus of pilgrims traveled in a large group, along well-marked trails. None but the very brave, or the very foolish, ever ventured off the beaten paths. That Billy Bob had done just that had had a lot to do with his being branded a scallywag, a no-gooder, and a scoundrel. The townies could think of no reason why an honest, upright gent, should be out wandering in places where he shouldn't have been.

But, Billy Bob had persuaded Betty Mae to come with him.

"We'll make a new life for ourselves, away from all this bullshit these townies are trying to lay on us," he had told her. And, she had come with him if for no other reason than that there wasn't much of a life for her in the town. She had been "had" by more of the local lads than *just* Billy Bob. Everyone knew that, too, even her parents—thus, her nickname: the Whore of City Pegal. So why hadn't her parents been damned happy— instead of so damned uppity—when Billy Bob had come along, willing to take their daughter, soiled as she was by her history of promiscuity, off their hands? Billy Bob suspected that they had still held hope that Betty Mae would settle down and become a respectable housewife. Betty Mae had once confessed that it had been her parents' eagerness to get her married that had sent her off on her whoring in the first place.

So, what had Billy Bob done to deserve all of this? Betty Mae's parents had been such shitheads, surely the First Astronaut Captain couldn't have meant for them to be in any way "honored". Certainly, the First Astronaut Captain wouldn't have instituted any such practice if he had ever met the two of them.

On the other hand, Billy Bob—even discounting any punishment being dealt to him for not honoring Betty Mae's parents—could still think of plenty of reasons why he had ended up in Hell. There was the way he had beaten up his mother after his old man had died. There was the way he had raped the poor Getling girl, and, then, had everyone convinced that she was delusional. There was the stranger he had killed in the woods and robbed of his poke. There was…

Yes, there was no doubt in Billy Bob's mind why *he* was where he was. Knowing the why of it didn't make his suffering any more bearable.

"You may be allowed another chance to redeem your wicked life," the voice said, penetrating the gloom. "Be prepared to make your decision, and quickly, when asked, my son, because a positive answer may be the only way for you to redeem your sorry ill-begotten life."

Was he imagining the voice? He hoped not! Oh, he did hope not. Hell was worse than he could have ever imagined it. If he had to go back and describe to everyone on Antheer-D just what was awaiting them if they didn't repent, he would willingly be the messenger. He would willingly do anything—if only he could have a chance to end his suffering.

"Not yet…not yet," the voice disappointed. "But soon. Very… very soon. You will think about it, won't you, Billy Bob?" Think about it? Think about it? Billy Bob didn't need to think about anything! He had his answer, right then and there.

He tried to open his mouth to give his heart-felt affirmative, but he couldn't get the word out.

"You think about it," the voice said, fading.

"Don't go!" Billy Bob tried to scream, but no sound came out.

Suddenly, there was nothing, again, but the silence—and the pain.

"Ohhhhhh, pleaseeeeese, nooooo!" Billy Bob silently screamed.

The Dzi Scholar watched the naked humanoid jerking in the tormo-tube. He found Billy Bob's muscled body extremely repulsive. All that brown hair covering the young man's chest, abdomen, crotch, and legs, reminded The Dzi Scholar more of an animal than anything else. And for male humanoids to have their genitals so exposed and unprotected was more than a little obscene.

"You're sure you have his pain levels registered correctly?" The Dzi Scholar asked, turning away. He was feeling slightly nauseous.

"You're thinking that it might be a little late for us to come across another recruit at this late date, so let's not spoil this one?" Murlock asked, not duplicating his associate's keen aversion to the creature captured from Antheer-D. He secretly held suspicions that The Dzi Scholars of Rysox thought themselves unduly superior to everyone else. Of course, he didn't say as much. Common causes were often known to make for strange bedfellows. Besides, in the final analysis, this Dzi Scholar was less obnoxious than most.

"It does seem obvious it would be a little difficult to lift another male from Antheer-D at this point in the game, even if we were lucky enough to find another in an isolated area. Organa can show up at any time."

As The Dzi Scholar spoke, he attempted to visualize humanoids (specifically Betty Mae and Billy Bob) mating. How disgusting that must be—primitive beyond comprehension! And, in the end, so much uncertainty as regarded any issue of progeny. Luckily, the plan in operation hadn't counted upon impregnation of the female by the male by way of inept normal humanoid rut.

"We have his pain threshold gauged to the very edge of his limits," Murlock assured, "although we've computed a safety margin to assure there's no stepping over that mark."

"He looks even more revolting than the female."

"He's usually clothed, remember," Murlock answered, wondering why he was defensive. "He's hardly at his best with the steady chemical currents injected throughout him, either."

"The more I see of these paltry creatures, the more assured I am that The Beast plays games with us," The Dzi Scholar said, walking away from the tormo-tube and the writhing male humanoid stretched out inside it

Murlock followed, having his own doubts about the validity of The Suicide's transmitted image.

CHAPTER NINE

Runes from undecipherable tablets found in wreckage of prehistoric spacecraft on asteroid Bega-Mo, Sector variants 2-2-1-4.6ABCZ. Origins of source material unknown at this time.

And forthwith, he came to Jesus and said, "Hail, master!", and kissed him.

"FOOLS!" THE SHAMAL GORF said and grunted, letting the leather flap drop behind him. The flap did very little to muffle the ecstatic shouts and groans of the frenzied multitude outside the sacred enclosure.

His hands were sticky with blood. His robe was splattered with it. His flared nostrils were filled with the sickening sweet smell of it.

He went to a stool and sat down, knowing that his role in this particular charade wasn't over. He would soon go out, again, lift the broadsword, made of the metal come through the flames with the First Astronaut Captain, and offer up another human sacrifice to Dielum. The people would become even more joyous, more excited, and more out of control.

"These stupid, ignorant, and gullible slobs!" Gorf mumbled, knowing his father would have delivered a severe blow to the side of Gorf's head if he'd ever heard his son utter such a blasphemy within the sacred enclosure. But, then, Shamal Yonk, father to Shamal Gorf, had really believed in all of this bullshit.

The poor, stupid, blind, short-sighted schmook!

On his part, Gorf wasn't sure he had ever believed. If he had, he had certainly been cured of any such belief at an early age. Oh, he could continue going through the motions. He could slaughter a whole nursery of Antheerinean children to Dielum, The Child Eater, if that was what these stupid people desired of him. But believe, along with them? Not likely!

Gorf was too close to the inner mechanics of religion to be awed by it. He knew there had been cracks in the statue of Dielum before this new upswing of fanaticism had added enough funds to temple coffers to repair those cracks, wash out the rat shit, put on a new shine. Also, he knew the origins of this religion.

He knew Dielum was no god, and he knew the First Astronaut Stone Hanlic had been nothing more than a man. And the god-seer Mave Stilter was nothing more than a loony bitch caught up in some kind of game that possibly had less to do with the Antheerinean deity than it did with a creature called Murlock from Rysox.

Murlock—although he had come from the sky, like the First Astronaut—wasn't a god, either; he'd never professed to be.

"You are not alone in the universe," Murlock had told Gorf. "Did you really think that you were?"

How many years ago had that been? Gorf had been but eight, not yet even gone through the initiation of manhood—certainly not yet been introduced to "the mysteries". He had been just a child. He might have been malleable enough to have believed Murlock a god, if that creature had set out to convince him of the lie.

"There are worlds out there, amongst the stars, you could never hope to imagine, landlocked on this planet as you are," Murlock had said. "All of those worlds have been created by creatures that might quickly be considered gods by people as primitive and as ignorant as you and yours. But, in fact, there is nothing really so special about any of them."

"And Dielum?" Gorf had asked. For being only eight, at the

time, and the son and heir apparent to the Shamal robes of his father, he was probably as susceptible to believe in a god, then, as he had ever been, or had been ever since.

"I spit on your god Dielum!" Murlock had proclaimed.

The slang expression "spit on" was obviously suggestive enough for the occasion of supreme disgust, but it was a misnomer as far as Murlock was concerned. For Gorf couldn't imagine from where Murlock would have produced any spittle for spitting. The creature had no mouth, his voice coming from a circular diaphragm located in the center of his face, which pulsed noticeably whenever Murlock spoke. His body was shielded by a long cape-like cloak that brushed the ground, so Gorf never had seen what Murlock's body looked like, except that it was connected to the pale green head by a throat that was as thin as a reed where it emerged from the garment neckline.

"Your Dielum is nothing but a form-changer who happened by for repairs on her disabled spacecraft and was spotted by your ancestors while she was in the humanoid guise she'd adopted in order to survive your atmosphere. *She*—for your form-changer was a female, I might emphasize—"

"A female!" Gorf had responded, horror stricken in having initially missed that point.

Dielum, The Child Eater—a woman! A thing, an alien, called a form-changer, a life form for which Murlock seemed to have very little respect.

"Of course, she was quite amused by the adulation of your ancestors, who had immediately taken to groveling in the dirt at her feet. However, there was nothing to keep her here. Even a form-changer wasn't prepared to look upon Antheer-D as suitable for anything but a forced layover."

So, from Murlock of Rysox, Gorf had learned the facts of life, the facts that his people were so ignorant as to have made a god of something as insignificant in the universe as a form-changer.

"Mostly, I must tell you," Murlock had informed, "your race is considered really quite hopeless by the higher intelligences of the universe. On the other hand, I'm convinced your condition is more one of environment than of genetic restrictions. In fact, I'm prepared to prove my theory by educating you, and showing you the wonders of the stars, if, that is, you're prepared to forfeit the price I'm asking. For, nowhere in the universe is something had for nothing."

"And how do I know I'm not just dreaming you?"

"One's dreams are but aspects of the real world in which one lives. Even nightmares are but distortions of the dreamer's reality. When, in your experiences, or in your wildest dreams, have you come upon the likes of me?"

Gorf had boarded Murlock's spacecraft and been lifted far enough to see Antheer-D from the air, to see how insignificant its oblong shape was within the immensity of space.

He had been sworn to secrecy and given The Plan.

"But that is years from now," Gorf had exclaimed in childish dismay. "I will have grown old."

"Twenty-five is hardly old," Murlock had countered. "Certainly, not too old to appreciate the wonders I'm willing to heap upon you for your cooperation. Besides, beyond the boundaries of this planet on which you live, even age can be manipulated, if one only knows the means of doing so."

"But, twenty-five!" Gorf had complained, yet again. When one is only eight, twenty-five is at least another two lifetimes in distance: an eternity when knowing that there were actually creatures in the universe not bound by gravity, or by atmosphere, to the surfaces of a planet like Antheer-D.

"The time will pass fast," Murlock had assured, "and can be well spent preparing you for what you must first do to gain access to the stars. When the time comes, there can be no mistakes whatsoever, or our bargain will be annulled. Do you understand?"

Murlock had left but returned to Antheer-D when Gorf had been eighteen—initiated into manhood—shown the mysteries of Dielum—discovered rat feces in the hollow image of the planet's oldest god.

"You seem surprised to see me, Gorf," Murlock had said, having locked the young man as easily into a stationary state as he had the first time. "Did you, perhaps, suspect you might have dreamed me after all?"

Now, Gorf was twenty-five, and, just as Murlock had predicted, the scenario was being played out as if no one had ever really divined the script years before.

He looked at his hands, again, seeing the red blood that stained them.

"A time will come," Murlock had said, "when you will look at your hands and see them colored a deep vermillion…will look outside your sacred enclosure and see your people dancing in a frenzied whirl around a hollow structure polished and cleaned of its rat shit…and you'll know your life is only beginning."

The flap came open, allowing the moving shadows from the flames outside to dance the inside walls of the small enclosure.

The Assistal Elnic came through, dressed in the guise of the mocdeer, his head sheathed in a mask that sprouted two twelve-pointed horns, his body in skins smelling of blood and booze.

"Dielum is calling for you!" the Assistal Elnic proclaimed, his fervor having dilated his pupils to saucer-size.

"Dielum will call you," Murlock had said, long ago. "There will be fires and dancing, and sacrifices on Antheer-D once again. But you must always remember that Dielum is just a female form-changer who stopped off, here, to repair her space-pod. All she became was a result of what your people have made of her. Of *her*, Gorf. They have made a deity out of a female who stopped off briefly, having assumed a male humanoid image as if she were off to some drag masquerade. Have the strength, then, to rise above any ignorant wonder that makes such a perversion something to be worshiped!"

CHAPTER TEN

"Ayra Organa: Accumulator" from THE HIERARCHY OF TYNBOTHIAN SANCTO-STRUCTURE:

Mylanta, the form-changer, was much surprised to find the Antheerineans had begun a cult in her honor. For, she had completely forgotten, at the time Ayra Organa came to bargain, that she had ever had occasion to set down her pod on that primitive planet.

Mylanta saw no possible use for the worshiping adulations of such a primitive culture (or, of any culture, for that matter), and was eager to accept the bars of Klintosos which Ayra Organa offered in exchange.

It was in this way that Ayra Organa did come to supplant Mylanta, the form-changer, as Dielum (later known as The Child Eater) on the planet Antheer-D, number six in the System Karl, in the Galx-V.

ANTHEER-D GREW SMALLER on the view-screen.

Galun leaned back in the pilo-seat.

He wanted to shut his eyes, but he didn't—not yet. Soon, there would be sleep enough—more complete sleep than even Deep-10 could offer him. And he was ready for it.

He felt old. He felt tired. He felt drained.

It was hard to fathom that it was almost over—at least as far as he was concerned. He had done his part, done it well, if he did say so himself. If he wasn't going to be around to see any sudden realization of the grand plan (would anyone be alive that long?), then, he had never suspected that he would be.

All in all, he figured he had lived a pretty full life. It had been an interesting life to boot; one made livelier by the dangers encountered along the way, although those dangers had—towards the end—become just a bit more of a strain than they were a stimulus.

He activated the scanner, bombarding the planet still on the view-screen. He was confident he had eliminated all evidence of his existence on Antheer-D, but he had to be positive. At this late date, he wanted nothing to put a blot on his record.

The scan came back clean. Antheer-D had once again been left entirely to the Antheerineans. Good riddance to bad rubbish: how Galun looked upon his jettisoning of the planet (for he did consider he was jettisoning it and not vice versa). His dealings with the humanoids had left him vaguely uneasy. They were too close to animal levels for his particular sensitivities. They were too volatile. They were too driven by primitive emotions and instincts which, tireum ago, had been bred out of more civilized species.

How could Ayra Organa have been related to those poor creatures?

Galun shut his eyes, then, opened them; shut them, and opened them again.

He was so tired.

In the old days, when he was searching for the Quass roots on Rysox, he had never gotten tired, or so it had seemed.

He wondered if it was a sign of progressing madness that his mind was more and more taking him back to those early days when he had actually been made more alive by the danger.

He had fought the Miral Bird, back in those old days. He had endured the intrigues of the Rysox Palace Complex, back in those old days. He had tricked the Priestess Paula Wyane into supplying him with the location of a Quass root, back in those old days. He had been recruited to the grand plan by The Dzi Scholar, back in those old days.

All of the good things he could remember happened back in those old days. So, when had it all gone sour? When had his old age crept up on him and made what had once been feelings of courage convert into feelings of genuine fear?

Had it started to go bad after he'd sampled the Quass root? Oh, yes, a long time after that. When he'd sampled the Quass root, he had been willing to risk everything for such adventures offered by The Dzi Scholar's tripping of him into the High Cascade.

Back then, all promises had come true!

Galun had gone back to Delcan Prime. He had spoken in tongues. He had gathered disciples and worshipers. He had seen a religious cult grow up around him. He had collected souls, feeling just a hint of the power possible to those, like The Beast, who collected souls uncountable. He had gone into the Wilderness, like the Stilter woman would soon go into hers. He had seen The Beast transmogrified into the form of Zurl. Galun had been tempted, offered kingdoms to rule as The Beast's vassal, offered fortunes, the likes of which he could have never spent in ten of his lifetimes, offered erotic and exotic pleasures beyond imagination. All offered in exchange for the few souls he had, according to The Beast, stolen from their rightful owner.

What would have happened if he had succumbed to temptation? Taken the offered vassalages? Taken the fortunes? Indulged in hidden passions? Forgotten completely the grand plan which The Dzi Scholar had laid at his feet? Where would he have been today? Surely, not on a spaceship heading for the iono-storm off Forrsim-B!

He shook his head, trying to clear it. His mind was wandering, and he knew it. He was an old Delcan Primenian, gone old before his time, going over his life like one of those legendary Aquailians who were rumored to have re-lived their whole lives in a few sesocndes of drowning. He was analyzing, as old people did, wondering if decisions had been right decisions, wondering how things might have changed if he had reacted differently. It was an old man's habit, a bad habit, at that, because nothing would ever be changed by mentally re-living it. And the chances were more than good that if he had reacted differently to past situations, his fate would have turned out to be far worse than it had. There were, after all, those who said The Beast eventually attempted to renege on every deal it ever made.

"It may offer you treasures beyond your imagination, pleasures untold, cities, or whole planets even, to lord over in its name," The Dzi Scholar had briefed Galun of Delcan Prime, during the days when The Dzi Scholar was the chief Advisor to the Rellixinian Cult on Delcan Prime, in those days when Galun was stealing Delcan Primenian souls from The Beast's coffer, "but be not deceived into thinking that anything offered by it will allow you better than the laboratory needed for the success of the grand plan."

Galun had been gullible. Galun had been sucked in. Galun had become as much of a pawn of The Dzi Scholar as he might have become the pawn of The Beast. Yet, should he complain? Didn't every man have a master? Was there anyone out there in the big wide universe who was completely in charge of his own destiny—with the possible exception of Ayra Organa, The God Killer, The Beast, herself/itself/himself?

Oh, what adventures Galun had known! What heights of ecstasy and courage, and triumphant exhilaration!

He had, after all, confronted The Beast. Not even The Dzi Scholar had done that, at least as far as Galun knew.

Even if The Dzi Scholar had manipulated the strings, it had been Galun who had stood his ground, calling forth inner reserves to say no to the kingdoms, no to the sensuous delights, no to the fortunes. Then, when The Beast had undoubtedly been contemplating more extreme measures to wrest from Galun the souls that The Beast was insisting Galun had stolen, Galun had asked for the laboratory.

Could The Dzi Scholar have successfully gauged the right moment to make that request? Could The Dzi Scholar have carried it off as well Galun had?

In a way, Galun could consider himself far luckier than The

Dzi Scholar, even though The Dzi Scholar might have laughed at any such suggestion. The truth of the matter was that the whole worth of The Dzi Scholar had to be boiled down to the total worth of the individual pieces he was moving on whatever game board he was using. The Dzi Scholar really had little life of his own. When all of his pieces were removed from play, he would be a mere cipher, while Galun, at least, had lived a life to be envied by any who wished for adventure, and danger, and intrigue. Galun had done his thing, and even with The Dzi Scholar whispering cues from the wings, Galun could have muffed his lines. Galun could have—quite on his own—made errors which would have taken him out of the play long before now and completely ruined the plan.

What was he thinking? Did any of these thoughts make any real sense? His mind wasn't functioning accurately as of late. It had been deprived of Deep-10 far too long to be fully functional.

Where was The Dzi Scholar now? What other pieces were moving on the board, other than this piece, now that Galun Rellix of Delcan Prime was about to leave the play?

Galun had never known how his part combined with all the other parts to make The Dzi Scholar an eventual winner. When it came right down to it, Galun didn't even know for sure if The Dzi Scholar wasn't just another puppet, The Dzi Scholar's strings pulled by some other.

Maybe, somewhere along the line, Galun should have stopped to ask himself just who and what The Dzi Scholar really was. Not that it really mattered, one hell of an iota, at this stage.

Oh, it was all too complicated! In the long run, it was best just to coast along and not question too deeply the reasons for anything. Questions only brought more questions. And, there was never anyone readily available who could, or *would,* answer everything to everyone's satisfaction.

After all, what did it matter who The Beast was? Or, if The Beast was male or a female? Or, if Ayra Organa was The Beast in its original form—as the Suicide's transmitted image had indicated? Or, if higher life-forms had ever evolved from humanoids as primitive as those on Antheer-D?

What *was* important was that an individual lived his life as best he could, enjoying it as best he could, realizing there were certain limitations to what could, or could not, be done within the short time span allowed him.

Galun had done that, hadn't he? Loved life. Enjoyed life. Realized limitations. And, if he had done so in ignorance, then what did that matter in the final analysis?

He shut his eyes, despite all of his efforts not to. Maybe it wouldn't really hurt for him to rest for just a moment.

He was so, so tired!

CHAPTER ELEVEN

"On the Birth of the Hero Hercleos" from RECORDED MYTHS AND LEGENDS OF THE MULCONUCULS:

At each Festival of the Mantan Moons, Dryon did assume the form of a gyrlyort and came down from Mt. Oleos to abide for a time in the temple of his name, accepting offerings made there.

And Herla, a priestess of his cult, knowing of the legend that said a child of Dryon by a Mulconuculs female would someday rule Far Lant, and desiring to conceive by Dryon, did bribe the sculptor Minelos to construct a gyrlyort of hollow bronze.

Of such superb workmanship was the gyrlyort by Minelos, it excited Dryon into a lustful frenzy that coupled him with the bronze and with Herla who was hidden within it.

So it was that Hercleos was conceived; the same who slew the Tempte Dragons, performed the Famous Feats, and deposed the Gurleon Kings to assure his heirs the blood-splattered diadem of Far Lant.

MAVE STILTER BID GOOD-BYE to her handmaidens (thirteen at the time) and to her worshipers (countless), telling them they must abide her leaving and await her return. For the time had come, she told them, when she had to retire to the Forest wilderness to pray and fast, as she had been instructed to do by the First Astronaut Stone Hanlic during his Visitation with her.

Her send-off was on a grand scale, attended by The Shamal

Gorf who personally offered sacrifices to Dielum, The Child Eater, and who baptized two more swords from the Stilter basement. There was much wine, and much food, much celebration. Many handmaidens and worshipers got drunk and boisterous.

Mave went bare-breasted and wore a white skirt. She went barefoot and carried a willow wand with which she occasionally reached behind to whip her own back.

She chanted wise sayings of the First Astronaut Captain as she went, sure doing so would make her strong to face the temptations that lay before her in the wilderness. She had to be strong, for although she came to Dielum as someone who had not yet proclaimed her desire to ascend to the godhead, it would be natural of Dielum to assume that was her purpose in gathering followers.

"He will see you as a threat," the First Astronaut Captain had told her. "His worship was in decline in my time, although at no time did I solicit worshippers to deify my person. He will see you as someone likely purposely out to dilute his authority. Therefore, it is of the utmost importance that you seek the blessings of The Shamal Gorf before you go into the wilderness. You must have The Shamal make sacrifices in the old tradition. That way, you can approach Dielum with assurances that you are not his rival, and he will be better disposed toward listening to your proposition without thinking you have ulterior motives. For a god, like Dielum, is apt to get what he wants by bullying, not letting the other side (you) get in much by way of argument. If he immediately bombards you with offers of gifts, treasures, and pleasures, you must merely avoid those temptations, and don't be fooled into assuming you won't be tempted. Eventually, his own proposals rejected, he will become curious to see if you have anything specific in mind. Do not delay too long, though, in telling him. After all, you will have little power against him, for he has others who worship him, under other guises, on other planets, from whom he has received much power. If he feels you can't be bought, or can't be bribed, he will move on to more subtle trickeries that will soon have your mind jumbled and your soul lost forever. For Dielum is most clever."

Night came, and still Mave continued through the Forest. She didn't know where she was going. After a while, she didn't even know where she had been. However, she wasn't afraid, knowing it was the destiny of things that she be there. It seemed completely inconceivable that anything as mundane as a Forest creature would come out and interfere with these workings of a higher, religious plane.

Finally, she did stop, sleeping right where she collapsed in her exhaustion, her head resting on a bed of red moss.

For thirty days and thirty nights, Mave roamed the wilderness. She neither ate berries from the bushes, nor did she drink liquid from the streams, for she had been told fasting would give her the strength she would need to survive her intended rendezvous with Dielum.

"Don't be concerned over the loss of your physical strength, brought on by your ordeal," the First Astronaut Captain had told her. "For no humanoid can ever possess the physical strength necessary to stand up against the likes of Dielum. You must, therefore, store up spiritual, inner strength. In the end, that will be what helps you in successfully achieving your important objective. Do know how much the salvation of your people depends upon your sexual seduction of Dielum, Mave? Dielum is a cruel god who, if allowed, will eventually turn all of the inhabitants of this planet to carrion. For he has long been brooding over how many of his worshipers deserted him for the cult raised up around me. Had he not been occupied on other worlds, he would have been here sooner, doling out his vengeance. Your people have probably survived this long only because he has waited until now before coming."

Mave lost weight, grew so wispy that a strong breeze would have most likely blown her away. Her hair grew matted. Her back and her breast became streaked with welts from self-flagellation and from the whippings given by bush branches when she passed too near.

In the same instance, her beauty was actually enhanced by

her new frailty; her skin almost translucent; her cheekbones accented; her eyes with an inner fire from the religious zeal that burned full-force.

On the evening of the thirty-first day, Dielum—or, rather, Ayra Organa (who was The Beast come in the guise in which the form-changer Mylanta had originally caused the primitives to fall down and worship her on Antheer-D)—did materialize.

The form of Dielum was the form of a man, slightly distorted in that Mylanta hadn't been all that familiar with humanoid anatomy. After all, she had merely been passing through that section of the universe at the time, and she had only heard computa-readings of humanoids as they had once existed on the planet Atla.

In result of Mylanta's on-the-spot and improvised efforts, Dielum was more animal than humanoid in appearance. He stood on two legs, had two arms, two eyes, two ears, one nose, and one mouth. He even had exposed and vulnerable genitalia, but he was animal-like, anyway.

He was hairier than the basest humanoid, the black strands so thick and so numerous that they actually caused a furring of his body from head to foot, with the exception of his face and his buttocks, where his skin was bare. His nose was flattened across the bridge and possessed large and flared nostrils. His lips were thick and could be pulled back, and were, to reveal large teeth with dominant canines. He had a high forehead.

He was large, certainly weighing more than any real humanoid. When he walked, he had a tendency to lean forward, his knuckles at times dragging the ground.

He had first been spotted by the Antheerineans as he had been sampling a local fruit that grew on tall plants with waxy, green, frond-like leaves. The fruit was yellow and called *minoso cradlica,* because it did, in fact, resemble baby cradles of those days, as weaved from the leaves of the plant on which the fruit grew in inverted clusters. The creature was, thus, called *Dielum eactle minoso cradlica;* or, God Eater of Baby Cradles.

He was the first god the Antheerineans knew who was of

living substance and could be converted, via carving (and, later, sculpture) into graven images.

Before Dielum, it was the wind, the rain, the thunder, the lightning, the sun, the moon, the stars that Antheerineans worshiped. They far preferred this new god, which could be so easily duplicated and bowed down to.

In time, Dielum assimilated all the powers attributable to the elemental gods that had come before him. After that, whenever there was a destructive wind, the people prayed to Dielum to stop it. Whenever there was devastating flood, the people prayed to Dielum to contain it. Whenever there was noise from the sky, the people prayed to Dielum to keep it from growing so loud as to permanently deafen them. Whenever the sun was swallowed by the darkness, the people prayed for Dielum to give them back the light. Whenever the moon disappeared from the sky, the people prayed to Dielum to make it return.

When the horror-plague whipped the planet with its sting, killing one Antheerinean in every four, someone recalled that his father had told him how Dielum had originally been known as The Baby Eater (the "Cradle" not remembered). Was it possible Dielum was angry, having sent the plague, because his followers had for so long forgotten his feedings?

Thus, it was that the first Shamal was selected to sacrifice the first child to Dielum, The Baby Eater. Shortly thereafter, the first frost came, and with it a lessening of the killing sickness. The Antheerineans gave thanks to Dielum, not to the cooling weather.

With the emergence of the First Astronaut Captain from the flames, during the Great Visitation, the sacrifices to Dielum ceased, for the Antheerineans, then, had a living god amongst them. Although Stone Hanlic insisted to his deathbed that he was merely a human being, he resembled Dielum just enough so that the Antheerineans couldn't help but suspect him of being the real thing. So, when he said, as one of his wise statements, that one shouldn't kill, the sacrifices were stopped. The Shamal retreated into the Forest, but he didn't protest his exile or the sudden change in religious doctrines, because he, too, could well-note the resemblance, albeit vague, of Stone Hanlic to the original, and he was reluctant to risk heresy by open rebellion.

After the First Astronaut Captain's death, there were no great catastrophes to jerk the Antheerineans out of the more civilized vein wherein the First Astronaut Captain's teachings—and, by then, his mingling genes—had elevated them. Granted, there were a few who were attracted to the more secret and mysterious aspects of worshipping with The Shamal in the woods, but there was little chastisement for those who drifted either one way or the other, since all believed that Dielum and the Great Astronaut Captain were one and the same; which the god-seer, Mave Stilter, had since seemed to confirm.

For Mave had proclaimed (stating it as a direct message from the First Astronaut Captain himself) that The Shamal Gorf should be called from the Forest to begin, again, sacrificing infants.

The Beast, before this, its latest transmogrification into Dielum, had spent many days observing this latest usurper of its power. It was not much impressed by what it saw. If its adversaries had been weak-minded enough to believe that The Beast would take pity on this weak female creature who (because of an infusion of the dominant genes of long-ago Atlan, Stone Hanlic) was now called a humanoid form, they were sadly mistaken. The Beast saw no sign of itself (as Ayra Organa) in the likes of this wretched subspecies. Ayra Organa had been a pure-blood Atlan, human from the very beginnings of her family tree. This barbaric god-seer was human only because her species had mutated into some semblance of that form because of the mating of one civilized man with prehistoric Antheerinean females. Had not Stone Hanlic's desires for survival of his species been as strong within him, as his race's eventual desires for destruction, Antheerineans today wouldn't haven't been humanoid at all.

As far as The Beast was concerned, Mave Stilter could hope for no access to the godhead through it, although it was curious that adversaries, as clever as these had proved themselves to be, in the past, would be so anxious to lay claim to an eyesore in space like Antheer-D. The place was so primitive that power derived from the combined worship of the whole population of the planet was hardly worth the efforts made to secure it.

Did The Beast's enemies see Antheer-D as merely the foot they needed in the door? As something upon which to build? After all, they had proved that they were willing to wait, extending their battle plan over generations. Whatever, The Beast somehow doubted they had as much patience as it did.

It was actually tempted to allow Mave Stilter ascension to the godhead, just to see where The Beast's enemies went from there. It would be quite easy for it to move in later and steal back from this creature whatever The Beast now handed over to her on a silver platter.

Before transmogrification to Dielum, The Beast had scanned the planet with termic probes, searching for the possible introduction of myron cubes, or other such forms of genetic interference on Antheer-D. It had found none.

It had scanned for foreign life-forms, it had found none of those, either, although there were certain memory fragments within some Antheerinean minds, in general, on the genes of the Stilter woman, specifically, that recalled blue-skinned monsters once appeared on the planet's surface, although those memories seemingly were hold-over from ancestors so far removed from Mave's generation that they could be accountable to several benign sources.

One: to pure imagination—primitive minds were known for their susceptibility. Conjurations of the id could, in fact, seem so real that they were possibly accepted as such. Two: to an alien life-form present at one time or another, since many life-forms had once gathered samples for planetal zoos from just such out-of-the-way planets as this one—before, that is, there was the Lantytic Counsel to lay down prohibitions. Three: to conspirators who had begun setting the stage for this performance many, many tireum ago, which, since The Beast had detected suspicions of conspiracy long before now, might well have been the case.

Number three could certainly not be discarded, not at this point in the game.

If Mave Stilter were a vital part of some active conspiracy, she certainly looked the part that had been written for her. The Beast had to deal with countless of these so-called Messiahs, over the years; creatures so mentally unbalanced they thought they were hearing the call to deification. In most cases, they were easily handled, their religious zeal cooling when it was seen just what they could achieve without being bothered by the power politics of gathering souls. Since so few of them could hardly know of the erktic energy radiated by each existing life-form, or how that energy could be captured, harnessed, and put to use, they were usually quite willing to barter those souls in their possession, receiving in payment more tangible items, like gold, silver, Klintosos bars…

If they were interested in power, it was usually on a lesser plane; a need easily satisfied by giving them rule over physical shells and physical structures, while they forfeited the spiritual by becoming vassals to The Beast.

On occasion, rarities would turn up who—like Galun of Delcan Prime—intuitively seemed to know the value of power to be had by accumulating followers, while simultaneously knowing they weren't really equipped to play in the big-league battle for souls. These special players entered the game merely to barter with those who had the power for things wanted but which would have been unobtainable under normal circum-stances. In Galun's case, he had surrendered his expanding cult of followers on Delcan Prime in order to obtain his laboratory.

In regard to this latter group (Galun of Delcan Prime included therein), The Beast had taken to thinking that, maybe, a sudden appreciation of power to be had, and used for bartering, had nothing whatsoever to do with intuition. Was there, in fact, someone, someplace, cluing in the likes of Galun of Delcan Prime, in order to collect tools, along the way, with which to launch an attack against The Beast that had some chance of victory? If so, who?

Oh, The Beast could enter the Calyxine Crystal and have the answer spelled out in no uncertain terms, but there was danger inside the Calyxine Crystal, even for the Beast. Besides, at that moment of his materialization on Antheer-D as Dielum, The Child Eater, The Beast was confident that his knowledge, had from the Gorda Bank, would be more than sufficient to put this latest challenge to rest.

Mave Stilter wasn't surprised to witness the appearance of Dielum. After all, she had been expecting him. The First Astronaut Captain had said he would come.

Nor was she as revolted by his appearance as she might have been before her fasting and prayers (the latter made to the First Astronaut Captain) had filled her with the religious fervor that could make even Dielum appear less horrendous than he really was.

"Well, how goes it with the thief, Mave Stilter?" Dielum asked, leaning back against a rock and facing the god-seer of Antheer-D. Simultaneously, he emitted tele-beams to make sure they were alone.

"I am no thief," she told him, although her voice came out hardly decipherable, since she had talked to no one for thirty-one days and had chapped and swollen lips as a result of taking neither food nor water.

"No matter what *you* call it, *I* call it robbery," Dielum said, waving one big-knuckled hand. "But you are lucky. I haven't come to debate semantics. I have come prepared to be magnanimous."

"But—" Mave began, but Dielum didn't let her finish.

"See what I'm prepared to give you for my property?" he said.

The scenery around Mave blurred. When it cleared, it had changed composition.

Mave found herself standing in a room surrounded on all sides by large tele-screens. Within the screens there appeared—

one after the other—all of the cities, towns, and villages on Antheer-D. Mave saw the buildings, everything that was in those buildings, including the people.

"You want these?" Dielum asked, for he was standing beside Mave in the room. "I'll give them to you. All of this can be yours, given so that you needn't go through the bother of stealing it. All you need to do is bow before me and kiss the ring on my hand. He showed her a ring on the middle finger of his hairy right hand which Mave hadn't noticed there before.

"Have I ever claimed that I wanted the adulations heaped upon me?" Mave asked.

At the same time, she was seeing, flashed on the screens, all the people who had ever slighted her, said mean things about, or to her, laughed at her, or mocked any member of her family. She saw Susan Smith, Barbara Jacoby, Sally Winn, who had never pretended to like her, or to believe she had the power in her to see gods, although those girls had since changed their tunes. They had caused much hurt in their time, and Mave was tempted to get her revenge on them.

"Just think," Dielum said, reading her reactions easily. "Now, you can finally repay old debts, right old wrongs, mend old hurts, via the power I'm offering, because all of those people, there, will be forced into doing your bidding. All of them, Mave. Even Susan, and Barbara, and Sally. They will finally know for sure that you had the power all along that they once doubted you as having. You'll be able to show them, once and for all, that they were fools!"

"Nooooo!" she moaned, realizing suddenly that she had been tempted by the offer. After all, what effort would it have taken to kiss Dielum's ring? Hardly any. To know such rewards! To know such satisfaction!

"Reconsider, Mave," Dielum persuaded. "It is power I can offer you, the likes of which you could have never dreamed possible when you started upon this little crusade of yours."

"Noooooooo!" Mave moaned again, struck cold to the very pit of her being, because she had thought herself so strong and had ended up so weak in the final testing.

How could she possibly hope to carry this through, when Dielum could so easily probe her mind and offer up gifts to tempt her avarice?

"No?" Dielum pondered. "Then, maybe, something more along these lines?"

The screens faded. The environment changed.

Mave was suddenly in the room of a luxurious house. There were rich rugs, crystal chandeliers, beautiful paintings, plush furniture.

Dielum pointed through glass doors that gave access to a swimming pool on the edge of a manicured lawn.

As Mave watched, a naked man came up out of the pool and reached for a towel on a nearby chaise longue.

Mave blushed, embarrassed by the sight of the handsome young man. On the other hand, she couldn't turn her gaze away from him. He had to be one of the best-looking men Mave had ever seen; the kind of man Mave used to dream about whenever she had begun running through the list of cousins available as prospective mates.

Dielum extended a hairy arm toward the glass doors. The doors slid open, and the young man by the pool turned, his light green eyes focused on the young girl beside Dielum.

"Mave," the young man said. "How very nice for you to have come."

He came toward her, into the house, dropping the towel on the flagstones behind him.

He had blond hair, like the sun. He had tanned skin stretched sensuously over his well-delineated physique.

He extended his hand, smiled. He had white teeth. He had a dimple in each cheek. He had a cleft in his chin.

"This is Jeffrey, Mave," Dielum said. "He's been waiting for you."

Mave reached out her right hand, letting Jeffrey have it. The handsome blond boy smiled at her, turning her hand to kiss its palm.

Mave was suddenly naked with him in a large bedroom with mirrors on its ceiling, walls, and, even, on its floor.

"I have so many wonderful things to show you, Mave," Jeffrey said, his body hard and warm against her flesh. "I've waited so, so long for this moment."

She didn't want to leave him, the bed, the bedroom, the luxurious house, even though she knew she—somehow—had to do just that.

She *had* to get away!

"Why?" Jeffrey asked. He had answered her thoughts, without her having had to voice them.

Certainly, as far as Mave knew, there was no one on Antheer-D who read minds, there was no one who looked quite like Jeffrey looked, there was no place that looked quite like this place....

"No!" she shouted, breaking away from the boy's encircling arms.

"Come on, Mave," Jeffrey cajoled. "Think of the fun the two of us can have; days and nights of sexual bliss. After all, what is the alternative?"

"No...no...no...no," she insisted and scrambled out of the bed, to cringe against a mirrored wall.

Jeffrey began to fade. The room began to fade.

Did Mave really want them gone?

His handsome form, and that of the room, began to strengthen in intensity.

Mave's thoughts, alone, were bringing them back.

She crossed her forearms over her face, shut her eyes.

"Leave me!" she commanded.

When her arms came down, the house, the bedroom, and Jeffrey were gone. She was back in the Forest.

Dielum was there, his hairy arms folded across his hairy chest. His thick lips were drawn back across his teeth, showing his canines to frightening advantage.

"Maybe, we could move things along a bit faster if you would come right on out and tell me just what it is you have in mind,"

Dielum suggested.

So, Mave told him.

CHAPTER TWELVE

Punch line from a sick joke making the rounds of Dicorium coffee houses:

"Congratulations! You're the father of a ten-pound head!"

FOR A LONG TIME NOW, Betty Mae had known no pain. Peacefulness had followed on the tail of her most painful period remembered. For days, weeks, months on end, she had felt as if her body was going to explode, to splatter her guts to the far winds. She had felt as if devils were literally in residence within her belly, living there, chewing away at her insides. Her stomach had felt like a boil, growing larger and larger, until, finally, in a peaking of her pain, Betty Mae assumed the canker could have only burst its accumulated pus out between her legs. With the exit of that pus had gone her pain. It hadn't returned—not yet, anyway. In fact, she was afraid to admit—even to herself—that the pain was over, for fear that it would come again.

She drifted. She enjoyed drifting. It was such a pleasure, after all she had gone through. In fact, if she hadn't known better, she might have assumed that she had completed her penance in Hell and had arrived finally in Haven Max.

Occasionally, she was aware of hands on her. But they were no longer probing hands, no longer wielding torture implements. They massaged her tired muscles. They bathed her flesh in soothing warm water and massaged it with sweet-smelling balm.

All the smells of the place had improved.

She thought she could sometimes hear birds.

Oh, but she would have done anything to keep her world just as it was. Then, though, one day, she opened her eyes and discovered a world even better.

She pulled back the lone sheet that covered her, and she sat up on the edge of the bed, looking around her.

The room was clean and simply furnished, like the bedroom she had known as a child in her parents' home in City Pegal. For a minute, she thought she was back in the home of her childhood.

All of this time, had she merely been experiencing a childhood nightmare?

Nope. Despite first impression, this wasn't any bedroom she'd known before.

"Billy Bob?" she questioned, finding it funny, after so long, to hear her own voice. "Billy Bob?"

She had heard a noise; not then, but at some other time, some other place, with Billy Bob who had heard the noise, too.

"That ain't no animal I ever heard!" Billy Bob had said. He had gotten up out of bed to go look.

Betty Mae had gotten up to go with him.

Together, they had crept down the stairs. Billy Bob had opened the back door.

They had died, right then and there, in a flooding of blinding blue light. Killed by whom? Killed by what? Betty Mae didn't know by whom, or by what. She did know that she had died and had gone to Hell, now to Haven Max. Didn't she?

At this very moment, she didn't feel dead. She pinched her arms, feeling pain. She didn't pinch for long. After all, she had endured too much pain, inflicted by others, to deliver agony to herself.

She spotted a robe on the back of a nearby chair. She reached for it, slipped it on.

She went to the window, pulling back the curtains.

It could have been Antheer-D, out there, but, somehow, she

knew with certainty that it wasn't.

* * * * * * *

"IS IT PERFECTLY CLEAR?" Murlock asked from behind a screen-shield.

"Perfectly," Billy Bob answered, on the other side.

"Do we have to go over it again?"

"I've got it," Billy Bob replied. "I've got it! I've got it!"

Murlock glanced nervously at The Dzi Scholar. He clicked off the PA system to Billy Bob in the other room.

"He seems a bit nervous, no?" The Dzi Scholar stated, checking through the transparent shield that allowed him a visual, but not vice versa. He would have said more, but, at this stage, there was little point in saying it. They were irrevocably committed with their cast of characters, Billy Bob included. There was no turning back.

"He's bound to be nervous," Murlock commented. "His salvation depends on this, as far as he's concerned, doesn't it?"

"Hmmmmm," The Dzi Scholar replied noncommittally. His opinion of Antheerineans over the last few days had declined considerably, and he had never thought all that much of them in the first place. He wasn't all that sure it had been smart to have so much of the grand plan hinge upon so many unstable Antheerineans. Granted, Mave Stilter had surprised by coming through with flying colors in her sexual seduction of and impregnation by Dielum. Even Betty Mae's pregnancy, via artificial insemination, and delivery had been pulled off without a hitch. But, there was the chance that expecting three out of three to go as well was expecting a little too much. The odds against Billy Bob succeeding had to be disproportionately one-sided—against!

"The readouts have given us nothing about which we need be overly concerned," Murlock assured.

"Let's get on with it, then," The Dzi Scholar said.

After all, there were other plans if this one didn't work. But those alternatives would take longer to carry out. Not that The Dzi Scholar had any real aspirations of seeing the whole grand plan through to its end. The prime disadvantage was having as an adversary someone (something?) whose life span and knowledge presently surpassed those of anyone and anything known to exist within these trying times.

CHAPTER THIRTEEN

Runes from undecipherable tablets found in wreckage of prehistoric spacecraft on asteroid Bega-Mo, Sector variants 2-2-1-4.6ABCZ. Origins of source material unknown at this time:

For God so loved the world....

IF BILLY BOB HAD DOUBTED, even for a moment, that he had died and gone to Hell, suffered, been offered salvation and passage to Haven Max (which he never doubted), then he would have been convinced, beyond a shadow of a doubt, by what had happened to him once returned to Antheer-D. For, how else, except via divine intervention, could he have found access to the sacred enclosure of The Shamal, and, then, had Shamal Gorf, himself, turn over a baby in exchange for the other?

That was exactly what had happened.

"We have set up this final trial for you, offering every chance of your succeeding," the voice in Hell had told him. "But do not think for a moment that there is no element of danger, because if you are discovered by anyone who doesn't know your mission, you will be mistaken for someone still alive, will die, yet again, horribly, as if you lived, and will be returned to Hell to begin penance all over again."

Billy Bob hadn't questioned this final trial chosen for him, although he hadn't helped wondering at its strangeness: one baby exchanged for another. But, then, his was not to reason why.

He had gone to sleep in Hell and had awakened on Antheer-D, in the strange bedchamber with the baby. It had been dark, as he had been told it would be. But, when living, he had been used to moving through the Forest in darkness. And, the way he had to follow with the baby, from that bedchamber, had been drummed into him in Hell, re-enforced each time by jolts of searing pain whenever he had failed to register the directions properly.

The baby had seemed dead, but he had checked it for a pulse and had been reassured. He had thought the baby possibly drugged. Whatever—it had made his job all that much easier. There would have been greater danger had it cried, although it was doubtful anyone would have heard its squeals once Billy Bob had drawn near The Shamal compound in the Forest.

There had been a celebration in progress. Billy Bob, who, before dying, had heard rumors that the god-seer was soon to instigate a return to giving human offerings to Dielum, had suspected what those festivities were about—which *would* have explained his delivery of the baby he had carried in the sling on his back—which *wouldn't* have explained the baby he had picked up in exchange.

On second thought, the explanation was probably that the babies really didn't matter at all. They were merely means to achieve an end. What mattered was that Billy Bob was being tested. He could just as easily have been asked to come back to Antheer-D and exchange coats or ceremonial rattles.

He had found the hidden passage right where he had been told it would be. He had entered it, walked until he had reached the wall. He had waited, had heard sounds, and had seen the wall slide back.

He had never seen The Shamal before, but he had known him immediately when he'd seen the blood-splattered robe, the blood-stained hands, the....

"Hurry, you fool!" Shamal Gorf had instructed, roughly turning Billy Bob around so the religious man could hurriedly remove the baby without Billy Bob having to remove the harness.

Billy Bob had felt the release of weight as the baby had been drawn free of the restraining straps. He had turned to see Shamal Gorf move quickly with the child to a far corner. When The Shamal had returned, he'd had another child, or, maybe, it was the same one—for all Billy Bob knew. Didn't all babies look alike?

"Turn around, damn it!" Shamal Gorf had commanded. He had been impatient.

The Shamal had positioned the baby in the straps; his fingers had been made clumsy by his nervousness. He'd had every reason to be nervous. If any of those frenzied worshipers, out by the fire, had known what he was doing, they would have torn him limb from limb.

"Go!" he had dismissed Billy Bob.

The young man passed back through the passageway, out through the exit into the Forest. Through the trees, he could see the festivities around the fire.

Who was the bare-breasted woman in the white skirt, collapsed by the altar, weeping? Why did she beat herself incessantly with a willow wand? What strangeness had apparently come to possess his people since Billy Bob's moment of dying? Already he felt completely separate from this world he had left behind him.

Soon, very soon, he would leave Hell behind him, too, having purchased his way to Haven Max.

He returned to the bedchamber in the Forest, placing the baby on the covers of the bed. He pushed all the proper buttons.

"Quite easy, Billy Bob, because the buttons will be alphabetically labeled," he had been told. "Just punch out your name: B-I-L-L-Y B-O-B."

He left the room, turned away from it.

"Do not turn back, Billy Bob. Do not look back. To do either will mean certain disaster for you. Understand?"

He headed back to The Shamal compound. He had two more

things to do, there, before he could achieve his long-awaited salvation.

Behind him, the spacecraft lifted, rising swiftly to seemingly nothingness in the darkness of the engulfing night sky.

CHAPTER FOURTEEN

From THE SAYINGS OF PHILOSOPHER GARY FELKS, edited by Harold Winesap, published in paperback by Feldspar Press:

"More lives have been lost in the name of religion than have been lost in the name of any other cause fathomable within the total expanse of our universe."

SUCCESSFULLY SUBSTITUTED for Mave Stilter and Dielum's baby, who had been scheduled to die, Betty Mae's baby died, instead.

The crowd went mad with excitement. The stupid fools thought the son of their god had just perished to obtain them forgiveness for all past sins.

Mave Stilter collapsed. Silly bitch! Had anyone bothered to tell her that she would be expected to offer up her son by the form-changer, after once having proclaimed her child the son of that god?

Shamal Gorf faced the crowd, showed them the bloody blade of the fourth sacred broadsword from the Stilter basement. The multitude went wild. If they, including Mave Stilter, only knew the baby sacrificed was the wrong one (or, the right one—depending, The Shamal supposed, upon whom had written he script)!

Where, Shamal Gorf wondered, had Murlock found the Antheerinean who had delivered the substitute baby to Gorf's doorstep? Or, had the young man really been an Antheerinean at all? Had he been a form-changer, made up to look Antheerinean? That was certainly one possibility, unless the courier had been offered much the same as Shamal Gorf to take part in this little charade.

Shamal Gorf had been tempted to ask the young man what the youth had been promised by Murlock. Had the courier, like Shamal Gorf, been informed that the whole religious ceremony was meaningless, anyway?

"Meaningless!" Murlock had emphasized to Shamal Gorf. And now Shamal Gorf believed it even more. How could there be any real religious significance to these present proceedings, when they had been written out—word for word, action for action—by creatures from another world?

After all, Shamal Gorf had known even before Mave Stilter that a god-seer would arise and go into the wilderness to return impregnated by Dielum.

That Dielum was a female, the form-changer, Mylanta, had admittedly caused Shamal Gorf a good deal of initial confusion.

"A form-changer achieves a complete physical change, for as long as that change lasts," Murlock had patiently explained. "As a humanoid male, she is quite capable of passing on her genes to any female of your species. You are confused only because you are not acquainted with the physiology of other, more complex life-forms than your own. But that familiarity will come to you, in time, after you have been removed from the smothering influence of your present environment. Trust me."

"But if the form-changer can, as a humanoid male, perform the male sexual role, is she *really* female?"

Murlock had sighed, as if dealing with a child who refused to accept the readily obvious.

"No matter what she becomes," Murlock had said, assuming the demeanor of a teacher ready to try one more time, "Mylanta must always revert to what she was in her beginning. Her being a male and humanoid for a minute, for an hour, for a day, for a year, for a tireum, for whatever the time span, doesn't make her a male or humanoid. In the final analysis, she is only what has been imprinted upon her original gene helix: a female form-changer. That is the one unavoidable constant."

"And she still lives?" Shamal Gorf had asked. The idea of someone living that long had boggled his imagination—still boggled it, for that matter.

"Have I not told you that age can be controlled by those who but have the key to make it so?" Murlock had said.

The screams of the crowd brought Shamal Gorf back from his momentary reverie.

He put down the broadsword. He nodded for the Assistal Elnic to prepare the sacrament for the crowd; flesh of their god's flesh; blood of their god's blood.

Shamal Gorf had many questions but had been assured there would be many answers as soon as this was over and done—which would soon be the case.

"He has died for your sins!" Shamal Gorf proclaimed.

The crowd went wild, animalistic. No wonder more civilized life-forms, like Murlock, looked upon Antheerineans as animals. That's what they were. Stupid animals, at that! How could any rational human being actually be led to believe he could receive salvation via the death and cannibalistic eating of a child—any child?

Then, again, having seen what he had seen, Shamal Gorf had no doubts, whatsoever, that a successful religious cult would bloom out of this, made more popular by the idea that god had sent down his son as living flesh and blood. Mave Stilter's supposed child had managed to unite the cult of her ancestor, the First Astronaut Captain, with the cult of Dielum, form-changer. And the bastard religion which had resulted would undoubtedly flourish, only a few knowing that it was based on a fraud.

What did Murlock want with the baby produced by Mave Stilter and the form-changer? Alas, that was yet another question whose answer would have to wait until Murlock rescued Shamal Gorf from this planet of ignorant, cannibalistic fools.

Shamal Gorf turned to leave the altar, taking one final look at Mave Stilter whose ancestor, the First Astronaut Captain, had said: *Do not kill.*

Puppets! All puppets! Mave Stilter would have been well to dry her tears. It was through no fault of hers what had happened. It was through no fault of any Antheerinean. They were all just pieces on the board, being moved here and here for the enjoyment of—

Shamal Gorf had a sudden shudder, caused by a disturbing thought. How superior could a race be who, purely for its own amusement, would maneuver primitives, like the Antheerineans, to such animalistic extremes?

The crowd danced in more frenzied disorder about the fire. Eyes glazed over, hair awry, mouths slobbering saliva, flesh sweaty and smelling of human sweat and human blood.

Gorf threw back the flap and entered the dimness of the sacred enclosure.

Billy Bob stabbed him, driving the blade of a sword deep into The Shamal Gorf's guts and all of the way out the other side.

While The Shamal danced his death spasms on the ground, Billy Bob took a dagger and quickly sliced a deep gash across his own throat, believing, as he did so, as he had been told, that he had just paid the final price for his entrance into Paradise.

CHAPTER FIFTEEN

Runes from the undecipherable tablets found in the wreckage of prehistoric spacecraft on asteroid Bega-Mo, Sector variants 2-2-1-4.6ABCZ. Origins of source material unknown at this time:

...And Jesus said unto her, Neither do I condemn thee; go, and sin no more.

BETTY MAE WAS HAPPY—happier than she had ever been in her life; happier than she had ever been with Billy Bob. But, then, she had come to wonder if she had ever really loved Billy Bob at all. In retrospect, he had merely offered her an escape from her parents who had never loved her, from boys who not only had no respect for her but who had never had any intentions of marrying her. Not even Billy Bob had offered marriage. What he had offered was a place where she could go and get away from everyone and everything—except for Billy Bob and *his* "thing".

Well, Betty Mae was away from everything now. She was away from parents, boys, City Pegal, and Billy Bob. She was even away from Antheer-D. She felt more content than she had ever felt. She felt protected and safe.

She knew her world was limited. She knew there were boundaries beyond which she couldn't go. Whenever she got close to those limits, a soothing voice would come from seemingly nowhere and say: "Please do not proceed farther." She never ventured to find out what would happen if she did proceed farther. She had plenty of space the way it was.

She wasn't lonely, because she had Parker.

She wasn't too sure from where Parker had come. One morning, he had just been there, lying in a crib by Betty Mae's bed when she had awakened. Betty Mae knew Parker was a little boy because...well, there was just no mistaking *his* thing. She knew his name was Parker, because he had a tiny wristband with his name printed clearly on it.

He was an extremely attractive little baby. He had blue eyes, although all babies had blue eyes, at first. Betty Mae really had no idea how old Parker was. He had a little pug nose, a cute little mouth, and was lean without being skinny, husky without being fat. He had dark black hair and a surprisingly large amount of it, too. His lush eyelashes and dark brows enhanced the light blue coloring of his eyes.

He was a good baby, hardly ever crying except when he was hungry. There was plenty of food. For some reason (Betty Mae merely accepting it as being one more miracle of the place), her breasts gave milk on which the baby seemed to thrive.

There were diapers, rattles, a bassinet, stuffed toys, all appearing during one night or another, as did the food.

There was plenty of sunshine, although Betty Mae could never really locate any source of the light. It seemed to appear from everywhere at once, illuminating a sky that stayed free of clouds during the day and free of all but a few stars at night. None of the stars looked in the least familiar—but, then, why should they? Betty Mae knew she was nowhere she had ever been before. It no longer worried or frightened her.

Even when she wasn't occupied with Parker (which admittedly wasn't very often), she was never at a loss as to what to do with herself. Every morning, she was like a kid, waking up on First Astronaut's Day to find gifts beneath every tree. There were needles and threads and materials with which to sew, and, soon, Betty Mae was making clothes for both herself and for the baby. There appeared a swing one morning on the limb of the big tree just outside the front door. Swinging always made little Parker laugh. He was such a happy little baby.

In the beginning, there were books, besides the ones stuffing the shelves downstairs. But, Betty Mae had never been very good at reading, and she glanced so briefly at the new offerings that the books quit appearing as suddenly as they had begun. At first, there were magazines, too, but all of them—from Antheer-D, as they were—were dated prior to Betty Mae's death, and there were no replacements. She really wasn't all that interested, anyway. Her whole world had shrunk to her home, her yard, the baby. What went on elsewhere in the universe, what went on back in Antheer-D—wherever Antheer-D now was—was of no consequence to her whatsoever.

She had even quit wondering where Billy Bob was, or what kind of penance he was being forced to go through, or if he had been allowed his own little slice of Paradise.

Sitting in the rocking chair, on the front porch, Parker's greedy mouth sucking up a storm on one teat, small birds singing in the trees, a warm breeze blowing in from the woods, Betty Mae could hardly recall that long, long period of time in which she had been subjected to such horrible torment and pain.

She felt clean. She felt revitalized. She felt reborn.

If she wasn't actually in Haven Max, she couldn't imagine that place being much better than where she had been allowed, finally, to find her peace.

CHAPTER SIXTEEN

Garulian truism; source unknown:

There is nothing new in the universe.

THE ROOM WAS ALL WHITE, with just a splash of gold—so white, so blinding, that when he opened his eyes, he, immediately, had to shut them.

There was a feeling of electricity in the air around him, the kind of electricity that caused clothes to stick to bodies, fur to stand on end, sparks to arc between metal and fingertips.

Iono-storm off Forssim-B?

No!

He had fallen asleep!

His eyes came open, again, successfully challenging the renewed assault of the glare. He was sitting in a chair, in no way physically bound, but, still, unable to move.

"Ah, Galun."

He turned toward the voice immediately recognized as the same has had been registered on the mind's-eye of Drawler, The Suicide.

"You!" he said, knowing it was Ayra Organa, even though he'd not seen her in this particular transmogrification.

"Yes," admitted Ayra Organa; The Beast; The God Killer; Dielum of Antheer-D; Zurl of Delcan Prime….

"We've met before," she reminded him of the time and place, although he didn't need reminding. "Maybe you prefer me as

Zurl," she said. "Your opinion of humanoid life-forms, I've come to realize, isn't all that high."

At that moment, she might appear as a humanoid, but she was a humanoid like none Galun had ever seen.

She had honey-colored hair that tumbled in cascades of flowing curls to parenthesize her oval face. She had golden eyes, flecked with black, that were shielded by thick blonde lashes. She had lips tinted a light gold. Her voluptuous body was draped in a sensuously clinging—and highly revealing—gown of rich and varied golden hues.

"Where am I?" he asked, although he wasn't at all sure he really wanted to know.

"Not in your laboratory," she assured him, with a laugh of genuine amusement that revealed an even row of white teeth. She shook her mane of honey-colored hair. It caught the light and held it, giving her head a deceptive nimbus. "Your laboratory stands empty, waiting for someone else to arrive to renew experimentations in selective breeding of Antheerineans."

Did she know, then? Had she probed his brain for its secrets? Had he failed, at the very last minute, by slipping into Deep-10?

"Yes, you *did* sleep soundly," Ayra Organa told him, able to read his every thought."

His head whirled with a thousand unasked questions, and Ayra Organa picked them, one by one from his brain, and read them.

"So many questions, Galun," she said, crossing her arms across her full breasts. She wore golden armbands, a golden collar around her neck, and golden starbursts in her ears. "And, you shall have your answer to every single one."

Nervously, he eyed her, detecting something in the tone of her voice that told him she was merely playing with him like a dac played with a moule. She could have killed him, long ago, drained his mind during Dream-10 and sent him into the iono-storm. He would have never known he had betrayed the grand plan. It would have been more humane had he not known. This way, he knew he had failed, and that, because of him, the whole plan was compromised.

"See what, other than I, is available to answer your questions?" Ayra Organa asked. She motioned toward the far wall which revolved a giant crystal cocoon into the room. The facets of the crystal immediately caught the light and refracted it into rainbows that splattered everything in sight.

Ayra Organa flashed another smile: triumphant, yet pitying in the same instance.

"You're not familiar with the Calyxine Crystal, though, are you?" she said. "You are possibly even surprised to learn that it, like I, survived Cataclys IX. Your knowledge of survivors seems presently limited to me and the Gorda Bank."

"A Gorda Bank has survived, then?" He thought of how much greater would be the chances of the plan succeeding if her enemies could get but one of their numbers plugged into the Gordo Bank and exposed to the knowledge made available to the early Atlans.

Ayra Organa read his thoughts and was amused by them.

"You think the Gorda Bank will help your cause?" she asked and laughed. "What if I were to tell you there will be a man, one day, who will willingly plug into the Gorda Bank? For, I have seen him."

"You've seen him?"

"I, too, sometimes have questions," she said. She walked— glided actually—back and forth in front of him. "Occasionally, I even come to the Calyxine Crystal for answers, although, I must admit, I'm envious of the insight you'll soon possess."

Galun would have commented on the strangeness of her comment, but he was distracted by a dramatic movement of Ayra Organa's right arm toward the crystal cocoon.

The Crystal halved, as if its front and back had been joined by invisible hinges. Inside was nothing but a crystal bench.

"Why don't you change seats, moving to the more informative one?" Ayra Organa suggested.

Galun's body responded without his ability to control it. It came up out of the chair and floated across the floor to, and into, the Calyxine Crystal, where, gently, but forcibly, it was deposited upon the crystal bench.

"We could sit and chat for awhile longer, but why waste any more time?" Ayra Organa said. "After all, all the answers I want from you, I've already scraped from your brain...."

He groaned in response. Ayra Organa only smiled indulgently, as if genuinely bemused that he might have thought it would be otherwise. Then, she continued.

"...and you shall soon have more answers than you have the capacity for."

Suddenly, she was gone, dissolved, disappeared, without a trace, without a sign, in the blink of an eye.

The door of the Calyxine Crystal came slowly shut, sealing Galun inside.

The interior was sprinkled with refracted light, as had been the room outside.

For awhile, Galun thought nothing was happening. After all, there were no evident sounds, no evident visuals.

Then, suddenly, he knew that The Beast knew everything. He didn't think, suspect, even fear that it knew. He *knew* it knew.

It knew about the experiments Galun had done in his lab, locating the Stilter family on Antheer-D whose selective breeding would finally deliver up a woman, Mave, whose gene makeup was as near as possible to the original contributor, Stone Hanlic.

It knew Mave had been purposely mated with The Beast (in The Beast's male form of Dielum of Antheer-D), in order to farther reach for a duplicate of that original Atlan species—all of whom had died except Ayra Organa.

It knew Betty Mae's baby had been substituted in the Antheerinean sacrifice of the god-child.

It knew the baby of The Beast and Mave was alive.

It knew...it knew...it knew....

It knew, and it had made plans all its own, because it was lonely for its own kind, lonely for those who had rushed to destruction in the lemming race that had left it behind.

It would use all of them!

And, Galun saw the how: the plans, the betrayals, the murders, the battles, the wars, and the generations yet to come that would spill their blood across the universe in pursuit of a cause they couldn't possibly achieve.

He saw even more than The Beast had ever seen, and, then, he died.

For something was ever had for nothing!

And, in the Calyxine Crystal, it was life itself which was the currency paid by those daring to experience total knowledge.

ABOUT THE AUTHOR

WILLIAM MALTESE, an international best-selling author of novels, short stories, including his popular Wildside Mystery Double, *Incident at Aberlene* and *Incident at Brimzinsky* (Spies & Lies #1-2), has published (under various pseudonyms) close to 200 books in genres ranging from straight and gay erotica, mystery, romance, western, adventure, espionage, cooking, wine, young adults and children, and twenty-four science fiction/fantasy/horror novels, beginning with *Five Roads to Tlen* in 1969 (as "William J. Lambert III") through *Bond-Shattering* (2007). For a comprehensive list of his literary output, see *Draqualian Silk: A Collector's and Bibliographical Guide to The Books of William Maltese, 1969-2010* (Borgo Press, 2010). With a Business/Advertising degree, Maltese enlisted in the U.S. Army, where he achieved and was honorably discharged with the rank of Sergeant (E-5). You can find him at:

www.williammaltese.com
www.facebook.com/williammaltese
www.myspace.com/williammaltese
williammaltese@yahoo.com (e-mail)

www.ingramcontent.com/pod-product-compliance
Lightning Source LLC
Chambersburg PA
CBHW050424260626
47156CB00003B/1149

WELCOME TO
YOUR UNIVERSE!

...Where religions hold a prominent place in providing societal cohesion, especially when the indigenous populations are making the transition from nomadic hunter-gatherers to more static lifestyles; and where the old faiths can also instigate major societal fragmentation....

On Bnth, religious fermentation suddenly comes to a boil, when diehard male-chauvanist zealots attempt to infiltrate the Beast's Fortress in one more attempt to defeat the transmogrified one-time humanoid female, Ayra Organa, who is obviously hell-bent on clandestinely supplanting every male god in every planet's pantheon. Will the schism fracture human society? Or will calmer, more reasoned minds prevail? A thrilling science-fiction adventure, the second of the Gods & Frauds Series!

Borgo Press Books by WILLIAM MALTESE

SCHISM ON BNTH

GODS & FRAUDS, BOOK 2:
A SCIENCE FICTION NOVEL

WILLIAM MALTESE

THE BORGO PRESS
MMXI

SCHISM ON BNTH

FIRST EDITION

Published by Wildside Press LLC

www.wildsidebooks.com

DEDICATION

For Pandora, sister and sci-fi fan.

CONTENTS

FROM THE FORBIDDEN TEXT OF THE HERETIC GIATH

"No god or goddess has created one creature, but creatures have created gods and goddesses. Lo, they have created them by the score. For creatures are somehow unable to admit to the reality that they are simply freaks of the elements and not some intricate parts of a divine plan."

WHAT, THEN, OF AYRA ORGANA?

CHAPTER ONE

Excerpt from THE BOOK OF RELLIX:

The door of the Calyxine Crystal came slowly shut, sealing Galun inside.

The interior was sprinkled with refracted light, as had been the room outside.

For awhile, Galun thought nothing was happening. After all, there were no evident sounds, no evident visuals.

Then, suddenly, he knew that The Beast knew everything. He didn't think, suspect, even fear that it knew. He *knew* it knew.

It knew about the experiments Galun had done in his lab, locating the Stilter family on Antheer-D whose selective breeding would finally deliver up a woman, Mave, whose gene makeup was as near as possible to the original contributor, Stone Hanlic.

It knew Mave had been purposely mated with The Beast (in The Beast's male form of Dielum of Antheer-D), in order to farther reach for a duplicate of that original Atlan species—all of whom had died except Ayra Organa.

It knew Betty Mae's baby had been substituted in the Antheerinean sacrifice of the god-child.

It knew the baby of The Beast and Mave was alive.

It knew…it knew…it knew….

It knew, and it had made plans all its own, because it was lonely for its own kind, lonely for those who had rushed to destruction in the lemming race that had left it behind.

It would use all of them!

And Galun saw how it would use them!

He saw it all: the plans, the betrayals, the murders, the battles, the wars, and the generations yet to come that would spill their blood across the universe in pursuit of a cause they couldn't possibly achieve.

He saw even more than The Beast had ever seen, and, then, he died.

For nothing was ever had for nothing!

And in the Calyxine Crystal, it was life itself which was the currency paid by those daring to experience total knowledge.

PARKER CAME AWAKE, sensing immediately that he was greeting a day like none other he had experienced in his eighteen tireum.

"Mother?" he called automatically, because it was the fact that he couldn't hear Betty Mae puttering around the kitchen downstairs which contributed to his sense of unease. "Mother?" he called again, throwing back his blanket and coming to a sitting position on the bed.

He heard nothing. Not the sounds of breakfast pots and pans, the sizzling of frying bacon...nothing. It was the utter silence that disturbed him. There were no bird calls outside his open bedroom window.

He came out of the bed, reaching for a pair of trousers thrown over the back of a nearby chair.

He was an exceptionally attractive young man. Well put together, as his mother often commented. He stood close to six-feet tall, his body naturally muscled to display finely chiseled pectorals and wash-boarded abdominals. He was well-endowed elsewhere, his mother hinting that Parker would have had any girl panting on far-off Antheer-D; although, Parker had little idea where Antheer-D might be. Parker's world gravitated entirely—these past eighteen tireum—around the farmhouse and the surrounding environs. He wasn't sure what a "girl" was, having never seen one except in books and magazines. He

assumed they were merely miniature versions of his mother.

Parker had dark hair and dark eyes. He had a square jaw line. He had a dimple in his right cheek. He had a cleft in his chin. He had a full and sensuous mouth. He had startlingly strong and white teeth. His chest and stomach were covered with a matting of curly black hair.

His pants on, he reached for his shirt and slipped it on as he headed for the stairs.

"Mother?"

The downstairs was empty. He went through it, room by room by room, coming up with no sign of his mother. Where could she be? She was usually up by now. She was usually in the kitchen. The kitchen was empty. There was no fire in the stove. The wood and kindling were still piled in the corner woodbin. The cupboards were closed, the dishes inside.

He remounted the stairs, pushing open his mother's bedroom door, after a loud knock brought no response. That room, like all the rooms downstairs, was empty. Oh, there was a bed, a chest of drawers, a chair, a footstool, a braided rug, but no sign of Parker's mother. The bed was made, which meant very little, since Parker's mother always made her bed immediately upon rising.

He quickly checked the remaining second floor rooms: the sewing room—empty, the bathroom—empty. All empty.

Parker descended the steps. He opened the front door and stepped out on the porch. He stopped, looked, listened. Something was wrong, very wrong, and he could feel that wrongness in his bones. He could see it, smell it, feel it, while being not quite able to define what it was—besides the fact that his mother was obviously missing.

Suddenly, he realized that everything had a different quality about it. The trees just stood there, like pieces of a stage setting. In fact, the whole place seemed suddenly like a stage setting.

Was he going mad? Was this a dream? Some kind of nightmare? He pinched his arm, feeling the pain. If he were in some kind of dream world, it was none too anxious to recede even

with the sting caused by squeezed flesh between index finger and thumb.

The bird caught his attention. A brown-feathered cornefell. Dead. Parker left the porch, kneeling on the ground. He cupped the dead bird in his hand, holding it closer for observation. Its lids were open, revealing its yellow eyes. The eyes were still in place, not yet eaten by ants or the other little insects who would normally have feasted on succulent, juicy, cornefell eyeballs. How strange the bird felt against his hand. But, then, when had he last held a dead bird? When had he *ever* held a dead anything? In his whole eighteen tireum, nothing had ever died around the farmhouse. He only knew of death, because his mother had once mentioned it as being part of the everyday existence on that place from where she had come.

"What was it like, mother? That place called Antheer-D?"

"In looks, very much like here," Betty Mae had replied, shivering at the memory. "Yet, in other ways, it was so different. It was an evil place, Parker, where men and women died for their transgressions."

Antheer-D: the place from where Betty Mae had come; although, she refused to admit that it was from where Parker had come. From where had Parker come from, then?

"You ask too many questions," Betty Mae would invariably say. Which Parker had always accepted—when he was younger. When he was older, of course, he pressed for more specifics. However, he was, then, to discover that his mother really knew very little about Parker's origins. One day, he had just been there. As to how Betty Mae had gotten there, Parker never did get that out of his mother, either.

"I was once a very wicked, wicked woman," Betty Mae had said. "I underwent penance and received salvation. I am here as my reward."

Betty Mae hadn't much liked discussing her life before the farmhouse. She didn't like the questions Parker was often apt to shoot at her. "Ours is not to reason why," she had told him when his questions, as they usually did, became quite unbearable for

her. "All we need to know will be made known to us—in time."

However, Parker was now eighteen. He still had no answers. Suddenly, he, now, had even more questions: Where was his mother? What was this strangeness he was feeling? Why was this bird dead? He dropped the bird back to the ground, coming to his feet.

How strange the sky looked: flat and gray like an empty canvas.

"Mother?" No answer. No apparent sound, but his own. Where could she be? Where could she have gone? "Mother?"

He began walking along the forest path, searching... searching...searching. Certainly, she wouldn't be hiding from him as part of some kind of game? No, hardly that! Betty Mae would know Parker was concerned.

Another dead bird. This one a camerrand, its eyes orange and staring. What was happening? What...was...happening? Quiet. The place was...deathly(?)...quiet. There was hardly even a sound as Parker's feet touched the forest trail.

He began to sweat. His body was growing damp beneath his arms, down his back between his shoulder blades. At his crotch.

It was hot, and he couldn't remember it being quite so hot before. Usually, it was a happy medium, a pleasant balance between hot and cold.

He walked farther, aware that he was approaching the boundary. The boundary: that place where a voice usually came from nowhere to request that he, *please, turn back and go no farther.* Only where was the voice this time? Parker stopped, knowing he should have heard the voice by now. Time and time again, the voice had bid him, *please, go no farther.* Twice, when Parker had been younger, he had disobeyed the voice. He had proceeded onward, despite the request. Each time, he had lost consciousness as a result, awakening in his own bed, back at the farmhouse. Each time, his mother had eyed him sorrowfully, even fearfully. "We have it so very, very good here, Parker," Betty Mae had said. "Why must you risk us losing it all?" Yet, now, there was no voice. Was the voice, like the birds, dropped

dead?

Parker walked on, realizing he was in territory he had never before entered. Or, if he had, he wasn't able to remember.

Was he sleepy? No, but that didn't mean anything, did it? Those other times, he hadn't been sleepy, either. One moment, he would be walking in the forest. The next moment, he would be struggling to wake in his bed, Betty Mae's chastising and fearful eyes there to greet him.

The trees began to thin, until finally, Parker was confronted by a painting. He reached out a hand and touched it, feeling the rough surface of the canvas that stretched left and right as far as the eye could see, curving inward. He looked up, following the trunk of one painted tree as it swept upward...upward... upward...the top of the canvas bending over him, heading back the way he had come.

It...was...a...dream! It had to be a dream.

He proceeded along the giant canvas, walking parallel to it. Suddenly, he stopped. He knelt. Like a burrowing animal, he used his hands to dig, continuing to do so until the lower edge of the canvas was reached about two feet below the level of the existing soil. If he had brought a knife, he would have sliced the canvas. But the closest knife was back in the farmhouse kitchen. If he went back for it, how could he know if he'd be allowed to penetrate to this distance again?

How had he been allowed to get this far now?

He continued to dig: three and then four feet below the level of the canvas. He would have dug farther, but he reached a smooth surface, beneath the dirt, that was hard and blue, but definitely not like any rock Parker had ever seen. He stuck his head into the hole, angling it under the canvas edge to see the other side. What he saw was a light bulb, ignited, in a ceiling.

He began widening the hole, since he could make it no deeper. After awhile, he sat back on his haunches to rest. He was sweating more profusely. Liquid from his pores drooled his forehead and his cheeks. His pants and shirt were soiled with perspiration and dirt.

He stripped off his shirt, tossing it to one side. What madness was this that suddenly had him seeing his whole eighteen tireum as having been lived in a canvas box? What existed beyond this canvas container? What kind of world was the whole of which Parker—up until that moment—had seen only as one light bulb?

His digging offered a slide way for his body. He sat on the ground, his back toward the wall, and slid head-first into the trench. He reached out behind his head, his fingers taking hold of the canvas under-edge. Using his feet, he braced and scooted his torso farther. Simultaneously, his hands pulled. The soil was rough and damp against his naked back. Dirt caught in his dark hair and clung there. He put his head beneath the canvas, once again looking upward at the light bulb. He wiggled and squirmed, working more and more of his body to the other side.

Where was the voice telling him to turn back? What secrets had it held before which it was suddenly so willing to reveal at this particular moment in time?

For the moment, Parker had completely forgotten his mother. When he did remember, it was only to wonder if she knew of the box within which the two of them had lived.

He came to a sitting position, his torso in the new world, and his legs in the old. He looked to his left and to his right, seeing a corridor lit by more bulbs. The corridor bent so that it formed a giant curve that seemed to parallel the back of the canvas. It had to be a dream sequence, didn't it? No one simply walked to the limit of their world, did he, finding nothing there but a painted canvas and another world beyond? The notion was simply too preposterous.

He pulled. He tugged. He squirmed. He came up and out the other side, his body caked with soil and sweat. Where was he? What was this place? Would the dream soon shatter, he awakening suddenly to find himself once again in his room, in his own bed?

He listened, hearing nothing but the sound of his own breathing, the result of his recent exertion. He came to his feet, stepping up onto a sidewalk that curved with the corridor. The

sidewalk seemed made of the same blue substance that existed beneath the soil. The material—whatever it was—was cool beneath the soles of Parker's bare feet.

There were no paintings on the reverse side of the canvas. There was nothing there but an expanse of rough, blue-colored material extending upward, angling away from him as it extended higher and higher.

He began to walk, after first depositing his handkerchief on the sidewalk to mark his beginning, should he return....

Should he return? *When* he returned! Was there any doubt that Parker would be returning to his old world? His mother was in that old world, wasn't she? *Somewhere* in that old world. Anyway, it seemed hardly possible his mother was in any way responsible for Parker having received entrance into this new landscape.

He hesitated, wondering if he should indeed go on. After all, there was fear in exploring the unknown. On the other hand, there was an almost sexual excitement Parker felt at that moment. It was a sense of delicious freedom in knowing that he had emerged, much like a butterfly from its cocoon, into a world far less confining than the one he had always know.

Who lived here? What lived here? Why had Parker and Betty Mae been forced to live on the other side, held captive, there, like animals in those zoos Parker had read about in the books at the farmhouse? Would this corridor merely circle the perimeter of Parker's old world, leading nowhere but back on itself? Would there be no entrances or exits? Was this merely the protective shell that kept Parker's world from the void?

He stopped. He turned toward the outer wall. He extended his fingers to feel of it. What he saw and what he felt was the same blue material upon which he walked. He doubled his fist and hit the surface with the heel of his hand. There was no resulting sound. There was no resulting dent. Immediately, it was obvious that this barrier was far more substantial than the canvas on the other side of the sidewalk. No knife, which would have easily sliced the canvas, would have sliced this blue wall

with a whispered sigh of parting material.

He turned, continuing on his way. Glancing back along the corridor, he could see that his handkerchief had already disappeared behind the curve of a bend. Ahead, the corridor continued its curve.

With each step, Parker was subjected to yet more corridor, and more bulbs, but very little else. After a time, it felt very much as if he was merely marking time without getting anywhere, rather like an animal might run forever in the same spot while the wheel in which it existed proceeded to turn around it. Still, he proceeded onward, knowing that—if this wheel did turn—his handkerchief had yet to appear before him in indication that a complete circle had been made.

He heard the hum long before he recognized it as such. When it finally reached a pitch that registered on his brain, Parker stopped, straining desperately to identify it. He couldn't. After all, Parker had nothing with which to compare it for easy reference. He had never heard anything quite like it before.

Animal? Vegetable? Mineral? Whatever was it, making the low, guttural sound? Was it friend or foe? The idea of the latter was disconcerting. After all, Parker had never had a foe. There was nothing seemingly harmful in the world in which he had lived, on the other side of the canvas. Yet, enemies had existed for many of the characters within the pages of the books in the library at the farmhouse. Also, in those books had been strange animals…strange creatures…strange beings.

Parker had often escaped into the fantasy worlds of the books; although, his mother had always seemed little concerned with worlds created by the printed page. In fact, Betty Mae had seemed so little concerned with the books in the library, beyond passing the time by an occasional flip-through for pictures, it seemed highly unlikely Parker would have learned to read if he had depended primarily upon his mother's tutelage. Fortunately, there had been the teach-box with its pictures and sounds.

"Where did the teach-box come from?" Parker had asked on more than one occasion, each time bringing a shrug from his

questioned mother.

"It, like you," she had told him, "just turned up one morning."

The teach-box was a wonderful plaything. Parker had quickly come to devote more and more of his time to it. In the same instance, he could tell that his mother frankly disapproved. Sometimes, Betty Mae would sit in on a lesson, frowning slightly and leaving before it was ever completed. Betty Mae, it seemed, was quite content with her life the way it was, without seeking to modify it in the slightest.

"I can't imagine what value they see in allowing you to learn such things," Betty Mae had once said.

Parker was continually curious about these *they* to whom his mother occasionally referred in conversations. After all, Parker had never seen anyone else but his mother. "They?" he always wanted to know.

"We are not alone in our universe," Betty Mae had said. "We are being watched over by others." By what others, Betty Mae never did say. Parker got the impression she couldn't say, because she didn't really know.

"Others, like those on Antheer-D?" Parker had asked.

"Leave it be!" Betty Mae had insisted.

Parker had had to let it be only because he'd had little choice in the matter. His mother never volunteered any information and successfully avoided his each and every query. So, was it *they* who existed out here, beyond the constricting boundaries of the canvas cage? If so, why had they suddenly allowed Parker access to their world?

The humming was getting louder…louder…louder. The corridor widened. The volume of the hum increased even more. Within the outer wall, there were suddenly cracks. Regular, not irregular cracks. Man-made cracks? Rectangular cracks. As if by pushing along the centers, Parker might shove out four-by-six segments of the blue-metal surface.

The hum: beyond the wall. Oozing through the cracks? He put his ear to the blue surface, listening to the hummmmmm. He pushed. Cracked or not, the blue surface didn't move.

A ding! Parker stepped back at the sound, simultaneously glancing up to see a green light had gone on within the wall over his head. There was a rasping sigh, and the blue surface, inside one of the rectangular cracks, slid to one side, revealing a small, empty space beyond.

A trap? A smaller cage?

Parker approached. He moved tentatively. Was he expecting someone or something to reach out, grab hold, pull him inside, and slide the door back into place? The light in the wall above Parker's head was still green. The hum seemed to become even louder.

Why was he so enticed by the opening? What drew him to it? There was nothing beyond but the small cubicle. No obvious doors, except for the one now open. No windows.

Parker stood on the edge of the crack that separated him from the small space beyond the corridor. Cautiously, he extended one foot over the boundary, shifting his weight forward.

What was he trying to prove? What was the point of tempting fate when there was nothing really to be achieved by entering this empty niche? Once in there, what did he expect? Maybe another slide of another wall to reveal yet another door, another space…even a room?

He scanned the remaining three walls of the cubicle, searching for telltale cracks that might give indication of additional hidden panels. He couldn't see any.

Corners seemed securely joined at their junctures. The ceiling seemed firmly anchored to the walls. The floor seemed firmly anchored to the walls: When—and if—the door were to slide back into place, there seemed no other existing exit. Yet, Parker was drawn deeper. He followed his first foot with his second. He was almost completely inside, now, leaning slightly back to make a quick retreat, if a retreat was suddenly necessary.

The door began to slide shut, reappearing from the slot into which it had disappeared. Parker reflexively jumped back into the corridor. As he did so, however, his arm bumped the leading edge of the sliding door, and the door reversed its direction;

soon, again, open.

He'd noticed how the door had seemingly responded to his touch. Knowing that, he felt more confident as he stepped back into the cubicle. As he did so, he noticed a series of buttons off to one side. One read "open", another read "close". He pushed the latter, and the door immediately emerged from concealment, en route to shutting Parker off from the corridor. Parker automatically stepped into the doorway, letting the door hit him. The contact, once again, sent the sliding door into disappearance.

Parker repeated the procedure three more times, each time verifying that the door opened and shut when he pushed the properly labeled button. Finally, the moment came when he allowed the door to slide completely closed. Immediately, made paranoid, even more than a little claustrophobic, he, reflexively, extended a finger to again allow him release from the cage. However, before his hand reached the button, this time, the small cage began to move.

He punched the open button with no result. To the left of open, various other buttons, lit up, then flicked off: 15, 14, 13, 12, 11, 10, 9....

Parker flattened himself against one wall, feeling gravity defied as the cage moved upward with him inside.

What...in...Hell...was...happening? The hum grew louder.

Suddenly, the movement of the small room stopped. Parker pressed himself tighter against the wall. He felt sweat drool his sides. His forehead was damp with additional perspiration.

The door slid open, revealing a room beyond. It was a room filled with equipment and strange machines. The space was alive with the hummmmm.

Parker waited. For what he waited, he wasn't certain. After awhile, the door slid shut again. However, there was no more movement of the cubicle. Where was he? What had happened? When would the dream end? This was nothing more than a dream, wasn't it?

Time passed in which Parker was able to muster his courage. He reminded himself that there had been no visible indication

of any genuine enemy. He reached out, putting his fingertip to the open button. He pressed. The door came open. Parker tentatively stepped out of the smaller room in the larger.

He was entranced by what he saw, probably because there was no way he could presently understand it. What were all of these machines, making all of their whirring sounds, all the while blinking blue, red, green, purple, and yellow lights?

How long had this place existed just beyond the limits of Parker's world? How long had the secret of this place been guarded by the voice, coming seemingly out of nowhere to tell Parker, *please, not to proceed any farther into the forest*?

Parker moved deeper into the room, turning nervously when the door to the smaller room behind him slid shut.

Turning back to the room at hand, he quickly saw that it wasn't the only room. At the opposite end, along the right wall, there was a doorway. As Parker approached, he could see the doorway led into yet another room filled with more strange machines. Room after room…after room…after room.

Where were the people who maintained this sophisticated equipment? Surely, it couldn't all function on its own. Yet, there were no signs of life. The rooms, except for their machines, were empty.

Parker finally reached a room that, at first glance, seemed to be another one with no apparent exit except for the doorway through which Parker entered it. He glanced toward the opposite wall where an exit, if, like most of the other rooms, should have been. What he saw was a slight triangular recess in the wall.

He approached, knowing now that appearances could be deceptive. Solid walls could unexpectedly slide to one side, giving access to spaces beyond.

He looked for any button which might, at a touch, set a door to sliding. Even as he looked, but did nothing else, there was a breathless sigh, and the door lifted.

Parker stepped through into a room different from the others. It had thick rugs on its floor, banks of deep couches, large scatter-

cushions, comfortable chairs, low tables of metal and glass.

The door dropped behind him.

The hum made by the machinery was suddenly gone, trapped behind the dropped metal. Was Parker as securely trapped on this side as the sounds were trapped on the other?

"Hello there," a voice said, startling Parker and making him jump.

He turned and saw her stretched out on one of the couches. He was quite sure she hadn't been there but moments before.

She had to be the most exquisite woman he had ever seen, even recognizing the fact that she was the *only* woman, besides Betty Mae, whom Parker had ever seen outside of books.

"I've been expecting you, Parker," she said.

She had honey-colored hair that tumbled in cascades of flowing curls to parenthesize her oval face. She had golden eyes, flecked with black, and shielded by thick blonde lashes. She had lips tinted light gold. Her voluptuous body was draped in a sensuously clinging—and highly revealing—gown of rich and variegated golden hues. She wore gold armbands, a golden collar around her neck, and golden starbursts in her ears.

CHAPTER TWO

Excerpt from THE BOOK OF RELLIX:

The Fortress on Bnth had physical boundaries that stretched from the Black Glass Sea of Torne to the Drandee Drop of Escarpment II. Its corridors and rooms honeycombed the mountain in which it sat, forming a labyrinth to which no one—but one—held the secrets or the keys.

QUORULU-MI WAS A STYROLEAN; Styrolea in the Star System Filii-3, knowing The Beast in its transmogrification of Simsimul: The Megatat-tat.

Quorulu-Mi had been in the service of The Beast for three tireum, having contracted for six tireum during a Fieal Ceremony at the full moons of Dyra and Syra-F.

He was handsome by Styrolean standards. Standing two-feet high at the shoulders, his rear legs, stubbier than the fore, dropped his rump to approximately one foot from the floor.

His tail was a bushing curve that formed a question mark above the small of his back.

His feet were four-toed pads that, when constricted, could extend sharp claws, each over two inches in length.

His compact, husky body was covered with long black fur that completely concealed the two small wings which—as on all Styroleans—had long since been genetically atrophied so as, now, to be quite useless in getting such weighty bodies airborne.

His ears, two of them, were long to the point where their

weight caused the upper half of each to droop to conceal all visuals of his auditory meati.

His eye sockets were squeezed to mere slits between his high, angular cheekbones and his short, overhanging forehead.

His eyes looked out from behind three membranes which were lowered to supplement night vision. Those eyes, seemingly black marbles of jet, gave no actual indication of the four individual pupils within each spherical viewing orb.

His three nostrils were slits in a triangular design within the beak-like jut of his upper lip. His lips, pliable now (as opposed to the hard horniness of such projections which had accompanied functional wings in the early tireum of Styrolean life-form development), had the upper completely over-biting the smaller, lower.

His teeth were small but sharp, designed more for tearing than for chewing. His complicated digestive tract, wound in lengthy vortexes of acid-oozing gut, allowed for most chunks of food to undergo complete breakdown before arriving in one of four stomachs designed for the assimilation of nutrients through a process known as absorbo-mechanics.

His sexual organs, quite impressive in engorgement, were now pulled completely to concealment within a protective pod secured within his lower body. His generative equipment was presently shrunken by the fear Quorulu-Mi was experiencing.

He was where he wasn't supposed to be. He could be in big trouble if he were discovered there. So much big trouble, he could shudder at the imagined consequences without really knowing exactly what such consequences might be.

It did little to alleviate Quorulu-Mi's apprehension that the rumor was out that The Beast was presently not in residence. Such scuttlebutt was of little consolation; one, because it could very well be false, and, two, because The Beast could return at any time to find one of its sycophants in an area normally not authorized.

Quorulu-Mi stopped, sniffing the air. What registered on sensitive nasal passages was a smell of damp decay.

The walls of the corridor around him oozed a wetness that came with a stench to equal sweat oozed from any pore.

It was pitch black. Not even Quorulu-Mi's adaptor membranes allowed for complete penetration.

He listened for sounds of other life-forms, glad when he received no indication of company within the immediate environs. After all, there were more things to be avoided within the Fortress than just The Beast.

Confident that he was alone, undiscovered, Quorulu-Mi proceeded down the corridor, down the stairs, and into deeper darkness.

How many corridors, just like this one, had Quorulu-Mi explored? He had a rough physical map, which outlined his ferreting progress, sequestered in a secret hiding place within his cubicle.

What a maze this place was! What a labyrinth. What a conglomeration of rooms and passageways seemingly constructed by a madman for a madman.

No one seemed to know what workforce had piled block upon block. It was rumored that the Fortress had been designed specifically to exact specifications provided by The Beast.

Designed for what purpose? The Beast had evolved to a state where physical boundaries weren't necessary to contain it. Granted, The Beast assumed various physical shapes for its roles of deities on those planets under its control, but those physical shapes were no longer necessary once The Beast retuned to the void.

Quorulu-Mi knew what The Dzi Scholar and Murlock *thought* was here—somewhere. The Gorda Bank, for one. The Dzi Scholar and Murlock were convinced a Gorda Bank had survived, along with The Beast, the mad lemming race which had siphoned Atla and its humanoids into the vortex of Cataclys IX, ejecting the residue beyond the veil.

Quorulu-Mi, though, had his doubts. He had been wandering this place for the total time he'd been here, and he had found nothing to give him any real indication that there was a Gorda

Bank, or anything else, that had survived the greatest catastrophe of recorded history.

It was more likely The Beast was playing games, having constructed this Fortress as a playground in which its enemies could waste valuable time searching for secrets not even there. Time which might have been better spent in activities far more detrimental to The Beast.

Quorulu-Mi descended another flight of stairs, wondering if these, too (like so many in the Fortress), led to a virtual blank wall. Not to a wall that concealed a secret passageway, either. Just a literal dead end. Or, maybe, the final step would be one a few miles long. Quorulu-Mi had encountered just such a final step during his search of the south wing of the Fortress. If it hadn't been for the visual aids offered by his three dark-penetrating membranes, Quorulu-Mi would have taken that final step, becoming of no possible use to either Murlock or The Dzi Scholar.

This stairway did not end in oblivion, nor did it end at a blank wall. It exited into yet another corridor. This meant Quorulu-Mi had no excuses for turning back. Actually, he would have welcomed the chance to do a quick about-face. There was something about this place which made him experience a running chill throughout his circulatory system.

In fact, it was during moments such as this that Quorulu-Mi wondered why he was even, here, doing what he was doing. What possible hope was there of him—or of anyone else, The Dzi Scholar and Murlock included—coming up with any plan to overthrow The Beast? The Beast was simply too, too powerful. It had been in existence before Quorulu-Mi was even born.

How had Quorulu-Mi been sucked into this campaign against the forces he couldn't even begin to understand? Was it madness which had compelled him? Had they brainwashed him? Had they scrambled his mind with conscious-bending drugs?

When had all of it happened—his joining up with a side which was surely destined to lose in the end?

He attempted to shake off his negative thoughts for three

reasons. One, any thoughts (negative or otherwise) about anything but the business immediately at hand, were dangerous to his well-being. Two, at this late date, it did very little to change the way things were. Three, he didn't want to begin wondering, again (as he had taken to doing too often lately), if he hadn't made one big mistake in being roped into an undertaking that could leave him dead along the wayside at any time during his stay at the Fortress on Bnth.

He did remember that, at one time in the distant past, he had had no qualms about what he was doing. He had embraced the excitement and adventure with the willingness of someone who didn't know better. Danger had been an aphrodisiac as powerful as any pheromone. However, too much danger, like too much sex, had obviously gone a good ways toward numbing the pleasure derived from it.

Oh, he had been a gallant advocate of the cause, hadn't he? He had thrilled at the idea of being the one selected to bargain with Simsimul: The Megatat-tat for riches beyond most Styrolean's dreams; forwarding a just cause, while simultaneously paid by the very entity his purpose it was to destroy.

Destroy? Could The Beast, in fact, be destroyed?

Since his initial recruitment into the band of rebels, Quorulu-Mi had come to realize that his enemy possessed far more power, had far more worshippers, than Quorulu-Mi had ever before dreamed possible. The representation given within the Fortress of The Beast's scope of influence was but the tip of the iceberg, for there were servants of The Beast who never got as far as this inner sanctum, who didn't even know the Fortress existed—as Quorulu-Mi had never known of its existence before being told of it by Murlock and The Dzi Scholar.

"We need contacts within the house of The Beast," The Dzi Scholar had said. "For it is there we believe The Beast is most vulnerable. Will you, for at least a time, be our eyes and ears in that place The Beast has constructed to hold his possessions secure from the outside world?"

Quorulu-Mi had come rushing in with his eyes wide open,

delighting in putting one over on The Beast in The Beast's transmogrification of Simsimul: The Megatat-tat on Styrolea. The question was, had he really put anything over on The Beast at all? He had served three tireum of his life in The Beast's employ, had been brought to do things (none of which he might refuse to do for fear of discovery), which would have been odious to any intelligent, civilized life-form, and for what? For a promised fortune of which he had yet to see a karpetic.

Had Quorulu-Mi been a fool? Had he become a tool of The Dzi Scholar and Murlock, who wanted him only for the information he might supply them? Had he become the tool of The Beast who would force him into doing more horrendous things, and, in the end, find some way of weaseling out of their bargain? The easiest way for The Beast to be removed of any obligation to Quorulu-Mi (as established in their agreement) was for The Beast to discover what Quorulu-Mi was really doing in the Fortress on Bnth. The Beast hadn't struck his bond with a known rebel spy but with what he assumed was but a lowly Styrolean. The very fact that Quorulu-Mi had had prior knowledge of what he as bargaining for could, in and of itself, make the transaction invalid.

Quorulu-Mi stopped. He listened. Having heard what?

His mind had been wandering. He hadn't been concentrating. He was losing his grip. Which was dangerous...dangerous... dangerous.

What was he doing here? What masochistic part of his character had allowed him to subject his system to such abuse as was being rendered by the gut-twisting fear running rampant through him now?

He knew what he probably should do. Oh, yes, he did certainly know that. He should have gotten out of there, fled back to his liv-cubicle as fast as his four legs could carry him. He should have given up this ridiculous notion that he could play an intricate part in the shaping of the power structure within the universe. After all, he could do nothing. He was simply too insignificant, too small, too ignorant. He had the most to gain by simply faith-

fully serving The Beast for the three remaining tireum of his indentured servitude, and receiving his just rewards for such service. Playing hero no longer held the enchantment it once did.

So, why didn't he turn back, since he had the shuddering sense of suspicion that there was some thing obscene waiting for him in the darkness up ahead? What was it that made his legs move in coordinated motions that propelled him low across the ground—forward, forward, ever forward?

His mind computed and analyzed, flashed references as to where Quorulu-Mi had been during the course of this most recent quest for information. His brain quickly began to formulate his escape route, a reverse of the route used in entry. There could be no mistakes if he were forced to retreat via any fast and furious scurry up stairs, along passageways, through tunnels....

There were sycophants of The Beast who were far better equipped for the darkness than even Quorulu-Mi of Styrolea. There was Misfa the Dila whose gaze could not only pierce the darkness but kill through it. There as Phmisft of Zorichlu who could sense a presence in total blackness and send out a net of glissner to entrap a victim at forty focci. Forty focci, for Zeepher's sake! Quorulu-Mi couldn't see that far in complete daylight. Very few life-forms could.

Quorulu-Mi was walking a tightrope. Tempting fate. Daring one of The Beast's entourage to catch him at his devious explorations.

If they hadn't discovered him already. It was not beyond the scope of reason that Quorulu-Mi had been discovered a long, long time ago, watched to see what he was up to, played with like a dynic played with a mulosin before pouncing on it for the final kill.

Such thoughts could, and did, chill Quorulu-Mi to the bone.

He computed time factors and mental mechanisms necessitated by no light entering these deep caverns from the outside. There weren't stars, moons, planets, or constellations on which to sight for any determination of time passage. Nor did Quorulu-Mi

wear a digital readout. If he could see the glow of numerals in the darkness, then others would have been able to see it, too. Besides, mechanical marvels were known to malfunction at inopportune moments. There was no way Quorulu-Mi was prepared to put his life in the hands of something constructed by someone other than himself, in pieces which could screw up without warning. His inner clock was sufficient enough to allow him more than adequate assessment of time available at the outset, time used as of date, time remaining to him.

He still had time to go on, even though intuition told him he had come quite far enough for one outing.

He was startled when his third membrane slid upward, leaving only two. It was sure indication that the darkness was paling.

Yes, it was lighter. Why, though? He could determine no apparent light source. Not yet anyway. Maybe if he went… just…a…little…bit…farther.

He figured he was deep beneath the Fortress, more near its center than near the perimeter of any of its wings.

Did he hear anything? No.

However, light of any kind at that depth had to indicate the presence of life-forms needing it, right?

The Beast didn't need light. The Beast didn't need dark. The Beast didn't need anything. The Beast was self-contained. It was a world unto itself.

The second membrane slid upward, leaving only the last of the dark-penetrating films in place.

Something down here needed light. Where was that something? Could it possibly exist without exuding some kind of aura? No. Only The Beast could do that. Even the diso-veils of the Vorleans could be detected if one knew for what to check.

Did Quorulu-Mi, though, know what he was looking for in this instance? He could detect the diso-veil of the Vorleans if he had to do so. His sensors were tuned not only for the diso-veils but for the iva-velocity concelatators of the Morficians. He could even detect the inviso-shields of the Xorsims. The latter's

existo-ocyclo would cause a tisle vibration, faint but unmistakable, on Quorulu-Mi's inner ears. Even the sophisticated dissolvo-shroud of the Auroliceans added a pale yellowish cast to the atmosphere concealing the body of the instigator. At least it did when one's visual plane, like that of Quorulu-Mi, was capable of registering the Dicton color scale.

There was no yellow presently being registered.

The ground underfoot became smoother, emerging blue-black within the increasing light. The walls, ceiling, too, took on the same smooth blue-black consistency. The corridor suddenly seemed less a passageway roughly hewn from solid stone by natural forces than it did a manually constructed slide way through the bowels of the mountain.

The decline became steeper and steeper. With each step, Quorulu-Mi reassured his footing. The last thing he wanted was to lose his balance and take the slide to some last destination from where it would be impossible for him to climb back to freedom.

The passageway curved toward the right, and, then, forked into three different directions. Each available choice of progression was lit to a varying degree of luminescence; although, Quorulu-Mi had yet to determine from just where the light was coming.

The corridor section that branched toward the left was the darkest. When Quorulu-Mi glanced in that direction, the two dark-penetrating membranes which had since disengaged, during his progression through the journey, immediately snapped back into place. Even then, it was almost impossible for Quorulu-Mi to discern more than a few metrolits into the gloomy tube.

The middle passageway was a little lighter. Quorulu-Mi would have had little difficulty seeing along that route, but he didn't particularly like the way the grade of the floor dropped even more sharply than the decline upon which he was now standing.

At first glance, the corridor to the right seemed to be the best

alternative. It was lit to a sufficient quotient to allow all three of Quorulu-Mi's dark-penetrating membranes to disengage. The decline of the floor remained pronounced, but it wasn't pronounced to the point where Quorulu-Mi felt he would have any real difficulty navigating.

However, it was the very attractiveness of the corridor on the right, those very attributes that made it most favorable over the other two available avenues, which had Quorulu-Mi think, maybe, it should be avoided at all costs. Traps were seldom successfully sprung by offering bait that wasn't enticing to an intended victim.

His chosen mission in life had made him very susceptible to paranoia. As well it might. This wasn't just a harmless children's game Quorulu-Mi was playing. The stakes could very well entail his loss of life-force.

Quorulu-Mi didn't want to die!

He chose the corridor on the right, rationalizing that what was possibly the perfect bait for him (i.e. an easy gradient and sufficient lighting), would hardly have been equally advantageous for just anyone passing this way. An Islefork would have had little difficulty with a decline dipped to one-hundred-eighty degrees. The suction cups arranged geometrically along its belly would have allowed substantial movement without slippage. The Monguels, or Tumptoffs, or any one of several life-forms indicative of any of the sunless solar systems, like Dindonola-D, or Kyrantillic-IV, would have found the light a painful assault on their visual sensors.

So, it seemed highly unlikely, in retrospect, that this trap had been baited specifically with Quorulu-Mi in mind. Unless, of course, all three passageways were traps prepared to deal with a whole gamut of life-forms—Styroleans being just one of them.

He could still turn back.

Was it partially, then, his insatiable curiosity which egged him on? The way he had it figured, he—more than about any other resident of the Fortress (except of course, for The Beast)— had the best comprehensive awareness of the layout of the place.

He knew for a fact that there were servants of The Beast who lived out their total periods of indentured servitude without moving beyond one small section of the Fortress. One sycophant—Miftoe the Queuel—had told Quorulu-Mi he had never been beyond the six walls of his (admittedly large) liv-space.

On the other hand, Quorulu-Mi had wandered hallways, tunnels, corridors, ramp ways, and even super highways (devoid of any visible means of vehicular movement)—all within the embrace of the Fortress and its foundation; none about which Quorulu-Mi's fellow inmates seemed to have a clue.

Here he was, now, about to enter into yet another arterial of this monstrous place which he often fantasized as having a life all of its own: its outer frame, its skeleton; its inner passageways, its guts.

There were places in this thing's bowels where Quorulu-Mi had heard sounds that gave all indication the whole mountain breathed. There were rivers of stuff in lower chambers (Quorulu-Mi had seen and smelled them), which gave all indication of nourishment in the process of being broken down in digestive juices.

There were places where violent winds pulsed through honeycombed chambers, as air pumped with bellow-like force through lungs and breathing mechanisms.

There were places where walls, ceilings, and floors had the consistency of living flesh—at least as Quorulu-Mi knew and thought of living flesh. Such places were punctuated with pore-like apertures that oozed moisture—like sweat. They grew grasses, like hair and fur. They sprouted growths, like teeth, fingernails, or pad claws.

Quorulu-Mi shook off his sense of having become some kind of insignificant parasite lost within the guts of some gargantuan life-form.

He moved forward, down a corridor which grew lighter… lighter…lighter.

He kept a careful check for spy holes, electronic beams to betray his step, tele-cameras to detect his presence and record

it for future replay within the memory banks of the giant computer, the latter something Quorulu-Mi had never seen but had heard existed somewhere within the maze.

From where was the light coming? Not from bulbs visible or recessed. Not even from radiation within the walls, ceilings, and floors which remained the same darkly tinted blue-black.

The light really seemed a part of the air through which Quorulu-Mi walked; although, he could feel no resistance to his passing, no caressing of his form as he progressed deeper... deeper...deeper.

Suddenly, he stopped, focusing on a section of the passageway up ahead.

There was color in movement up there, splattering the area with dancing blues, purples, yellows, and reds, as if the light source was shattered within a prism.

Quorulu-Mi moved closer, noticing, as he did, that the flitting colors were projected from a door-large opening in one side of the corridor.

How hypnotic those helixing colorful sworls that drew Quorulu-Mi nearer...nearer...nearer.

He sniffed the air, smelling nothing but the heady aroma of his own fear.

His skin tingled, puckered around fur roots to send the hair on his body standing one end.

His ears strained for a sound, hearing none except that of his own breathing.

Gingerly, he stepped into the color speckles—expecting what? Burns like acid? Brands to mark him forever with: Quorulu-Mi Was Here!

The colors continued their crawl over his body, over the walls, ceiling, and floor, leaving no trace of where they had been.

Did that make Quorulu-Mi feel safe? In fact, it didn't make him feel safe at all, because things could mark without leaving visible evidence. Right then and there, he could have already been striated with scar tissue visible only when subjected to special bosle, tyil, or phospholoc lighting.

Whether marked or not, Quorulu-Mi had already taken the risk. He was already exposed. Having risked so much to get this far, it would have been ridiculous not to see all there was to see, glean whatever bit of intelligence there was to be had.

By way of backdrop, the room was all white, with just a splash of gold detected through the moving rainbow hues splattered all about it by a now-seen giant crystal.

The crystal, a multi-faceted cocoon, was alive with the color shards caught and concentrated within it.

Was it simply what it appeared to be, or was it something elsc? It seemed inconceivable The Beast—despite the obvious value of any such gemstone—would have any real reason to hoard it.

Yet, if it wasn't just a crystal, then what was it? To what purposes could it be put? And by whom?

Was it the fabled Gorda Bank, survivor of Cataclys IX with The Beast? Quorulu-Mi thought not. The Dzi Scholar and Murlock had given a description of the Gorda Bank. There had been word-of-mouth remembrances of what that gadget had looked like, and they had described nothing like this.

Quorulu-Mi became aware of electricity in the air. It disturbed him that the sensation had crept up on him unawares. It moved over and through him like undulating waves. It was like a hand petting his fur, soothingly stroking...stroking... stroking...making him feel so...so...so...good.

He allowed himself a deeper entrance into the room. He had to see the crystal first-hand. He had to observe it carefully. He had to examine it thoroughly. The Dzi Scholar and Murlock would be most interested. Maybe, they would be able to make heads and tails of it. Maybe, they would...

The floor dropped out from beneath him. There, one minute, it was simply gone the next. With its removal, Quorulu-Mi was airborne, his useless wings flapping frantically (no doubt triggered by some prehistoric response mechanism not yet watered down in his genes)—to no avail. Styroleans hadn't flown in meg-mega-tireum. There was no way Quorulu-Mi was going

to fly now.

Like a rock, he dropped, completely under the control of gravity.

He plunged into a seemingly bottomless darkness. During the course of his fall, one, two, three of his dark-penetrating membranes fell automatically into place. Still, he fell, thinking that there possibly was no end, until....

He came to a jarring, teeth-shattering stop, wedged into a position from which he was unable to escape.

He had plugged into a V-shaped chasm at a point where he was well aware of its two slanting walls.

Above him, the open mouth of the V had either closed, or Quorulu-Mi had dropped so far down that whatever light was still provided by opening was no longer visible.

He couldn't move up. He couldn't move down. The force of his drop had inserted him so securely into his present slot that he couldn't move forward-to-back, or side-to-side, either

When he tried to move at all, the resulting pain hinted that he had possibly broken one or more bones. The pain, as his shock diminished, became more and more intense.

So, the game was finally over for him, was it? There was a sense of relief to be had in that. There would be no more sneaking around, no more fear of discovery, no more....

What was that smell? So sweet and, yet, so sour. All around him. Making his mind go hazy, making even the pain wane, making him unable to realize that being caught was possibly only the beginning of the horror destined to follow.

CHAPTER THREE

Excerpt from THE BOOK OF RELLIX:

They were headed through a walkway carved by lasers into the mountainside. The passage—as were all the parenthesizing rooms—was lined with cilysal; the whole underground complex was shot-through with thriene, all in an attempt to keep this small pocket in the universe secure from penetration. Whether the precautions were successful, or not, really couldn't be known for certain, since the factions responsible for Tilox— as the place was called—weren't really completely certain as to the scope of power had by their chief adversary. There were doubts that cilysal and thriene were sufficient in themselves. Pocket 12 and Pocket 120 (the former shielded just with cilysal, the later just with thriene) had both been penetrated. It still remained to be seen whether a combination of the two offered suitable shielding. Of course, there was always the possibility that a completely impenetrable forcefield was the last thing to be desired. It had been suggested by some that Organa's inability to scan certain areas of the universe with even her most sophisticated beams was enough, in and of itself, to set off alarm bells in her computer linkups. After all, who would erect such barriers if they didn't have something to hide from her?

THE BLAST WAS SO POWERFUL, its heat so strong, that the protecto-shield of the buffeted spacepod actually began to melt, setting off alarm buzzers that echoed within the interior

and sent lights flashing on the consoles of more than one control board.

The Dzi Scholar turned from the defense computer, where he was monitoring incoming projectile trajectories in an attempt to throw light on the location of their adversary; although, everyone alive now knew (most all of those dead having known before dying) just who it was that had lined Forlux up on the sites of space cannon and had blasted the small pocket of resistance out of existence. The Beast had somehow found them, pinpointed their hideaway among the space dust cluttering this segment of the galaxy.

Few had survived the last mega-lit bomb blast which had disintegrated everything and everyone who hadn't been airborne at the time. One of the space canon projectiles had made a direct hit on the dorlic energy piles, and that had been the end. Forlux was no more, and the crew of the spacepod Belun could shudder with the knowledge that their own continued existence hinged only on the fluke that had had them all in position, preparing for blast-off when the first bomb exploded on the asteroid's outer defense shield.

Now, Forlux was nothing but a glow of dust fanning outward from that point in space that had once contained it.

"Cannon projectile veering from the left sector!" someone announced. The Dzi Scholar thought it might be Murlock's voice but hardly took the time to verify, turning his full attention to the viso-screen. Just because their spacepod had attained lift-off before Forlux became no longer a form of habitable existence, didn't mean that their ship, or its crew, could heave any sighs of relief. Quite to the contrary, since cannon projectiles, having registered the main objective for destruct, were programmed to search out and destroy any life-forms which might have evaded the destruct cycle.

"Our forcefield is down in that area!" The Dzi Scholar announced, as if that wasn't already evident by the computer visual announcing their vulnerability via a series of blazing lights on the main control board.

"We'll have to take it out with a barrage of lentilic rays," Murlock informed, just as The Dzi Scholar announced there was yet another cannon projectile veering toward them from sector 16. "Is the forcefield up in that area?" Murlock asked, knowing if it was down in both areas of attack, they were probably doomed.

"Forcefield is up, but unlikely to survive a direct hit!" The Dzi Scholar informed, knowing that was better news than had there been nothing there, period. At least, this way, attention could be centered on eliminating the cannon projectile approaching the already vulnerable side. If the second forcefield was knocked out of commission, in the process, well, they would simply have to cross that bridge when they came to it.

"Give me manual override!" Murlock commanded. "I can't chance the main computer circuits becoming damaged to the point of miscalculation."

The Dzi Scholar obliged the request, watching the visoscreen while their spacepod was simultaneously attacked from two separate quadrants of near-space. He rechecked his safety factors in preparation for the destruction of the one forcefield.

In the meantime, Murlock busily tried to ascertain the best defense tactics against the more dangerous of the cannon projectiles en route to the ship. The Dzi Scholar silently wished him luck, since the impact of the one bomb against the existing forcefield would come first, possibly making all of Murlock's calculations come out wrong.

The Dzi Scholar prayed to whatever power existed beyond the void, just in case he would soon be making the journey. His god had no name, since The Dzi Scholar had long ago discovered that most named gods had no right to be called gods at all. The Beast, in its myriad forms, was the prime example. The Dzi Scholar had long ago refused to give worship to any throne that had what was left of a woman humanoid sitting on it.

The cannon projectile hit the forcefield, sending the spacepod into a vibrating state of shock. The Dzi Scholar, unable to function as he would have liked, only hoped Murlock was better

attuned to battle conditions. In Murlock's favor, he had survived the destruction of Pocket 16, although that pocket had been sabotaged from within, not.....

There was a blinding flash of light that momentarily eliminated all shadow, turning the world inside the spacepod into a bright sunburst. The Dzi Scholar thought for sure he was dead. Even the breath he managed to suck in through the filtering diaphramgmatic circle, that centered his green face, was possessed of a scalding heat that seemed to singe the interior lining of his air bellows.

However, the flash had heralded the successful destruct of the cannon projectile by the barrage of lentilic beams, and the shadows again returned to the ship interior. The Dzi Scholar realized—with no small degree of disbelief—that death had somehow missed him again. Considering the definite possibility that they were hardly safe, yet, that was only minor consolation, at most. Still, it was something, and The Dzi Scholar's reflexes were automatic in taking whatever continued action was necessary to maintain the functioning of his life-system. He quickly scanned the dials, lights, and messages within the visual and audio computer readouts.

"Cannon projectile scanning sector 40 but not yet locked in," he reflexively informed. "Another is in sector 6. Another is in sector 12, but, apparently, malfunctioning and en route into deep space." Then, he swirled his chair toward Murlock. "Good shooting," he congratulated, knowing that they weren't out of this yet.

"Yes, well, I don't know how many more good shots I've left in me," Murlock said, willing to admit to himself, if to no one else, that his success in taking out the cannon projectile had been a good deal luck, pure and simple, that he wasn't prepared to call upon twice in any short time span. The ship, now with two of its vital forcefields down, was particularly vulnerable. Just because none of the remaining cannon projectiles on visuals had locked in didn't mean they couldn't or wouldn't.

"I think you had better program us for Tilox," Murlock

instructed, "by a circuitous route to be sure. It may be the only outpost sufficiently equipped to offer us protection at the moment. If The Beast can take Forlux, it may well be able to take them all."

"Tilox included?" The Dzi Scholar had long worried that even the complicated defense mechanisms installed to protect Tilox were worthless when it came to giving protection against The Beast.

Murlock suspected The Dzi Scholar's thoughts, having experienced much the same at many times in the past. Often, it seemed they fought a losing battle, The Beast always one step ahead of them and waiting to pounce. Still, the war wasn't lost, yet, even if the loss of Forlux stacked up important points in the Beast's favor. The Beast's advantage would have been far greater had it been able to eliminate both Murlock and The Dzi Scholar in one swoop. Had The Beast known both Murlock and The Dzi Scholar would be there? Was that why the attack had been initiated on Forlux at this particular moment in time? That Murlock had handpicked the people on Forlux didn't mean there weren't spies amongst them. Life-forms, no matter how devoted they were to any cause, were often vulnerable, especially to the kinds of temptations The Beast might hold out to them as rewards. That was why Tilox had been gradually vacated to leave intact only its non-life-form overseers. That didn't mean computers weren't often vulnerable, in their own right. In some instances, they were even less trustworthy than life-forms, especially if one held the keys to them. But, there were only two people who now had the keys to the computer system on Tilox: Murlock and The Dzi Scholar. If either of them were traitors, then the whole game being played would have been lost a long time ago.

"We have a spacepod, category X-5, approaching from beyond the metolscan," Gungol Fox announced. Gungol was Melantite from one of the moons of Kyroxene-9. Murlock had known his father and his father's father. As far as he could trust anyone— and he trusted no one one-hundred percent—he trusted Gungol

Fox, son of Titian Fox, and grandson of the Great Fox of Barren World War VI.

"Can you identify the spacepod as an eject?" Murlock asked, already beginning to compute the figures necessary to put the oncoming craft in a deadly crossfire of lentilic rays. The Beast wasn't above disguising a detonation device as a spacepod having survived the apocalypse of Forlux.

"I.D. number X-4-oh-Oh-Sixer puts the craft assigned duty to bio-life system 7-Oh," Gungol answered, checking his computer readouts which had quickly sifted through files and produced the identification that corresponded to the now visible I.D. inscribed on the side of the incoming craft. However, Murlock still wasn't convinced. If The Beast knew of Forlux, it might well have known of a category X-5 spacepod, I.D. number X-4-oh-Oh-Sixer, assigned to bio-life-system 7-Oh.

"Attempt a life-scan," Murlock instructed, first checking to make sure all visible and wandering enemy cannon projectiles were out of lock-in range. He wasn't yet prepared to risk communication for fear one or more of them were sensitized for honing in on any transmits.

"Life-scan indicates one survivor on board. Type: undeterminable."

The Dzi Scholar knew the possibly negative predicament of allowing any closer approach by the category X-5, even if it, a fellow survivor, wasn't equipped for lengthy travel in deep space, and, now that Forlux had been disintegrated, needed to dock with the larger ship or perish. If it were was trap....

"Angle approach so that one of our remaining operational forcefields is between us and the craft," Murlock instructed. "If there is any veering of the X-5 to modify for an approach toward one of our more vulnerable sides, weapons-lock on for an immediate destruct."

The procedure was initiated, the larger spacepod rolling on its axis to present one of its operative shields to the oncoming smaller craft.

"It could be a trap," The Dzi Scholar pointed out the obvious.

All of Murlock's orders, thus far, had been given as if he acted under that very assumption.

Again, The Dzi Scholar scanned for any indication that one of the enemy cannon projectiles had registered their presence and begun pursuit. All sources indicated that both spacepods had apparently slipped free of the danger zone. A mere suspicion of escape, though, wasn't about to let The Dzi Scholar relax his visual. The Beast was famous for sneaking up unaware.

The X-5 continued its approach, apparently quite content to make contact with the larger ship on a protected side. Murlock was somewhat encouraged by the fact that, whatever the life-form on board, it had made no attempt at communication, possibly leery—as was Murlock—that the enemy cannon projectiles were programmed to pick up distress calls between surviving ships. Were the approaching ship one of the enemy, it seemed likely the easiest way to destroy the larger ship would be by calling in all the live ammunition wandering after the destruct of asteroid Forlux. On the other hand, Murlock was tempted to blast the smaller craft out of the sky merely as a safety precaution, especially since he had already ordered his ship to assume a circuitous course toward the highly sensitive pocket Tilox. An enemy on board the category X-5 might very well assume it could supply far more valuable information to its master by joining up with any survivors. Likewise, it seemed unlikely an enemy, unless a bona-fide martyr, was going to call in the bombs at this point.

"Shall we extend retracto-beams for docking?" Gungol Fox asked. The X-5 had reached the forcefield and was resting against it, like a globe resting against the leading edge of a barricading dam.

"Yes, extend retracto-beams," Murlock said. "Then, send an armed escort to supervise disembarkation of our guest. Paldon?" he said, turned toward The Dzi Scholar. "Will you join me in extending greetings?"

Murlock and The Dzi Scholar took the ele-tube to the docking area, arriving to find the X-5 docked, its hatch still closed.

Protecto-barriers had been activated and put into place in case the occupant turned out to be dangerous.

"Problems?" Murlock asked, moving into place behind a barrier and viewing the X-5 through a viso-shield that would have deflected all but a direct hit from the X-5's primary pholau-beams.

"Whoever is in there shows no inclination of coming out," one of the men said. "Our life-scan indicates a possible fading life-force. Perhaps, the rider is wounded and unable to disengage the hatch."

"On the other hand, the rider is possibly feigning injury, via mal-pip, and waiting to catch one or all of us," The Dzi Scholar said, although a mal-pip was hardly a standard piece of equipment on any X-5.

"Do we go in if it won't come out?" Murlock asked. "If its life-force is failing, as indicated, it would be a shame, I suppose, to have gotten it this far and, then, lose it before we can plug it into life-support." He picked up the microphone on the control board built into the side of the protecto-barrier. "Move in!" he said, his voice seeming to echo as it was played out through the speakers around the docking area.

Murlock and The Dzi Scholar kept out of the way. There were others in the zone better qualified at boarding the X-5 than they were; others who were certainly more expendable than either Murlock or The Dzi Scholar. As a matter of fact, the more The Dzi Scholar thought about it, the more he was determined to discuss the definite possibility with Murlock of how they were courting a setback to their plan by being where they were, even now, at one and the same time. What if The Dzi Scholar and Murlock had gone up in the same puff of smoke that had disintegrated Forlux? They really should be separated, considering the very good possibility that The Beast had already taken advantage of their pairing to attempt wiping them out.

Two crewmen used torc-flamers to sever, successfully, the still-closed hatch of the X-5.

"Life-scan indicates life-force in high-fade," someone

reported who was monitoring equipment that had rays beamed through the docked spacecraft. Whatever was inside, at least according to the equipment, was dying—and fast.

"Volunteers?" Murlock asked, immediately getting three who took to the hatch and tugged it off its sliced hinges. The metal hit the floor of the docking area with a loud reverberation, the volunteers moving in with weapons drawn.

"Standing by to assist!" Murlock promised.

"I have a straight line on the life-scan," the male at the monitoring equipment announced.

"Take in the life-support system. Now!" Murlock commanded, deciding the risk had to be taken. Whatever had escaped the explosion of Forlux, it was officially dead (according to the equipment), and it would remain dead if it didn't receive vital assist within a very short time.

"What do you think?" The Dzi Scholar asked, a few seconds later, having listened for any signs of hostility from within the X-5 and hearing none.

"I think we would have known by now if it was the enemy," Murlock said.

The survivor was female. Hydro-bi-sci Lylana Kore. A Dicelean. Murlock had recruited her and tagged her file while searching for a research assistant for the Dagil in the bio-life system of the Cilin-102 complex. He hadn't used her there, but he had remembered her when Forlux was initiated. Because of him, she had almost died on Forlux, and, then, she had almost died in the escape capsule in which she had, somehow, managed to flee the holocaust.

"What do you think?" The Dzi Scholar asked later, Murlock and he surveying the vital signs of the patient on the medo-board in the ship's hospit-cubicle. He wasn't familiar with the Dicelean anat-system, but the medo-board indicated life signs were, again, registering within the living quotient, even if the patient was still unconscious. Death, even for those few moments it had taken the life-support system to reach her and be attached, might well have done irreparable damage to impor-

tant cervo cells.

"We won't correctly be able to evaluate full damage until she regains consciousness and gives us a self-monitor," Murlock said with a shrug. "Until then, I'll be optimistic."

The two remained a few moments longer at the bedside of the Dicelean, at the medo-board, watching the female's three small breast swell and contract beneath the plasto-sheet spread over her.

"Only a Dicelean could love a Dicelean," someone had once told The Dzi Scholar. He remembered the statement now, even if he couldn't remember who had said it.

In truth, the species all looked pretty much the same to The Dzi Scholar, except for the three breasts of the females, compared to the two had by all males. Their heads were all uniformly round. Several Diceleans standing together always reminded The Dzi Scholar of a patch of fin-fin melons. The Dicelean skin pigment was almost the same shading of the fin-fin, right down to the scaly splotches that occurred with the fruits' prolonged exposure to sunlight. The Dicelean eyes, continually shielded by yellow membranes, and positioned triangularly within the center of the face, looked very much as if a Kyka bird had landed in the fin-fin patch and beak-tapped three identical holes, exposing melon flesh on each circular ball.

"We have to talk," The Dzi Scholar told Murlock, remembering that The Beast on Dicelean was called Dikela, one of The Beast's few manifestations as an inanimate object; the Dikela a species of tree that grew in the Syan Swamps and whose decaying bark caused a fatal gas that, when caught within the stiff Walwawa Winds—as it so often was—still periodically wiped out half that planet's population.

On how many planets—if any—had The Beast ever deigned manifest itself in some *magnanimous* form?

"Your right, of course," Murlock said, leading the way out of the hospit-cubicle and into the hallway that would eventually lead them to the ele-tubes and the liv-cubicles, "if you're thinking this latest move by The Beast took us off-guard."

"What *if* we had both died?"

"If you're suggesting a necessity of taking one of us important eggs from this particular basket, I'm inclined to agree," Murlock said. "However, we can't indiscriminately dump one us, or the other, into unfriendly space, can we?"

"I've checked the star charts," The Dzi Scholar said. "I could jettison in Quadrant V-429."

"For Siphion-6, you mean?" Murlock said, surprising The Dzi Scholar with his accuracy. Granted, there were only four possible alternatives for such a jettisoning, but it seemed more than luck that Murlock should have specifically pinpointed Siphion-6. "An unobtrusive exit would require utilization of a perto-craft during a garbage release. You'd be cramped to be sure, and any misfiring of jets en route would leave you considerably short of the mark."

"Be that as it may…."

"Of course, if you're willing to take the risk…."

"The Beast could very well know we escaped the holocaust on Forlux."

"The Beast could very well know *everything*," Murlock reminded. "It might even know when you jettison in a perto-craft, smelling of garbage."

That gave The Dzi Scholar a renewed feeling of apprehension, if just because Murlock was right. The Beast *might* very well know everything, having known it all along. The Dzi Scholar often had the distinct impression he was nothing more than The Beast's plaything. He often had the distinct feeling they were *all* nothing more than The Beast's playthings.

They took the ele-tube to the liv-cubicles. Murlock laid his handprint on the release mechanism to open the door of his apartment. He and The Dzi Scholar stepped inside, sliding the door closed behind them.

"Will you stay with Tindala on Siphion-6?" Murlock asked, sitting. He turned his full attention on his companion. He could sense The Dzi Scholar's surprise, even if it was impossible to read anything much in the blandness of a green face whose

diaphramgmatic circle pulsed even when The Dzi Scholar wasn't speaking.

"You know about Tindala," The Dzi Scholar said. It wasn't a question only because Murlock had already verified his knowledge.

"If you had been anyone but who you are, we wouldn't have stood for it," Murlock said. "I always marveled that you, of all people, would chance a security leak by teaming with a Category-9 female."

"Tindala is unclassified," The Dzi Scholar argued. Actually, he should have known better. If Murlock knew about her, then, of course, she had been classified.

"A Category-9 female," Murlock insisted. "Had she been a Category-10, we would have terminated her and saved us all a lot of bother. As it happens, though, she might surprise all of us by being of some use."

The Dzi Scholar sat down, pulling his robe securely about him. He had questions. Since Murlock intuitively sensed them, he proceeded to answer most of them before The Dzi Scholar needed bother asking.

"You really can't be too surprised that we not only know of her but went to the bother of running up an extensive categorical profile," Murlock said. "You've admitted that you and I are important clogs in this war we're fighting. How can you, then, expect everybody involved not to be a little concerned when you take up with this female who—at the time—was a common... ah, how should I phrase it, politely?"

"She was from a good family, fallen on hard times," The Dzi Scholar said, immediately coming to Tindala's defense.

"You checked on that, did you?" Murlock said. His question was superfluous. He knew from his own checks that The Dzi Scholar's checks on his mistress had been (lust-based?) superficial at best. "No? Well, as it turns out, she *was* from a good family, fallen on hard times; although, she's removed from that good family by at least three generations. Her ancestors fought on the wrong side of the Spice Wars on Rajah-D."

"She's not betrayed us!" The Dzi Scholar said. Then, lest Murlock read something into that statement that he shouldn't, he quickly added, "Not that I ever discuss such matters with her."

"Yes, luckily for you, she's genuinely only interested in pleasure and material things," Murlock said. "That probably reverts to the fact that her great grandfather was genetically altered to assure he would never again choose sides in a war—to possibly, once again, choose the losing side. However, whether interested in your business or not, whether capable of analyzing any such information or not, it can still be possible for some things to register on her brain, yes? All brains are like sponges, indiscriminately soaking up everything and releasing everything—when squeezed."

The Dzi Scholar knew the squeezing mechanism to which Murlock probably referred was the mind-leech. It could squeeze out every thought a brain had ever absorbed, sort them all out, and, via computer, play them all back to a viewer in living color. Someone like Tindala, if fallen into the wrong hands, could prove a viable information source to the enemy even if she— quite genuinely—hadn't the faintest notion as to what pertinent information her brain cells might have stored up without her knowing.

One of the disadvantages of the mind-leech was that once the information had been gathered and computerized, there was no returning it to the brain. As a result, the brain came through completely wiped clean.

The Dzi Scholar sought stringently to remember if, when in all-consuming rut, he had ever—EVER—let drop anything about his activities in front of Tindala. Having done so accidentally had become an even greater possibility once he had realized she had no interest whatsoever in what happened beyond the perimeters of her liv-space, in general, her sleeping-cubicle, in particular. Why be guarded around someone who obviously doesn't care or understand? Except that The Dzi Scholar had always known of the distinct possibilities of the mind-leech

being used.

"You do realize just how vulnerable Tindala would be if our enemies were to use certain electronic probing devises on her, don't you?" Murlock asked, knowing intuitively where The Dzi Scholar's mind was presently wandering. Not that Murlock need go so far as to explain to The Dzi Scholar just how concerned everyone had been who had been let in on the little secret that The Dzi Scholar's sexual impulses had suddenly kicked in and become a potential security problem. Not that The Dzi Scholar's advanced age had ever crossed off the potential for his having sexual liaisons. His species' sexual functions were hardly ever upset by the mere process of aging. It was just that Murlock would have hoped The Dzi Scholar had a bit more control and common sense. "I actually wouldn't have figured the Tindala woman as your type."

The Dzi Scholar recognized that as the put-down it was, and he was embarrassed and enraged by it. Probably because, before he had ever met that ravishing creature, with her slender pencil-thin figure, and her emerald-hued skin, he had never thought she was his type, either. He had always rather fancied himself as being more attracted to inner qualities (i.e. brain complexities and maturation, rather than the delicate circulatory tracings on a female's hands and feet).

"At least, she's a variation of my own species!" The Dzi Scholar attacked. Murlock's sexual associations with the Klinbears of Grinkc were legion. The Klinbears had even less resemblance to a civilized life-form than even the present-day humanoids. In fact, the Klinbears were primitive to the point where their sexual drives were of paramount importance, at all times, and not for the purpose of procreation. Like bees who only pollinated by accident, having no real plan to bring life to one kind of flower or another, the Klinbears were indiscriminate as regarded with whom or what they mated.

"At least Klinbears can hardly become a danger via mind-leech," Murlock reminded, knowing exactly what The Dzi Scholar had been insinuating. The Klinbears were ideal for

mating on two counts. One, it was highly doubtful they had minds to be leeched. Two, they died immediately upon completion of a sexual coupling (their death throes making for some damned exhilarating orgasms for anyone on board at the time, as Murlock could verify), leaving no chance of their divulging anything that their primitive cell structures might have picked up being whispered in any fits of passion by their partners. As far as Murlock was concerned, The Dzi Scholar would have been doing the cause a tremendous benefit had he channeled his sudden upsurge of sexual drives into mere releases with a Klinbear instead of risking the emotional strings so often formed between any male and female of the same species— even if the female in point computes out as having a metat-capacity somewhere very near that of a Klinbear.

"My apologies," The Dzi Scholar said hurriedly. "It's certainly not my place, now, nor has it ever been, to judge another's preference in certain physical departments."

Murlock knew The Dzi Scholar's apology was nothing more than an attempt to channel the conversation into another direction, after insinuating The Dzi Scholars "physical departments" were of no business to anyone but him.

"Your suggestion, as regards the Tindala woman, to use her as your cover, is one I find to have merit," Murlock admitted, "especially since you and I have gone to such extremes to keep her existence a secret. At the moment, I foresee no safer place for you than with her, since we've both agreed it does seem imperative the two of us part, as soon as possible."

"You agree, then, that I should jettison in a perto-craft in Quadrant V-429?"

"Yes."

"Then, I suppose I should begin making immediate preparations for that eject."

"After which, I will proceed to Tilox, and, if everything is as it should be, there, make arrangements to contact you and bring you up to date on the situation. If I do not get to you within a reasonable time frame, you should suspect the worst and work

from there, accordingly."

"I shall be optimistic," The Dzi Scholar said, coming to his feet.

"Yes," Murlock said, "there is certainly no harm in pretending we have just as good a chance of coming through this as The Beast has."

The Dzi Scholar went to the door, preparing to open it as Murlock voiced an apparent afterthought.

"You do know," Murlock said, "that it might be a bit too optimistic for either of us to believe Tindala might not have to be sacrificed, eventually, don't you?"

"Yes, of course I do!" The Dzi Scholar said, trying to control his temper. He was angry, because he had, from the beginning of his affair with Tindala, assured himself that she might eventually have to be terminated, while deep down he had refused to believe that would ever become the reality.

"That goes for the whelp, too," Murlock said, his sensors registering The Dzi Scholar's evident shock.

"What whelp?"

"Yours and Tindala's," Murlock said. "It seems she was so caught up in her passion the last time you two met, she forgot her dosage of quinquala. She should be whelping about the time you get there. Forewarned is forearmed."

CHAPTER FOUR

Excerpt from THE BOOK OF RELLIX:

"No!" she shouted, breaking away from the boy's encircling arms.

"Come on, Mave," Jeffrey cajoled. "Think of the fun the two of us can have; days and nights of sexual bliss. After all, what is the alternative?"

"No…no…no…no," she insisted, and scrambled out of the bed, to cringe against a mirrored wall.

Jeffrey began to fade. The room began to fade.

Did Mave really want Jeffrey and the room gone?

His handsome form, and that of the room, began to strengthen in intensity.

Mave's thoughts, alone, were bringing them back.

She crossed her forearms over her face, shut her eyes.

"Leave me!" she commanded.

When her arms came down, the house, the bedroom, and Jeffrey were gone. She was back in the Forest. Dielum was there, his hairy arms folded across his hairy chest. His thick lips were drawn back across his teeth, showing his canines to frightening advantage.

"Maybe, we could move things along a bit faster if you would come right on out and tell me just what it is you have in mind," Dielum suggested.

So, Mave told him.

IT SOUNDED TOO FANTASTIC to be true. So, why did Parker persuade himself to believe it? He did so, because it was flattering to believe he had a more important role to play than merely the son of Betty Mae.

Damn, what a tale Organa had spun of his being the real son of Mave Stilter, a god-seer on Antheer-D, and of Dielum, the Antheerinean God. Of his being kidnapped and brought here, passed off as Betty Mae's son, held captive in this cage that had him believing this small pocket of the universe was all that there was.

"As the son of Dielum, they feared having you remain on Antheer-D," Organa said. God, she was a beauty: all that honey-colored hair; golden eyes, flecked with black; golden gown, flowing in sensuous folds around the curves of her voluptuous body! "Yet, what with you the son of Dielum, they were reluctant to kill you. Deiticide has been known to bring down all sorts of unwanted bad luck on the participants. So, they brought you here."

"Who brought me here?" Parker wanted to know. There was so much he wanted to know.

"Oh, it is all so horribly complicated," Organa said with a low sigh that began deep in her throat and exited as a sweet breath of air. "You must not expect to understand it in a minute, certainly not in a day. You must merely absorb what you can, a bit at a time, and, in the end, all will, hopefully, surprise you by becoming clear."

Parker's ego was bolstered by his being the son of a god-seer and a god. He had always known, deep down, that there would be more for him in life than wandering the small space which had turned out to be surrounded by a canvas painting that defined the perimeters of his miniature cage.

"You mustn't be overly impressed with yourself, however," Organa warned, smiling. Her sensuous lips pulled back to reveal a row of even, white teeth. Literally, her eyes twinkled. "In the hierarchy of the gods and goddesses, Dielum of Antheer-D is but a minor deity. His subjects are so primitive that they are

often spurned by those who exist elsewhere in the universe."

"Are you not from Antheer-D, then?" Parker asked. He was sitting on the couch across from her, embarrassedly trying to hide, with his hands, the extreme state of his sexual arousal.

"I, from Antheer-D?" Organa asked and laughed. The youth was really more than she had expected. He was strong, and he was handsome. His mind was still uncluttered by a knowledge of the machinations that had taken place in the universe beyond Tilox. Organa felt certain inner stirrings that told her she wanted this young man's body as surely as she had wanted no one else's since the last of her kind had returned to Atla and perished when that planet had been destroyed in the vortex of Cataclys IX. Yet, she had to control her lust, her needs, and her desires. To surrender to them, now, and take this young man, prematurely, would be like plucking a tinial fruit from its vine before it was ripe: never to see a sweet and mature fruit, but, only, watch it wither and die. "Definitely, I am not from Antheer-D," she told him.

She had to be careful what she did tell him. He was such an innocent. They had apparently kept him ignorant of most everything, even the fact that his whole universe had been a space that could have easily been contained in a mere corner of but one of the many Bisoluitic spacecrafts which had plied the space lanes at the time of the Great Atlan Conflux.

"I am from Planet Atla," Organa said. They had probably kept him ignorant, because they'd wished his mind pliable when they thought it mature enough to be molded for use as a weapon against her. Organa had beaten them to the punch. She had arrived to find Parker's mind not yet programmed against her; so, she could imprint upon it what *she* wanted.

"Where is Atla?" Parker asked. Oh, but it was all so new to him! It was hard to believe that just the previous evening he had gone to bed in the farmhouse, only, now, to find all these new horizons opened to him.

"It was destroyed in the upheaval of Cataclys IX," Organa explained, "leaving very few of us Atlans left in the universe."

What would he say to learn that there was only *one* full-blooded Atlan left alive? What would he say to learn that the time mechanism inside Organa's brain, the same as which had sent all of her kind racing, lemming-like, to destruction, had somehow malfunctioned and allowed her—but no other Atlan—to survive?

"What was the upheaval of Cataclys IX?" Parker queried. There was so much to know.

"All will be clear to you, in time," Organa promised. "Now, you must simply trust me. I have come to rescue you from your prison. I have come to…"

"Why," Parker interrupted, "have you come to rescue me?" He was confused. The woman wasn't even from Antheer-D.

"We are distantly related," Organa said, amused by the way Parker's dark eyes lit up at that. Oh, she was going to have a marvelous time molding this pliable boy into the man she would someday take to her bed to father her child. "Our common ancestor was Captain Stone Hanlic, an Atlan astronaut, who crashed on Antheer-D and took to wife a distant relative of your mother, implanting within her the seed that made her offspring, by him, humanoid, where before all Antheerineans had been below the line."

"I am part Atlan?"

"Yes," Organa said. For the moment, that was all she told him, certainly nothing as to how he had been the end result of genetic experiments conducted by her enemy, the now-dead scientist Galun Rellix. An experiment which had been geared to produce the closest equivalent possible to Captain Stone Hanlic, that man who, upon crash-landing on Antheer-D, became a god in his own time. Of course, there was no way the end product, which was Parker, could be one-hundred percent pure, because the Atlan genes had been so diluted the moment Stone Hanlic had mated with a subhuman. But, of all the Atlans who had once been, Parker Stilter was as close as any living life-form could come to the original—save, of course, for Ayra Organa who had, through no conscious control of her own, thwarted the

holocaust which had robbed her of her kith and kin.

"What will you do with me now that you have rescued me?" Parker asked. Also, he was wondering just where his captors were at the moment. He had never seen them.

"Oh, there is much to be done when we leave here," Organa said, using gold-lacquered fingernails to push back a tumble of honey-colored hair which had fallen over her eyes, "if you but have the courage to take part in the adventure. Have you the courage, Parker of Antheer-D?"

"Yes!" he told her, although he knew that his courage had never been tested, because there had been no apparent enemies within the world from which Organa had rescued him. There were enemies, now, though, weren't there? If he could but be put to the test, then, he would prove his courage to this woman. For even without visible enemies, he had always felt courage was an inherent quality he possessed.

"On the other hand, maybe, you are content with the life you have known up until now," Organa said, knowing the young man would be a fool if he could think what he had was preferable to the life she was offering. "You needn't embark upon this new pathway. I can leave you here, just as you were before I came."

He was going to respond that he could never go back to his cage now that he had recognized it as the cage it was, but Organa raised a hand to silence him for the moment.

"I shall show you more of what has governed your life here," she said, standing. "Come with me."

He followed her out of that room and into the adjoining room with its hum of exotic machinery. The triangular door had slid open to let them through, dropping into place behind them.

She walked him down a line of the humming, blinking machines, stopping before one stretch of wall that was, now, where it hadn't been before, pockmarked with rectangles of opaque glass. If there was anything beyond the glass, Parker couldn't determine it through the milkiness of the screens.

Organa adjusted several mechanisms. Parker wondered how

she knew what she was doing; he wouldn't have known where to begin.

All the screens, nine in all, suddenly filled with light. Parker jumped back, made even more nervous by a resulting crackle that accompanied the ensuing flickering.

The screens filled with pictures familiar to Parker, because they were of scenes in and around the farmhouse. There was his bedroom…his mother's bedroom…the kitchen….

"I watched you on these monitors, earlier," Organa informed. "Looking for Betty Mae, were you?"

"Yes," Parker said, suddenly guilty he had completely forgotten Betty Mae.

"She's quite all right, by the way."

Parker had pretty much removed Betty Mae from his mind the minute he had discovered that she definitely wasn't his real mother. Strange, how quickly he had discarded her. Whether she was his real mother or not, she was the only mother he had ever known. Yet, there had always been that certain something missing between them. That *something* was now merely definable.

Organa turned to him, smiling as if she had somehow known all along what he was thinking. "Here." She fingered one of the dials on the control board. One of the screens zoomed in on a section of forest floor. "Recognize the bird?"

It was the camerrand with orange eyes. Dead.

"Not dead," Morgan disagreed. She *was* reading segments of his mind! "Do you know why?" She smiled a secret little smile that somehow made the desire in Parker's loins swell to even greater proportions.

"Why?" Parker asked, anxious to know the secret.

"Because, it was never alive," Organa said. "Nothing in your old world was alive, except you and Betty Mae. The rest merely provided the illusion."

Parker wondered if he'd really been so gullible as to have lived his eighteen tireum unable to distinguish reality from fantasy.

"Watch," Organa said. She touched several dials on the control board, and the camerrand came alive; or, at least, it seemed to do so, in that it hopped, flapped its wings, flew, even sang. Parker was made to hear its song—three shrill whistles—when Organa adjusted certain other dials to feed audio into the room.

Organa pinpointed the cornefell on another screen, and, then, she proceeded to resurrect it, following with a blue galuso. She started and stopped ants crawling, butterflies fluttering their wings, showing Parker—beyond a shadow of a doubt—that he had lived in a world only as real as the machines had made it.

"Who operates these when you're not here?" Parker asked, it having struck him, once again, that he had never met, even seen, his keepers.

"No one operates them when I'm not here," Organa said. "They have been programmed to operate themselves. They have been operating themselves most of the time you've been here. They would have undoubtedly continued to do so if I had not manually overridden them."

"All of these operate themselves?"

"Actually, they fill quite an impressive little pocket in space," Organa said. "Your enemies have spared no expense by way of duplicating a piece of Antheer-D as nearly as possible."

"I'm still not sure I understand just why anyone would go to the bother."

"Because, there is a marketplace, out there, that deals in souls," Organa said, cryptically. "As the son of a god-seer and a god, you could command souls that others would have for themselves."

"Souls?"

"Souls are power," Organa said. "You'll see that in time. You'll see why you were sequestered, here, away from prying eyes, in all hope that you would never realize who you were and what you might do with that knowledge."

"You'll show me the way?"

"I have come, haven't I?" Organa said. "The question, then,

is not whether I will show you the way, but whether you will follow the way I show you. Are you afraid to follow, Parker Stilter? Are you afraid of what you might find in the world into which I would take you?"

He would have lied to impress her, except, there was something about her that insinuated she knew the answer already and wouldn't have appreciated his lie.

"Yes, I'm afraid," he admitted, frankly.

"Good!" Organa exclaimed, her smile flashing wider. "For only a fool faces the unknown without fear. You are no fool, are you, Parker of Antheer-D?"

Her question was rhetorical, and Parker recognized it as such.

"Now, aren't you wondering what has become of Betty Mae?" Organa asked, changing the subject. At the same time, her expression gave every indication that she very well knew that Betty Mae had, once again, become the last thing in Parker's thoughts. "She has merely fallen asleep in the wild flowers out behind the barn. Flowers, by the way, which aren't flowers at all."

"She *is* real?" Parker asked, suddenly seeing the only mother he had ever known flashed on one of the viso-screens. Just as Organa had said she would be, Betty Mae was curled in the wild flowers—which weren't wild flowers—out in a segment of meadow—which wasn't a meadow—behind the barn—which wasn't a barn.

"Didn't I already tell you she was real?" Organa said, twisting a dial to bring Betty Mae's image into close-up. "Your enemies didn't want to chance you suckled by a robot with synthetic milk. Your captors found Betty Mae, having lost a child of her own, ideally suited to be your wet-nurse. No one was willing to risk your well-being, since there was always the chance that your father might someday discover their ruse."

"Where is my father?" Parker asked. "How does it happen that you're here with me and he isn't?"

"Your father thinks you're dead," Organa lied. "As for my part in all of this, well, as I have said, before, and, as I will

say again, it will all become clearer to you as time goes on." She doubted Parker could understand, at least not yet, how it was her, in her manifestation of Dielum of Antheer-D, who had fathered him on Mave Stilter, the god-seer. He was hardly aware of his own sexuality without complicating matters with tales of transmogrification beyond his present scope of comprehension. Yet, possibly, in his present child-like state of innocence, he might be more able to accept things on Organa's mere say-so, and…No. She wasn't prepared to bring him too suddenly into the reality of her world—which was now his world. She would coax him along, one step at a time, until, one day, he would well understand how his father on Antheer-D could, indeed, become his female lover within the Fortress on Bnth. "Your father is off doing whatever it is that gods must do."

Parker glanced back to the viso-screen and to Betty Mae still on it. "She looks so…dead," he said, trying to determine any signs of life in Betty Mae's slumbering form.

"'She has merely been temporarily disabled," Organa informed, "by a quite harmless gas. It leaves no trace of an aftereffect, duplicating natural sleep as nearly as any synthetic is capable."

"What will happen to her if I should escape this place without her?" Parker asked, more from a sense of protective obligation than from any real suspicion that he might actually choose to stay there, rather than indulge the temptations Organa was holding out to him.

"Happen?" Organa asked curiously. "Nothing much will happen, as I see it. She shall continue to live as she has always lived; mournful, at first, that you are gone, but adjusting to that tragedy as she has adjusted to other tragedies in her life. The cage shall take charge of her well-being as it always has. It is programmed for that function, you know?"

"Perhaps, she could be persuaded to flee with us?" Parker suggested, unable to imagine Betty Mae receptive to whatever the mysteries and dangers existing beyond the safe confines of her cage.

"No," Organa said, although she was positive that Parker had known the answer before voicing the question. "There is no chance of her coming with us, in that it isn't wise to remove certain hothouse flowers from their controlled environments and expect them to survive."

"Am I not even more of a hothouse flower than Betty Mae?"

"Certainly, there is the possibility that you might not survive the transplant," Organa admitted. Then, she hurried on, for fear she might scare him off. "However, some are stronger than others, more prepared to mutate, when necessary, in order to adjust to any changes in their environments. It helps when they're young, strong, and not grown so tightly into their pots that they are destroyed in the attempt to pry them free. If you are too afraid, I shall not force you to come with me. If you feel you're not suited to the adventure, you should feel free to remain."

Organa knew what she projected for him within her mind's-eye, but such pictures weren't always one-hundred percent accurate. Maybe, this wasn't the Chosen One of her dreams, the one who would be her consort and be the father of a power that would pale even the forces at the disposal of The Beast. If not, he would have to be destroyed. His unsuitability would make him worthless to her, but too much of possible worth as a pawn of her enemies.

"Perhaps, you would like a preview of what awaits you in the future, should you leave here?" Organa suggested. She could easily feed his mind inconsequential things which would still be enough to awe him in his innocence.

"A preview?" Parker asked, doubting he heard correctly. How could anyone give him a preview of events which hadn't yet happened?

"They'll be mere reflections upon mental glass but, nonetheless, viable threads of that final tapestry yet to be weaved."

Again, she wondered if she weren't moving too quickly. Even the watered-down mental projections she might summon for him might prove to be too much for a mind that had registered

so very little in eighteen tireum except a farmhouse, a barn, the contents of a few books....

"Show me a glimpse of my future," Parker begged, knowing he was caught securely within the web of enchantment that this beautiful woman had thrown out to ensnare him.

"Yes," Organa consented, fading before him. "Let it be so."

And, he saw the battles to be waged for control of men's souls. He merged into those battles to become a part of them, seduced completely by the eroticism of fear and his attempts to triumph over it.

CHAPTER FIVE

Excerpt from THE BOOK OF RELLIX:

She was searching for him, flinging her mental sensors over spaces unfathomable to those simple folk housed on this planet of Antheer-D. These beings didn't even know she existed—not in a body evolved long ago from real flesh and blood like their own. In fact, they worshipped her as Dielum: The Child Eater; as countless people—on countless planets, in countless solar systems, in countless galaxies—called her by other names, saw her in other forms: Txn, The Dead One; Boxer, The Draxl; Porun, The Taker of Men Child; Hexca, The Mother; on and on and on.

But to Galun Rellix, she was Ayra Organa, The Beast.

And she was out to kill him!

MURLOCK ORDERED THE CREW to prepare for suspended animation. He was taking them into SensaSpace in order to cover more quickly the distance between them and Tilox. He had to get to Tilox as soon as possible, fearing the worst, even though it seemed inconceivable that so much time and effort could have been put into a project, only to have it suddenly go against them. What would Galun Rellix have said to learn that his sacrifices, his life included, had been for nothing? Not just Galun Rellix, either, but Drawler, The Suicide; Quan Knoba, The Form-Changer; Saintal Ann; and so many, many more: all dead! For what? So The Beast could stop everything

now?

Oh, there were contingent plans, but none held out the hope of success that this one had. What better way to conquer The Beast than to give it an opponent of its own makeup; anyway the makeup of its original form, since The Beast had long since mutated into something far more complex than the humanoid Ayra Organa of Atla? While there had been no Atlans remaining that Murlock could grab up, convert to the cause, and thrust into the arena with The Beast, he had recruited Galun Rellix to make him one, or at least the next-best thing. Galun Rellix had experimented with the Antheerineans, without their knowledge, to breed, as nearly as possible, the equivalent of an Atlan male. For Atlan Astronaut Captain Stone Hanlic had mated with an Antheerinean subhuman and had, thus, shared with her his genes. His genes were the same as hopefully some still had by The Beast.

What if The Beast, now, had the result of Rellix's labors? What was worse, what if it had known of Tilox, all along, just waiting, as its enemies had waited for the boy to become a man? Wasn't that a gut-shuddering suspicion! That Galun Rellix might have obliged The Beast by giving it as near a kinsman as it was liable to find in the universe after the holocaust of Cataclys IX. Would The Beast be able to mold the raw material given it by Galun Rellix's genetic experiments? Or was the Antheerinean anat-system too polluted with the contributing genes of the original subhuman to be of much good?

They should have worked faster to program the boy. They should have begun as soon as his tynal cells had appeared in his brain. They had waited, knowing it would be of more benefit to have him programmed after the onset of puberty, after the tynal cells had jelled for absorbing all of the information they intended to feed them. So, what had they gained by waiting, but, possibly, a monster of their own making, destined to be turned against them by a power that Parker Stilter had no suspicion was evil incarnate.

WHY HAD THEY WAITED?! HOW HAD THEY

DELUDED THEMSELVES INTO BELIEVING THE BEAST COULD BE KEPT IGNORANT OF THE CAGE AT TILOX, WHEN IT SEEMED TO KNOW ALL ELSE IN THE UNIVERSE?

Murlock told himself he was paranoid. How could he know the Beast had sacked Tilox until he got there? All might still be all right.

Except...he...had...this...feeling...in his gut.

He leaned against the wall of plasti-metal, feeling the resulting vibrations as the perto-craft, The Dzi Scholar enclosed, was ejected with the garbage. Simultaneously, he wished his fellow Rysoxnian luck. The Dzi Scholar was undoubtedly going to need it. Certainly, Murlock wouldn't have given odds on the survival of a perto-craft in a mad dash for Siphion-6 when any trouble—ANY TROUBLE—would have meant coming up short of the mark. There was no communications equipment on board with which to signal for help, either.

Damn, but why were things always going wrong for them? Was there never a time when things went wrong for The Beast? Had there, in fact, ever been a time when The Beast didn't have an upper hand?

Murlock's great-great grandfather had said, yes, but no one had listened to him at the time. Everyone had been too busy struggling to survive in the aftermath of the lemming race that had seen the Atlan species siphoned back to its home planet. It had seemed a reverse of the Big Bang. Atla, the planet which had civilized and colonized a whole galaxy, suddenly siren-called back its Atlans, leaving behind whole worlds dependent upon machines that local populations couldn't operate to this very day.

"One of them lives!" Murlock's great-great grandfather had said on his deathbed. "Lo, but it would have been better for my seed, and my seed's seed, should all Atlans have perished in the vortex of Cataclys IX. At least to have been left two, to do battle amongst themselves. But one? *Just* one?"

Ayra Organa, Atlan female, humanoid, had survived the

holocaust. How, or why, nobody seemed to know. No one had even known for sure The Beast was a woman until Drawler: The Suicide paid with his life for that piece of information.

"One of them lives!" a dying Rysoxnian had once proclaimed. He had been an entomologist, an expert on insects, not humans. Everyone had forgotten it until Murlock, tireum later, found the tele-plate that recorded the death scene. Oh, what Murlock would now give to have that old man back, to be able to ask him how he—above all others—had come by his information that there had been an Atlan survivor of Cataclys IX? How had he prophesized disaster as a result?

Ayra Organa had, since, metamorphosed into something besides her initial humanoid state, but exactly what had she become? If Murlock's great-great grandfather once had the answer, no one seemed to have it now.

Murlock started down the hallway en route to the control deck. Now that The Dzi Scholar was on his way, the quicker the spacepod entered SensaSpace, the quicker Murlock would reach Tilox—for better of or for worse.

He was met by Gungol Fox in the corridor.

"The crew is completely bedded, sir," Gungol informed, "except for me, you, and The Dzi Scholar. I can't seem to raise The Dzi Scholar on the tele-communicator."

"He's bedded in his sleep-cubicle," Murlock lied, purely from reflex. Surely, Gungol Fox wasn't a spy. The Melantite's grandfather had been the Great Fox of Barren World War VI. The Foxes were certainly to be trusted. "I wired the Dicelean female for suspension, but the medic-doctor recommends a periodic check as she hasn't yet regained consciousness. I've left instructions that all of us reviving for instrument checks should make sweeps of her vital signs and revive the medic-doctor for assistance if circumstances seem to warrant it."

"You seem to have things well under control," Murlock complimented. So much so, it made Murlock tired. Lately, he had been getting more and more tired. Old age was creeping

up on him. He was approaching death-cycle, no closer to overthrowing The Beast than he had ever been. Where youth had allowed him the luxury of overlooking setbacks, with hopes for successes yet to come, his increasing age, now, told him there were very few "more tomorrows" on his horizon.

Damn, but the time had sped by since his recruitment. Who would carry on after he was gone? All of his peers were slowly but surely dying off, or being killed. There were so few young left who really even cared that the primary deity in the universe was a woman who had metamorphosed into something else and who could, now, change sex and physical structure at will, with the same ease with which she once changed wearing apparel.

Deities, appearing male, should not be humanoid females, in origin! At least not those deities worshipped by any male who was truly a man.

Had Murlock deluded himself into believing that it really mattered, in the long run? As he grew older, it seemed less and less a solid basis upon which to have launched a whole crusade, even if it had been all that had been needed to recruit him. The very idea that a female deity was pulling the wool over everyone's eyes, often masquerading as a male in order to fool worshippers, had been so horrible a premise for Murlock to accept, he had jumped on the bandwagon to rectify the horror. Others, of course, had been persuaded by other reasons, but Murlock had always known his prime enticement in joining had been male chauvinistic, born of his indignation that any female of any species would connive to trick men into kowtowing before her. The whole notion of it bordered on the obscene and became even more so when Murlock first realized just how much power one female had come to wield in the universe. It was staggering! Time after time, delving had uncovered age-old male gods, of so many planets, not being male gods at all but this woman in disguise. She was kicking the true male image out of all godheads! Murlock had been determined, and probably still was, to fight that blasphemy to the bitter end.

He ceased his self-analysis of his motives, probably because

he had taken to doing just such thinking more and more often, always ending up with the same conclusion, right or wrong, that he had devoted his whole life to prove (1) males were superior too females, and (2) no male Rysoxnian, himself included, was inferior to a mere woman from Atla.

"Why are you one of us, Gungol Fox?" Murlock asked, stopping his walk down the hallway and turning to his companion.

How surprised the young man looked. Would anyone have looked as surprised?

Murlock really did want an answer to his question. It was surprising how little he really knew about what motivated other solders fighting on his side of this war. Identifying motivations was the business of recruiters. The only time it usually concerned Murlock was when he acted as a recruiter in his own right. Which, considering his position in the hierarchy, wasn't very often.

He had played a key role in the recruitment of Galun Rellix. Yes, he and The Dzi Scholar had been necks-deep in that one. What arguments had they used to bring Rellix around? It was so hard to remember, especially since one had a tendency—at least Murlock had the tendency—to try and forget arguments used to seduce a life-form to its death. Galun Rellix was dead, because Murlock and The Dzi Scholar had enticed him with promises of....

Not of money...nor of fame...nor of power. The Beast offered those. The Beast gave away whole worlds to sycophants who would but bow down just to give it worship. What they had offered Galun Rellix was a chance to fight against Evil—with a capital "E". It was surprising how many people could be charged up by the idea that they—and they alone—were possibly all that stood between chaos (a.k.a. Evil), and peace and goodness with mercy prevailing. In the same instance, it was surprising how many of those same high-minded idealists could be compromised once The Beast started throwing around the goodies. Every life-form had its own price. Who had said that? Whoever it had been, Murlock agreed with him one-hundred percent.

Even Murlock could have been bought if it had been possible for a certain female ever to convert—genuinely—into a male.

It helped, of course, when The Beast wasn't aware of just with whom it was dealing, and if a bargainer never knew just how much The Beast could be persuaded to offer once the bargainer's true leanings became obvious.

Galun Rellix had confronted The Beast in its manifestation of Zurl on Delcon Prime, Galun trading gathered souls for a laboratory when, had The Beast but known who had put Galun up to that request, it would have offered much more than it had to bring Galun Rellix over to its side.

Gungol Fox had been taken aback by Murlock's question, there in the corridor. Additionally, he was taken aback by the way Murlock obviously retreated into his own thoughts immediately upon asking the question. Gungol took advantage of Murlock's retreat into himself to try and come up with an answer that would satisfy. He ended up providing an old standard.

"There has to be a few of us to take a stand against Evil," Gungol said finally. By that time, Murlock had been so involved in retrospection that Gungol wondered whether or nor Murlock had really wanted an answer.

"Yes, there does have to be a few of us, doesn't there?" Murlock said, coming back from his thoughts at the sound of Gungol's voice.

He started off down the hallway, leaving Gungol to catch up with him. He didn't know what was getting into him. The whole organization was liable to tumble if it started to rot at its brain centers. If Murlock had had any serious doubts about his present mission in life, he should have had them worked out a long time ago. It…was…simply…way…too…late…now!

Gungol was worried by Murlock's strangeness. It was unexpected and not at all typical. Stopping in the corridor of the spacecraft to ask a fellow member of the cause to expound upon his motivations just wasn't something Murlock was apt to do. Unless…

It couldn't be that Murlock suspected anything, or he would

have done more than merely ask a question!

By the time they reached the control deck, Gungol had time to recover his cool. The rest of the crew was laid out in suspended animation. Murlock walked to his own wire-up and did a quick check to make sure everything was in proper working order.

"Who's assigned first watch?" Murlock asked, as soon as he was satisfied with the equipment that would soon suspend his body functions until the craft tripped out of SensaSpace around Tilox.

"I am, sir," Gungol replied, knowing that if Murlock did suspect anything, it would likely be now that Murlock would act upon it.

"Very good!" Murlock said, allowing Gungol an almost audible sigh of relief.

"Allow me to help you with hook-up, sir," Gungol volunteered. The sooner he got Murlock under, the better he was going to feel. Murlock made him nervous, if just because Murlock was nobody's fool.

Why had Murlock asked a question regarding Gungol's motivations?

"Yes, hook me up, will you?" Murlock said, slipping into the contoured chair. "The sooner I'm under, the sooner I'll know the better or worse of our present situation."

Gungol didn't press for specifics. He might have chanced it under other circumstances, but the queerness of the episode in the hallway left him paranoid. He didn't want Murlock to think he was overly curious.

Actually, Gungol was trembling when his hand poised above the activation switch.

"Ready, sir?" he asked, not wanting Murlock to see that he was so overly anxious.

"Yes," Murlock said absently. "I'm ready."

Gungol flipped the switch.

What had he expected? That the suspended animation device wasn't going to work? If he had suspected that, he was worried for nothing. The device worked perfectly. Almost immediately,

Murlock was under. It was highly unlikely he would have so willingly gone under if he suspected anything.

Hell, why should he suspect anything? Certainly, Gungol hadn't given any outward appearances of having any advantage when the cannon projectiles had penetrated the Forlux facility. In truth, there were times when he had even wondered if his promise of safety from The Beast might have been overlooked by his benefactor; except, just as The Beast had promised, he had come through in one piece.

He rechecked the systems, making sure they were all operational. When he was content that he was the only one on board who wasn't in suspended animation, he began a thorough examination of the area to discern whether there were any recording devices or cameras clandestinely planted to somehow take advantage of the moment to record his betrayal. He came up with nothing.

He went to his contour chair and sat in it. He didn't put himself into suspended animation. He didn't put the ship into SensaSpace. Either move would have made it impossible for him to conduct mental communication with his master.

Quickly, he located and isolated the beta-1 needed for mental-link. Only then, did he remember that The Dzi Scholar had been suspended not on the main control deck but in a liv-cubicle. Not that that was unusual; one of the prerogatives of rank. Still, it would have been unwise to announce, with any assurance, that the ship was en route with a full contingent when he didn't know for a fact that The Dzi Scholar was bedded out elsewhere.

He isolated and confined the beta-1, left his contour chair, and headed down the hallway to make doubly sure The Dzi Scholar was where Murlock said he would be.

CHAPTER SIX

Excerpt from THE BOOK OF RELLIX:

Hanlic's injection of superior seed, and resulting evolution, hadn't much improved the stock. After more than a quantiuminium having passed since Atla had been siphoned into the vortex and ejected as space dust into the void beyond the veil, the Antheerineans were still hardly impressive in either their physical or intellectual makeup.

They were primitives in the most literal sense. Even with the assist of the myron cube, they could be trained to do only the simplest tasks.

Nor was the Antheerinean girl, Mave—even with the generations of selective breeding which had gone into her being—anything of great exception.

But, then, Galun had never found the humanoid form, or its brain, to be worth any special note—which had provided the main source of his surprise when he'd learned from The Dzi Scholar that Ayra Organa had evolved from such unlikely beginnings.

"You judge humanoids purely by what you have of them to be seen around you today," The Dzi Scholar had chided. "The best examples, though, have all evolved out of their original matrix. We see today's Terarlians, the Antheerineans, the Etharians, and we make value judgments based upon that. The fault is not grasping that these were never the epitome of what their humanoid form once had to offer. During the Great Atlan

Conflux, your and my ancestors were as backward to the Atlans as the Antheerineans are to us today."

TINDALA MEUSEEMA HAD WHELPED twice before. The other two, though, had been preemies. She had gone to the Fos-woman Muloc to assure that they would be preemies. This was the first full-term she had whelped. It would certainly be her last.

She checked herself in the reflecto-glass, admiring her pencil-thin body, running her hands, streaked as they were with their lacy network of veins, up and down her midsection, hoping there was no whelping bulge but thinking there might very well be one that remained. Well, at least she wouldn't have to be as slim as she had been, since she no longer needed to rely on her body for her livelihood. She was well-fixed now. Not that she planned to give up the little pleasures. The Dzi Scholar really wasn't all that bad.

Would The Dzi Scholar notice the whelping bulge that remained after delivery? She hoped not. She had no desire to make any explanations. Not that she would have to do so. Since The Dzi Scholar was such an infrequent visitor, she would probably be back in tip-top form upon his next arrival, and he would be none the wiser.

What, she wondered, would The Dzi Scholar think if he knew such a very few minutes of his passion had brought such a high price on the marketplace? Who would have ever dreamed…?

It certainly didn't turn out this lucky for some females in Tandala's trade. Borsuna whelped two full-terms and had gotten not a penny, only heartache and a whelp bulge that made her so ugly that few high-payers ever looked at her again. Borsuna should have gone to the Fos-woman Muloc and assured herself of preemies. Some females were plain stupid!

Tindala draped her body in her new robe of soft cream that showed off the emerald green of her skin to exceptional advantage. More than once, she had heard it said that there was no female on Siphion-6 who had skin that compared to hers, by

way of fine coloring. Usually, emerald green was the color attributed to the aristocracy. She had no doubt but that her ancestors' genes could be thanked for her good looks, even if they had fought on the wrong side of the Spice Wars, and, thus, given her very little else. Well, she had amended their mistakes, hadn't she? Now, she had a bank account that would have her on easy street for a very long time.

"Oh, thank-you, thank-you, Paldon, The Dzi Scholar!" Tindala said, dancing over to the bed-square and falling down on it, stretching sensuously.

It did feel so…so…good being whelped, having all that excess weight finally spilled out of her belly. She felt so good that she would have welcomed a caller about now, if she didn't know that she should refrain from any such activity for at least three more denos

She shut her eyes, thinking, suddenly, that she had never even seen the little mite. She didn't even know if it was male or female. Not that it really mattered. It was probably for the best that she hadn't seen it. Mother's instinct was a tricky thing with which to contend, and she might have seen the whelp and gotten all weepy and possessive. Then, again, she thought that would have been highly unlikely. There was no way she pictured herself a mother, doing motherly things. She only saw herself as she was, now—lying on a luxurious bed-square, draped in a luxurious robe, knowing there was plenty in the bank to buy her all of the additional luxuries she could ever possibly want.

She didn't think too much about the Mammoosse, because she didn't like unpleasant thoughts. While there had certainly been nothing unusually unpleasant about the Mammoosse handing over the currency for the merchandise, there had still been something about the little creature—despite Mammoosses not all that uncommon on Siphion-6—which had sent Tindala's circulatory juices vortexing to the freezing point. At first, she thought he—she presumed it was a he, it being so damnedably difficult to tell the sex of the hairy things—had come to avail himself of her professional services. In no uncertain terms, she

had told him that he had stopped on the wrong doorstep, referring him to Borsuna who would have welcomed even a Mammoosse for a bed partner. But Jaccuue—that the Mammoosee's name—insisted that Tindala was, indeed, the very one he had specifically come to *see*. *Not* to bed. This allowed her a small breath of relief.

However, when she heard what he had come for, she had, immediately, gone back to being disturbed. Not that his offer of payment for her whelp wasn't a god-send, but Tindala had only just realized, the day before, that she was with whelp, and she had certainly not spread the word around anywhere the Mammoosse might have heard about it.

"Whatever gives you the impression that I'm with whelp?" Tindala had asked the hairy monstrosity on her doorstep. To have invited him in would have caused all kinds of nasty gossip. As it was, he could easily be mistaken for a salesperson if kept on the outside. Mammoosses, known to be persuasive talkers, were often found in the selling profession.

This Mammoosse, though, hadn't been selling anything. He had been buying....

"Let's not play games," he told her. "You're with whelp. You know you are. I know you are. I want to purchase the mite when it drops at full-term."

...and they had sealed the deal.

"Don't bother asking any questions," he told her, each time he checked by to see how things were progressing.

When her condition began to show, she retired to her bedroom, having everything she needed delivered to her, and scaring away everyone by announcing, through the porch tele-communicator, that she had something contagious and had been quarantined by the local medi-installation.

She whelped herself—no big deal!—squatted over a sterile combis pail and, then, handed the results, without even bothering to look inside, over to Jaccuue who was there almost to the very moment Tindala finished the chore. He couldn't have turned up at a better time, either, since his punctuality prevented

Tindala from having had the time to be tempted into peeking at the result of her and The Dzi Scholar's few moments of heated passion.

In retrospect, she did wonder if the whelp had come out in its mother's shade of exquisite green, or whether it was the inferior shade of its sire. If it was with her shade, the Mammoosse had possibly made himself a good bargain, especially if he had plans to sell the child's favors to those who always got such a big charge out of young things AND couplings with a possible aristocrat. Tindala had certainly had to deal with both those kinds of customers in her lifetime.

Yet, the Mammoosse had bought the whelp sight unseen, not even bothering to peek into the pail on the doorstep to see if he had his monies' worth. He merely handed over the credit cube for payment due and went hurriedly down the street with the combis pail hefted over one hairy shoulder.

Oh, well, whatever the Mammoosse wanted with the whelp, he now had it, and Tindala couldn't be bothered. Her mind drifted to planning her long overdue vacation: a pastime that never bored her, especially now that she actually had the finances to go wherever she pleased, whenever she pleased.

"Maybe to Mimosa-F," she told herself aloud. There was a very expensive rejuvenation farm on Mimosa-F which could certainly remove any telltale bulge remaining from Tindala's dropping of the whelp. Or, maybe she would....

Her thoughts were interrupted by a signal from the telecommunicator in indication that someone was on the porch. Her immediate reaction was to think that it was the Mammoosse, who, having finally discovered the whelp was of the wrong color, was bringing it back for a refund. If that were the case, he would have another think coming. She had deposited her credit cube in a very safe place, and no one was going to pry it out of her.

Once again, the indicator sounded evidence of some visitor, and Tindala decided she would just remain silent in the hope that whoever it was would simply give up and go away. However,

what happened, after the third try to raise her, was that whoever was out there inserted an entro-key-release into the reflecto-lock and sent the front door sliding open to reveal the startled Tindala who was standing in the middle of the liv-space.

"My God, Paldon!" she exclaimed. Who, after all, had she been expecting? There was only the one male, The Dzi Scholar, to whom she had given an entro-key-release, and here he was.

"I thought you were out," The Dzi Scholar said, partly in accusation, partly in relief that he had been wrong.

"I've had a headache all morning," she said, gliding toward him, giving him an enticing peek of one lacy-veined leg through the slit in the right side of her robe. "I thought you were one of the girls come to bore me into distraction with small talk."

"Obviously, I'm not one of the girls," The Dzi Scholar said, a little piqued; although, Tindala saw no reason whatsoever why he should be. He should have had the common decency to call before coming, instead of dropping in out of the blue. Had he come expecting to find her coupled with someone else? Well, if he had, hadn't she fooled him? Since the evening she'd given him his own entro-key-release, she had made it a point to do most of her entertaining in a small liv-cubicle she rented across town.

Still, she was glad to see him. Hadn't she just been fanta-sizing a male caller but minutes before? Here was one of the best of her regulars. He was always such a spirited lover, too, after his usually long absences. This last absence had been such an exceptionally long one that Tindala had actually wondered if he was ever coming back.

"How quickly the sight of you has made my headache fly," she said. She lifted her face to his sensuously vibrating diaphragm as it touched hers. She got a thrilling all of the way down to her big toes.

Apparently, she was more ready for The Dzi Scholar than even she had been able to gauge. Her extended period of being with whelp had been the longest dry run she could remember, since she had stumbled onto the facts of life at a vey early age.

"Here, come with me into the bedroom," she said, finding his hand hidden within the folds of his robe. She pulled him toward her. She knew she should wait those three more denos, but she knew giving any excuses why she couldn't comply would only arouse The Dzi Scholar's suspicions. Besides, she had just about decided, for certain, that she would vacation on Mimosa-F, confident the facilities, there, would be able to take care of any mending necessitated by her surrendering, now, to any premature indulgences.

Sure enough, The Dzi Scholar followed her, but Tindala couldn't help sensing that all wasn't what it was supposed to be. Then, maybe, she was imagining it. The Dzi Scholar was always a little uptight whenever he came in from the field. It probably never helped him that he never talked about where he'd been, or what he'd been doing. Tindala had often wondered what it was that kept The Dzi Scholar from even hinting about the nature of his profession. However, she never did wonder for too long, because—in the long-run—she didn't much care. As long as any male had the money to keep her in the manner to which she had grown accustomed, it didn't much matter what he had to do to get the currency. For as long as Tindala had known him, The Dzi Scholar had been exceedingly generous.

"Here, I shall even put on siphon sheets," Tindala said, turning a switch which automatically replaced the sheets on the bed-square with the new, more sensuous ones. "I only wish I'd known you were coming so I could have had some Kalalil delivered. I do remember how you love Kalalil, especially when pitted and soaked overnight in sim-sim."

She adjusted the lighting so it was softer and would better conceal, rather than emphasize, the possible bulge from her recent full-term whelping.

"There," she said, dropping languidly to the bed-square, allowing one thin leg seductively to escape the robe. Simultaneously, she was sure some material kept her stomach concealed. "Take off your robe and make yourself more comfortable."

However, The Dzi Scholar showed no indication that he had any immediate intentions of disrobing or joining Tindala on the bed-square. He paced the room from one side to the other, taking in all the space at a glance.

"Where is it?" he asked, stopping and nailing her with a stare.

"What?" she asked. She didn't know to what he referred. It never crossed her mind that he might know about her whelping. Except for thoughts regarding her figure, she had almost forgotten, already, that she'd dropped the mite.

"You know *what!*" The Dzi Scholar accused. It was obvious she had whelped. Her figure, beneath the clinging folds of her robe, despite the tiniest evident bulge of her belly, was simply too thin for her still to be holding the whelp inside of her.

For a moment, it passed through his mind that Murlock might have been wrong. Quickly, he rejected that notion, since there was no reason for Murlock to have made it up. However, there was every reason for Tindala to lie. She knew he wanted no offspring. He had made that perfectly clear at the outset of their relationship.

"Honestly, I don't know what you're on about," Tindala insisted.

No way, though, did The Dzi Scholar believe she didn't, by now, have some clue.

"Did you actually think you were going to keep it a secret?" he asked. He was angry, not only at himself, for having allowed his getting into this mess, but at Tindala for trying to deny there *was* a mess.

Again, he visually checked the space—carefully. No sign of the whelp.

"Did you see a Fos-woman?" he asked. At the same time, he remembered that Murlock had mentioned nothing about a Fos-woman. Murlock had distinctly insinuated that Tindala was going to whelp a full-term. If Murdock had known Tindala's condition, it was hardly likely he would have overlooked her having decided for a preemie.

"Yes," Tindala said, gathering herself up to the head of the

bed-square and pulling her robe protectively around her. "I saw a Fos-woman."

Yet, she knew, the moment she said it, that it was the wrong thing to say. Once she had embarked upon the lie that she hadn't been with whelp, she should have stuck with it. It was bound to seem funny that she would have denied whelping if it had been a preemie. As a preemie, the whelp would have offered The Dzi Scholar no threat, so Tindala should have, from the start, pretended a preemie instead of no whelp at all. Changing her story, in mid-stream, was not the correct tactic for her to have made.

Still, she didn't know why The Dzi Scholar was so upset, or why he might feel threatened by an absent full-term whelp in the first place. It wasn't as if Tindala had come crying to him about how he had made her with whelp and how she, therefore, needed money and assistance from him. She had handled it all herself. Neither he nor she was liable to be bothered with it ever again. It was gone, disappeared into the combis pail carted off by the Mammoosse.

"You needn't worry," Tindala assured. "It is all taken care of."

"But I *do* worry!" The Dzi Scholar told her; although, even he wasn't yet sure just why he was so worried. Surely, he wasn't beset by sire instincts, was he?

"I have made all the disposal arrangements," Tindala bragged. "I didn't wish to bother you with them, knowing your feelings about such things. So, why must you bother with them, now?"

"We agreed there would be no whelp from our couplings," The Dzi Scholar reminded. "You said you never had any desire to whelp and knew how to prevent one. That is what you told me, isn't it?"

"Yes, I did," Tindala admitted. "I should be very angry with you for having excited me to the point of my forgetting my dosage of quinquala," she added, thinking that it might be best to put the blame on him. Actually, it was more than a little tiresome blaming anyone. Why, oh why, was he making such a

needless fuss?

"That doesn't tell me why you went ahead and whelped," The Dzi Scholar said. "It certainly doesn't explain why, upon discovering you were with whelp, you didn't immediately consult a Fos-woman to arrange for a preemie."

"I simply couldn't bring myself to see the Fos-woman," she lied, wishing he would quit all this nonsense and come onto the bed-square with her.

"You didn't seem to have any trouble going to a Fos-woman on those two other occasions," The Dzi Scholar said. He noted her surprise. "Oh, you, perhaps, thought I was ignorant of your other two preemies? Well, in fact, I know a good deal about you, Tindala, except why decided to carry my whelp to full-term."

Indeed, Tindala was surprised that The Dzi Scholar knew about the other two preemies.

"That you so willingly went to the Fos-woman twice before reassured me that, should an accident ever happen between us, you would have the common sense to go the Fos-woman, again, to take care of it."

"But I *did* take care of it!" Tindala insisted. Whether with the Fos-woman, or in some other manner, what can it possibly matter to you?"

"What other way are we talking?" The Dzi Scholar demanded.

"You're being ridiculous!" Tindala said, coming off the bed. She had quite tired of The Dzi Scholar's cross-examination. He was simply going to have to take her word for the matter having been taken care of to everyone's satisfaction. She couldn't' tell him that she had sold the inconsequential whelp for a credit cube, because that confession would possibly have The Dzi Scholar asking for his half of the profit. Oh, she knew The Dzi Scholar was already well-fixed, but did anyone ever have enough currency—or ever be too thin?

She refused to share her profit from this deal, especially when he, by his own admission, would have preferred she'd paid a Fos-woman for a preemie.

"I have said my last on the matter!" she insisted.

"Have you, now?" he said, grabbing her arm and tossing her back onto the bed-square. He threw open his robe and reached inside one of the inside pockets.

She knew what he produced from there, even though it was a miniature version of the more popular model portrayed in horror comics. The sight of it made her tell him everything. In the end, though, he used the mind-leech anyway—in order to verify.

Then, he dissolved her in a combis pail similar to the one the Mammoosse had used to cart away the whelp. He used a delitiun gun-ray brought from the ship especially for just a contingency. When he was finished melting her to gelatinous mass, she didn't even completely fill the bucket with green slime.

He was glad to have her gone, and not only because she had sold their whelp to an agent of The Beast. Oh, yes, The Dzi Scholar knew that Jaccuue was no ordinary Mammoosse. For what would an ordinary Mammoosse want with the whelp of The Dzi Scholar? But, The Beast would possibly have a use for it, even though it would be sorely surprised were it to believe that The Dzi Scholar would be persuaded into anything with threats toward a mite that should have never been whelped in the first place. He was glad to have Tindala gone, because he had always resented the fact that he had succumbed to the temptation to couple with her. He had never quite gotten over the frightening something that had happened to him in that bar, there on Siphion-6, when he had first seen her and been informed she was available. How could he have lusted for such a woman? Murlock had been right: she was a Category-9 female. It made no difference that her coloring was emerald green. Her claim to that color had not been through her own merits but through the gene contributions of ancestors dead and buried before her time.

She had been a Category-9, and a fool to boot, satisfied for a credit cube when The Beast might well have offered her whole worlds—if she had but had the sense to ask for them. The Dzi Scholar was actually insulted that The Beast had the whelp so cheaply. Not that The Beast would find the whelp worth even

what little it had paid for it.

The Dzi Scholar carried Tindala's residue to the nearest sewer drain, seeing her emerald coloring cling momentarily to the grating before slithering into the depths. He rinsed the rest of her out in the river, and then set the bucket to float. Possibly, he had been seen, either going in, or coming out of Tindala's liv-space, maybe both, but he doubted she would be missed for quite awhile. It was doubtful she had done much socializing, leading up to her whelping—she had been way too vain to expose her bloated body to her fellow working females. Even if someone had seen The Dzi Scholar arrive or leave, what did it matter? Death was the ongoing risk of every girl in Tindala's trade.

CHAPTER SEVEN

Excerpt from THE BOOK OF RELLIX:

"It may offer you treasures beyond your imagination, pleasures untold, cities, or whole planets even, to lord over in its
name," The Dzi Scholar had briefed Galun of Delcan Prime,
during the days when The Dzi Scholar, was the chief Advisor to
the Rellixian Cult on Delcan Prime, in those days when Galun
was stealing Delcan Primenian souls from The Beast's coffer,
"but be not deceived...."

PARKER WAS BATTLING with a computer which projected
a shadow opponent into the room. They—Parker and the three-
dimensional apparition—were fighting with scima-knives and
small, circular wrist shields. When shield hit shield, or knife
hit knife, or knife hit shield in parry, the sound effects were
realistic enough to have Parker believing he was engaged in
actual close combat. When the apparition's knife made contact
against Parker's flesh, there was no drawing of blood but a
resulting electric shock to Parker. When Parker scored a touch,
the phantom—who, when struck, had the apparent consistency
of real flesh and bone—immediately spotted red. A successful
thrust to a vital spot by the apparition had Parker feeling an
extra strong jolt; if such a thrust was by Parker, the apparition vanished. In either case, there was an audio announcement
by the computer: i.e. Kill by Parker of Antheer-D. The apparition was termed by the computer as "opponent Y-1-Y". Parker

had been assured that opponent Y-1-Y was only one of several programmed into the extensive electronic complex. However, it was opponent Y-1-Y which would give Parker the training he needed to meet the challenge in the offing.

"A challenge?" Parker had asked, simultaneously disturbed and thrilled by Organa's pronouncement that there had been one. "Why would anyone want to challenge me to battle?"

"Word has already leaked out that you have been freed of your cage," Organa said. "Your enemies have already begun to tremble and have sent a pawn to be sacrificed in testing your metal. When you have faced several of these insignificant challenges, and been victorious in each one, your enemies will be less anxious to sacrifice even their pawns, since your victories will be beneficial to your reputation in that there are some who will always flock only to a winner. You will be the one seemingly winning against all odds."

She must have read his mind, for she smiled.

"You needn't worry of dying, Parker," she told him. "Anyway, not right now. The true test of your worth will come much later, when you are face to face with your real enemies. Those who come now are but peons."

"I've never fought before," he confessed.

"Do you think I would send you into any battle, even against peons, unprepared to conquer?" Organa asked with a delightful laugh. "No way would I have you go to such battle without every chance of you being victorious."

Therefore, she had sent him to training with the computer which, she told him, was a far more skillful opponent than the Styrolean who had challenged him would be.

"Styrolean?" Parker had wanted to know. There was so very much he wanted to know. Things had moved almost too fast since Organa had put him into a strange craft that had actually traveled among the stars, bringing him to this place that had rooms huge enough to dwarf all of Tilox. Tilox, he had since learned, was nothing more than an asteroid, a mere speck in space.

Styrolea is a planet in the Star System Filii-3," Organa said. "See, you have enemies in worlds of which you now know nothing. At the moment, be not too concerned regarding your ignorance of such matters, because—before long—I shall expose you to a learning devise from before Cataclys IX. It will so cleverly stuff your mind with necessary information that it will seem as if you always knew it."

There were to be tests, first, though, before Organa subjected Parker to the miracles of the Gorda Bank. There was information in the Gorda Bank which Organa wouldn't want to fall into the hands of the enemy. She was fairly convinced that she had gotten to Parker before he had been programmed against her, but this group of adversaries had proved surprisingly capable in the past, and Organa wanted to be positive that Parker was an ally rather than an enemy mole.

Besides, it was imperative Organa have a man who wouldn't be afraid to kill or to die, a man who could be trained in the ways of battle. For Parker's survival might very well depend upon his ability to defend himself with traditional weaponry, in that he wasn't a pure-blooded Atlan, and, thus, could never possess all of those powers Organa had at her personal disposal to assure the safety of her person. She wanted a partner, not someone she would be forced to baby-sit and look over at all times. It was imperative that Parker prove himself as a man of courage before she pulled him even more deeply into her secret world.

Not that she was in any way prepared to risk losing him at this early date, certainly not to the claws of a traitor Styrolean. The battle, unbeknownst to Parker, would be rigged in his favor. Yet, since the young man could hardly know the outcome was already ordained, he would react as if his life were at stake, and Organa would be able to tell much by observing that. So would the computer, for the computer was storing up all of Parker's movements, all of his responses, to better act as his teacher.

Parker parried, faded back, turned, stabbed a fatal penetration; the apparition disappeared.

"Kill by Parker of Antheer-D," the computer announced in its metallic monotone.

"Hey, are you sure you weren't born with a scima-knife in your hand?" Organa called encouragement.

She saw him beam with his success. Of course, the computer was programmed to let him win, on occasion, which had now happened. As in any training program, one had to win sometimes for incentive to continue. Unknown to Parker, the computer was unbeatable.

"Ready to try again?" Organa asked, deciding, once again, that he was an extremely handsome member of his species, especially stripped as he was to the waist and sweating.

"Not content to see me quit on a win?" Parker asked. Actually, he enjoyed these workouts.

"Maybe, we'll let you quit on your next win," Organa bantered. "Until then, I'll leave you for a few moments so that you're not distracted."

Suddenly, the apparition reappeared, and immediately thrust for a kill. However, Parker had already learned to expect the unexpected. He was there to deflect the scima-knife with his wrist shield. Organa left him to his instruction.

Immediately beyond the door, she faded. She had become too jaded with other modes of movement far more convenient than the rather outmoded walking or running required of her in her Atlan form, although she was growing a bit more used to it, again, since she moved everywhere with Parker in that manner, since he hadn't yet mastered those means of space trip-ping which were within his power. She couldn't yet risk a fade in his presence, nor a transmogrification, because Parker, in his present naïve state, hardly could be expected to understand. Everything in its own time!

She arrived at her intended destination within the Fortress, but she didn't materialize until she had taken the opportunity to observe her prisoner. She was pleased to see that his inju-ries were pretty much healed. Admittedly, he still moved with a definite, uncharacteristic, stiffness, as a result of his extensive

battering during his fall, but it was doubtful Parker—having never seen a Styrolean—would recognize he was battling someone who was a long ways from being in prime condition.

When she did materialize, it was, again, in the form Ayra Organa. She found that form as pleasing as most, and even more so, these days, since she had first recognized the desire it sparked in Parker's eyes. She had almost forgotten what it was like to see admiration exhibited by someone more her original matrix than the other life-forms with which she had been forced into contact since her kind had run madly to their destruction without her.

"Ah, Quorulu-Mi," she said by way of greeting. Momentarily, she was uncertain whether he recognized her in a form other than Simsimul: The Megatat-tat, which was how she had conducted earlier dealings with him. She needn't have worried, though, since whom else, but The Beast, would he have been expecting to see appear suddenly in his cell?

"What are you planning to do with me?" Quorulu-Mi asked. He had feared a mind-leech ever since he had been retrieved from the hole into which he'd been dropped during his clandestine explorations of the Fortress.

"Why should I use a mind-leech?" Organa asked, so obviously surprising Quorulu-Mi with her insight that she couldn't help laughing. "To me, your mind is already an open book. As it always has been."

Quorulu-Mi refused to believe that. Surely, she couldn't have known from the very beginning.

"Oh, yes," Organa said, contradicting his thoughts, "from the *very* beginning. Back when you were pretending to be naught but a lowly Styrolean, bargaining with Simsimul: The Megatat-tat for a fortune in exchange for a few tireum of servitude."

The mere possibility of that being true caused Quorulu-Mi shudders to the depths of his very bones. How could his side possibly win if they were battling a creature who could read their very thoughts?

"Not the thoughts of *all* life-forms," Organa said magnanimously. She could give the poor thing that much, considering he wasn't long for this world. "Not yet, anyway, but I have certainly mastered the thoughts of the lowly Styroleans. Very soon, I must admit, I shall have mastered adding the thoughts of even those life-forms who have successfully resisted me this long."

"Why have you kept me alive?" Quorulu-Mi asked, remembering how much information he had passed on to Murlock and The Dzi Scholar, wondering how much of it had been planted for his transmission.

"Oh, yes, Murlock and The Dzi Scholar," Organa said, once again surprising Quorulu-Mi by her infringement upon his thought patterns. "Perhaps, you'll be interested to learn that neither of those Rysoxnians will be around much longer to receive your output or anyone else's?"

Quorulu-Mi didn't buy that.

"Oh, I assure you, it's quite true!" Organa said. "At this very moment, Murlock is en route to a prison that's just part of the considerable holdings Gungol Fox was given by me in payment for a shift to my side."

"Impossible!" Quorulu-Mi said, positive that she was lying. Everyone knew that Gungol Fox was the son of Titian Fox, and the grandson of The Great Fox of Barren World War VI. Gungol Fox a traitor to the cause? No way!

"Believe it, or not," Organa said, "I do assure you that it is quite true. I haven't yet decided just what I must do with Murlock. You may be relieved, though…or, maybe not…." She gave him a wide smile. "…to learn that I've everything worked out as far as the dispositions of you and The Dzi Scholar."

Surprisingly, hearing that gave Quorulu-Mi a senses of relief—whatever his fate might be. Now, that he was caught, with no chance of rescue, or escape, there was greater strain, going from day to day, not knowing when his end would come, than there was in simply facing the inevitable crisis head-on and getting it over and done, once and for all.

"Unfortunately, The Dzi Scholar's arrival here won't coincide with your continued residence," Organa said.

"He's coming here?"

"Would you be surprised to learn that you are aware of that fact even before he is?"

Considering everything, Quorulu-Mi wasn't likely to be surprised by much of anything, ever again. Besides which, something had snapped inside of him, a kind of explosion of utter helplessness, and he truly found himself looking forward to ending it all. He would welcome blessed peace of death in the offing.

"I'm glad you're so resigned to the way things must be," Organa said, already in fade. "Death will certainly give you the blessed peace for which you're looking."

It was only later that Quorulu-Mi learned the nature of his fate, mainly because Organa had waited for Parker to become proficient enough with the scima-knife so that he could logically assume that he triumphed without any outside help.

When Quorulu-Mi did find out what was expected of him, a fight to the death with some humanoid, he decided to spoil The Beast's fun and games. He was determined, since he rightly assumed he would die, whether he won or lost, to simply submit willingly to his slaughter. He would refuse to put up the spectacle The Beast seemed determined to make of him.

En route to the arena, Quorulu-Mi couldn't help wondering what had brought his opponent to this madhouse. Was the humanoid, like Quorulu-Mi, somehow caught up in a conspiracy, destined to death because he had been found out by his adversary?

He was escorted by two Dyoleen, big, brutish characters without a hair on their muscled bodies. Quorulu-Mi knew the one, although not intimately. Friendships weren't encouraged by the occupants of the Fortress on Bnth. The general motto was, "Every life-form for itself!" Mainly, life-forms were, here, fulfilling contractual obligations incurred during deals made with The Beast for fortune, power, or fame; although, there

was the whole section of the lower Fortress wherein there were the poor creatures, like Quorulu-Mi, who had tried unsuccessfully to outwit The Beast and had been outwitted in the process. Quorulu-Mi, though, had never run upon any of his fellow unfortunates in any of his travels.

"You are a fool!" Sanglo the Dyoleen told him when Sanglo's fellow guard momentarily left them to announce their arrival to The Beast awaiting in the area.

Quorulu-Mi didn't bother with a reply. What could he answer? By that time, he wasn't all that sure he hadn't been a fool, except he wasn't about to admit that to anyone but himself. Let these followers of The Beast, Sanglo the Dyoleen included, wonder—if just a bit—what it had been that had ever possessed Quorulu-Mi to rebel and renege on his part of the bargain.

The other Dyoleen, the one Quorulu-Mi had never seen, prior to the escorts' arrival at Quorulu-Mi's cell, returned with instructions that the prisoner was to enter alone. Apparently, The Beast had decided that the Dyoleens weren't up to witnessing the fun and games. Or, perhaps, The Beast, suspecting that Quorulu-Mi was planning to go out docilely, didn't want to disappoint two more guests.

The Dyoleens escorted him to the entry door. Expecting him to do what? Make a break for it, he supposed.

What exactly, he wondered, would they do if he *did* attempt to make an escape? What kind of instructions had they received? Kill him? Wouldn't that have ended all chance of the fun and games The Beast had planned in the arena? In the same instance, their harming him, in any way, would make him hardly the opponent for the humanoid that The Beast was expecting.

He did not test his theory by trying to escape, because how could an escape be an escape when there was nowhere for him to escape to but into the maze of the Fortress? The Beast knew this labyrinth far better than Quorulu-Mi did. The place had most likely been constructed to The Beast's specifications. If it hadn't, then, The Beast had been around long enough to know each nook and cranny of it. Quorulu-Mi had no intentions of

spending his last hours playing dynic and mulosin, with him in the role of mulosin.

"You two Dyoleens are the fools!" Quorulu-Mi said, activating the lock release that sent the door sliding upward. He stepped inside, the door sliding shut behind him to leave his escorts out in the hall.

He had never before seen the arena. He didn't even know that there were many arenas in the Fortress, this one of the smallest.

It was round, with a single gallery that horseshoed three-fourths of its circle, absent of gallery only in that part wherein the door gave access to, or exit from, the room.

The Beast, in its manifestation of Ayra Organa, sat in the primary chair which—as was probably fitting—was like unto a throne. She was alone. Quorulu-Mi, looking for his opponent, couldn't find him. Was The Beast, then, the humanoid with whom he was supposed to give battle?

"What kind of a competition would that be?" Organa asked, once again shocking with her ability to hear him without his having to speak. "It isn't I whom you'll be fighting, for we have already fought, and you have lost. That is what brings you to this arena in the first place. Rather, you shall do battle with the humanoid, Parker of Antheer-D."

"Of Antheer-D?" Quorulu-Mi was surprised by that revelation. However, in retrospect, what had he expected? How many pure-blood humanoids were there left in the universe since the vortex of Cataclys IX had sucked them all to disaster? All that remained were traces of watered-down genes like those deposited on the planet Antheer-D by the likes of a downed Atlan astronaut whose sex drives were so pronounced he had taken to rutting with barbarians.

Organa was actually planning to pit him against an Antheerinean? Was she mad? What chance was an Antheerinean going to have against him, even with Quorulu-Mi in such a run-down state?

"Oh, yes, I see how you might think that," Organa said, smiling at the Styrolean's jump to conclusions. "You've heard

of the humanoids of Antheer-D, have you? How they are an ungainly lot whose only claim to being human can be traced to one oversexed Atlan astronaut?"

Mentally, Quorulu-Mi computed his chances of defeating the Antheerinean, and they still seemed very good to him.

"Wrong!" Organa informed. "You have no chance of defeating this particular Antheerinean. Even if you did, don't you suspect I would find some other way of disposing of you?"

Yes, that was how he had it figured, too, wasn't it?

"You are quite wrong, too, in assuming that you will stand idly by while the Antheerinean slits your throat with his scima-knife" Organa said.

Immediately, Quorulu-Mi knew his plans for a convenient suicide by Antheerinean were nothing more than wishful thinking. Organa had no sooner confessed her knowledge of his planned complacency than Quorulu-Mi felt the icy sensations running through his entire body.

Without any conscious control, his hair began to rise all along his spine. His body dropped into a low crouch, his claws slid from their concealment. He growled in challenge, the sound loud within the room.

"See?" Organa said.

Quorulu-Mi knew, then, that The Beast had somehow locked on his mind and was in complete control of it. Quorulu-Mi had become nothing more than a puppet, Organa pulling all of his strings. If Organa wanted Quorulu-Mi to fight, then, he would fight.

"Let's hear that magnificent growl, again, shall we?" Organa said with a smile. As if she were the ventriloquist, Quorulu-Mi the dummy, he growled for her on command, unable to keep the sound from erupting from deep within his throat.

The door behind him slid open. Quorulu-Mi heard himself growl again. Then, he felt himself retreating deeper into the arena. Center stage, he came up on his hind legs, like a trained monoquis. He pawed at the air, his sharp claws unsheathed and looking very deadly.

In the open doorway, Parker was struck by the scene. He had never seen anything like this fierce little creature, nor had he ever read anything about such a thing in the library at the farmhouse. Nothing Organa had ever said had quite prepared him for this, either.

If Parker thought of escape—and he didn't—then the sudden dropping of the door behind him would have prevented his exit.

Quorulu-Mi growled again, made another swipe at thin air with his talon-like claws.

Was the Antheerinean so stupid that he couldn't see that Quorulu-Mi was merely an animal performing on cue?

In fact, Parker didn't see it. He saw a creature that seemed likely intent, from the very beginning, on having Parker's life. Parker was made even less apt to suspect Organa in control when, once the battle was begun, Quorulu-Mi delivered a slashing blow that striated Parker's muscled chest with bloody scratch marks. How could Parker know that Organa remembered enough about Atlan men to know how they had once basked in the glory of their battle scars? Organa had given Parker his first battle scar, to see, hereafter, in any reflecto-glass every time he stripped off his shirt, and remember his first battle, where his enemy had taken first blood, but Parker had taken first life.

Organa let them fight until Parker was nearly exhausted. She had remembered that few Atlan men had ever appreciated a victory too easily won. Besides, she was aroused by the combination of sweat and blood that glossed Parker's exceptional body.

She couldn't recall a time she had seen a Styrolean fight quite as well as Quorulu-Mi managed under her expert guidance. She was required to run Quorulu-Mi through such an impressive battle routine, because Parker really turned out to be quite good with the scima-knife. Actually, Parker turned out to be more than *just* good. Organa was impressed as to how much technique he had absorbed from his sessions with the computer.

In a surprise move that left Organa gasping, and left Quorulu-Mi with a slit throat, Parker had Organa wondering if

he might not have been able to take care of the Styrolean even without her having been at Quorulu-Mi's controls.

She went to Parker who trembled, partially as a result of the purely physical exertion which had been required of him, partly from the eroticism Organa always noted most men derived from excelling on the battlefield.

He was standing on a floor slicked by his and the Styrolean's life fluids. His eyes were dilated. He was breathing hard.

She touched him, her fingers gently tracing the ridges of coagulating blood caused by the slash marks from Quorulu-Mi's claws.

She sensed his physical arousal, remembering how it had been the first time she had coupled with fellow Atlan Ramij Jai when he had killed the Krysor Balic in the Atlan Games on Omega-D.

CHAPTER EIGHT

Excerpt from THE BOOK OF RELLIX:

"Well, how goes it with the thief, Mave Stilter?" Dielum asked, leaning back against a rock and facing the god-seer of Antheer-D. Simultaneously, he emitted tele-beams to make sure they were alone.

"I am no thief," she told him, although her voice came out hardly decipherable, since she had talked to no one for thirty-one days and had chapped and swollen lips as a result of taking neither food nor water.

"No matter what *you* call it, *I* call it robbery," Dielum said, waving one big-knuckled hand. "But you are lucky. I haven't come to debate semantics. I have come prepared to be magnani-mous."

"But—" Mave began, but Dielum didn't let her finish.

"See what I'm prepared to give you for my property?" he said.

The scenery around Mave blurred. When it cleared, it had changed composition.

Mave found herself standing in a room surrounded on all sides by large tele-screens. Within the screens there appeared— one after the other—all of the cities, towns, and villages on Antheer-D. Mave saw the buildings, everything that was in those buildings, including the people.

"You want these?" Dielum asked, for he was standing beside Mave in the room. "I'll give them to you. All of this can be yours,

given so that you needn't go through the bother of stealing it. All you need to do is bow before me and kiss the ring on my hand.

"WHY?" MURLOCK ASKED. If ever there was a super-fluous question, under the circumstances, that one surely had to be it.

Gungol Fox, if he thought the answer obvious, nevertheless decided to humor Murlock. He motioned him deeper into the room, after first dismissing the guards. He went to the large, circular window that was so convexed that one could actually stand within it, nothing below the supporting glass but the drop to the clouds which concealed the maze of traffic lanes far below.

"This is why," Gungol said, a sweep of his arm taking in all that could be seen—which was considerable from that height. "This, this planet, this whole solar system. All mine. And, you ask me, why?"

It had to be a sign of the times, sure evidence of Murlock's encroaching old age (if he hadn't arrived upon old age a long time ago), that he could actually comprehend Gungol Fox's rationale. There had been a time when Murlock would have refused to believe that someone could actually betray for material rewards. Oh, how naïve he had been. Now, it was quite easy to see how Gungol's rewards, seemingly so sizable (and, *indeed,* they were sizable until one stopped to consider what The Beast had to draw on), could have persuaded Gungol Fox to hand Murlock over into the power of The Beast. What was Murlock, anyway, to Gungol Fox but a life-form probably already beyond his time? Murlock's body, dissolved down to the mineral content of its total gelatinous mass, would have brought very little on the Elementals Marketplace.

What did Murlock have to show for his old age? Very little, especially by way of material things. Yet, here was Gungol Fox, four times Murlock's junior, and what did Gungol have to show as his own? Why he had a whole solar system, and everything therein, save for its souls, turned over to him by The Beast who

could well afford to part with it, since The Beast wasn't interested in merely physical things, only in the worshipping souls of the inhabitants of this solar system, because worshipping souls generated erktic energy which The Beast could use, but for which Gungol Fox, without the knowledge necessary, had no use. As far as Gungol Fox was concerned, he had gotten a good deal.

"You don't rule here," Murlock said. "The Beast does." Despite his ability to see the reasoning in Gungol Fox's mind, he refused to admit to any understanding of it.

"Every life-form has a master," Gungol Fox said with a shrug. "Possibly even The Beast does, for all we know. Don't shake your head, as if you—among some select few in the universe, stand alone as being somehow self-contained. A master need not be a physical thing, or even a theological entity. It can be an idea, a thought, or a cause. I was never so enslaved by The Beast as you have been enslaved by your idea that by conquering The Beast you will have somehow saved the universe—from what?"

"From Evil," Murlock said, automatically, bringing a look of amusement so obvious in Gungol Fox's features that Murlock could be embarrassed by having come forth with such a hackneyed reply, once even used by Gungol Fox as a lie.

"Evil," Gungol Fox echoed, as if he wanted Murlock to hear the ridiculousness of the word and be embarrassed even further by having come up with that time-worn catch-all. "Well, Murlock, if nothing else has been given me during my life, it is the ability to see that good and evil are relative."

"Your gross error!" Murlock said, mustering as much disgust as he could.

"I have seen the cause, for which you fight," Gungol Fox said, "in my grandfather's time, in my father's time, and in my time. In the end, I think there is a fairly even balance between murders perpetrated by your side, and murders perpetrated on the side of The Beast. In the final analysis, which side is righter for its murders, or is it merely a case of the pot calling the kettle black?"

"If you cannot see the difference, by now, I doubt that I shall ever be able to persuade you to see it," Murlock said.

He looked out over Gungol Fox's city, realizing that all this—hell, even *more*—could have been his in his lifetime if he had just, like Gungol Fox, shifted sides, or at least laid down his cause. He could have ruled whole solar systems, done great things (for there was more than soul-gathering by which a life-form's existence might be measured). He had said no to the temptation, and who would remember him after The Beast was through with him? Granted, there would be a few who would proclaim him a martyr—but certainly only a *very* few.

He remembered the assassination of Xxero of Tusiv. There was a man who had sold his soul and the souls of countless tirel-lium to The Beast. Yet, when he died, poets wrote poems in his praise, sculptors sculptured his likeness in stone and wood to be erected in public squares where people could come and weep over his untimely passing. Xxero of Tusiv was still considered one of the truly fine and great men of his solar systems. In reality, Xxero of Tusiv had been nothing more than a puppet of The Beast.

"It really isn't Evil you have been fighting all of these years, is it, Murlock?" Gungol Fox said, folding his arms over his chest and causing a rustling of his long robe. "Never Evil. What you've been fighting is merely a woman."

"Who told you that?" Murlock asked, wondering how long Gungol Fox had known, wondering how many of the other young recruits knew. It wasn't as easy now, as it had once been, for males to see why Murlock and The Dzi Scholar had such an abhorrence for even the idea of a female—an Atlan female, at that—being the chief deity of the universe. It was even harder to argue the point now that Ayra Organa had obviously mutated into something far beyond sexuality. Yet, it always boiled down, for Murlock, to the fact that The Beast started out a woman, and, therefore, no matter what form it took, was *still* inherently a woman.

"Times are changing," Gungol Fox said. "There are many of

us who simply fail to see the difference between bowing down to a deity that's male, or bowing down to one that's female, since—in the final reasoning—the sex of a god has nothing to do with power far greater than any the rest of us have. How *much* power is it before power becomes merely relative? So, why must we make such a big fuss?"

Murlock didn't answer, knowing that Gungol Fox, from another generation, could probably never be made to understand. What difference did it make, anyway? Murlock had been through too much really to care what Gungol Fox thought, especially now that all of Murlock's efforts had so obviously come to naught. If all Gungol Fox's peers were as easily able to rationalize, as he was, the triumph of Evil over Good, the triumph of Female over Male, it was only a matter of time before The Beast reigned supreme—if it didn't already.

"You older generation have always been too caught up in the religious aspects, anyway," Gungol Fox said. "When, in the end, religion is really no big thing."

"What a fool you are, Gungol Fox!" Murlock said. If the youth believed what he had just said about religion, he was, indeed, a fool. For if religion was no big deal, then why did The Beast devote so much time and energy to it? What was happening was merely the younger generation finding it easier to believe that religion was no big deal, simply because they—unlike The Beast—were unable to see how real power could be derived from it. Unable to understand the nuances of manipulating religion for power, they all too willingly allowed that power to slip through their fingers, telling themselves they were losing nothing of importance.

Murlock wasn't sure why he should any longer care—or if he *did* any longer care—that it was the Gungol Foxes of the universe who had already given The Beast so much *(supposedly insignificant)* power that The Beast could now probably never be stopped.

"What side of the war would you and The Dzi Scholar be on if it had turned out that the matrix of The Beast had been male,

rather than female?" Gungol Fox asked. "By the way, just where did The Dzi Scholar get himself off to when he left the ship?"

"You'll have to find him and ask him yourself," Murlock said. It was far too late for him to turn traitor. No matter what was offered him he doubted he would have had many tireum left to enjoy it.

"You know," Gungol Fox said, a sweeping glance of the panorama beyond the window reassuring him that he had done the right thing, "the chances are very good that The Beast already knows where The Dzi Scholar is hiding. It seemed hardly surprised when I informed it that he was missing from the spacecraft."

"Yes? Well, I'm really quite tired of hearing about the omnipotence of your *Mistress,*" Murlock said, wondering if he could end his life, now, at his own initiative, cheating The Beast, by heaving himself through the glass of the window. He didn't make the attempt. Such windows would hardly have been designed as they were if they could easily be shattered. "I think I would by far prefer the solitude of a cell."

"As you wish," Gungol Fox said. He turned and went to summon the guards.

Murlock took one final look at the view beyond the window, seeing what might well have been his had he but been as willing to pay the price that Gungol Fox had so willingly paid.

"Too late for regrets!" he told himself, aware that two guards had stepped in beside him.

He was taken to a cell to await the verdict of The Beast on what should be done with him.

CHAPTER NINE

Excerpt from THE BOOK OF RILLEX:

Who was it, on high, running the show? Who sat the other side of the game board? Ayra Organa? Or did The Beast sit on *both* sides of the board, compelled to play with himself/herself/itself, since there was no one remaining in the universes capable of offering up a challenge?

Not that it really mattered. Galun, while resenting his destiny had somehow been taken out of his hands (if it had ever been there to begin with), knew he had no viable alternative but to go on. After all, what purpose was there in living if one didn't have goals—whether those goals were self-originating or programmed by another? Galun's goals had been programmed for him a long, long time ago. Those goals re-enforced each step along the way: on Rysox, by The Dzi Scholar, through the Quass Root, that had tripped him into the High Cascade and into confrontation with Zurl on Delcan Prime.

HIS SPACEPOD TRIPPED out of SensaSpace, and The Dzi Scholar knew that by just reviving he would be able to see Tilox on the viewer screen. So, why didn't he really wish to revive? Why was he tired when suspended animation should have left him refreshed? Why had he dreamed of Tindala's emerald green clinging to the sewer grating, when he had never dreamt before when he was under for travel in deep space? Why did he look with dread upon his upcoming arrival on Tilox which

should have offered him that haven of safety he hadn't found on Siphion-6? Why was his intuition telling him that there was nothing for him on Tilox?

He revived. There it was: Tilox. He scanned for life-forms, finding none registered. This was really as it should have been. If screening mechanisms didn't shield the asteroid from the probe-sensors of The Beast, they certainly proved effective as regarded the probes on conventional spacecraft.

What gave The Dzi Scholar a queasy feeling was the possibility that the asteroid *was* deserted, just like his instruments told him. Yet, why should he confront that horrible possibility until it was absolutely necessary to do so? What he had to do was merely assume the best.

So...why...wasn't he assuming the best?

Something was wrong. He could feel it. It wasn't a mere matter of suspicion any longer. It had somehow gone beyond that.

His mind quickly calculated his alternatives. He could bypass the asteroid, pretending he was en route somewhere else. Then, go where? Oh, there were other outposts, but none close.

Hell, maybe, it *was* imagination! Where was his sense of adventure, his ability to take a few risks? He was growing conservative in his old age. Besides, there was always the possibility that his acute paranoia was simply steering him wrong. How foolish it would be to glide right on by, after having come so far, especially if Murlock was docked and waiting.

He turned on only one set of landing lights. That was the signal to Murlock and to the Tilox computer that a friendly craft was making an approach with all intentions of landing. The asteroid had extensive defense mechanisms. If The Dzi Scholar violated procedure, he was apt to get blasted out of the sky by the lazos of his own side.

He surveyed the area, checking for space flotsam and jetsam. There would have surely been some if there had been any kind of space battle. Murlock would have put up a fight in defense of the asteroid and what was on it. The survey, however, turned up

clean space.

He punched his approach path into the ship's computer. It was a complicated access that necessitated the ship pass along the narrow valley existing between two parallel mountain ridges, plus a sharp turn to the right to brush one nondescript mountaintop, before the trigger mechanism dropped one of three fake crater floors to provide a suitable docking area.

He sat back, the ship under control of the computer. Unless he shifted to manual override, he was committed to a landing.

"So far, so good, he told himself in an attempt to bolster his flagging confidence. The thing was to think only positive thoughts. There had once been a time when he had been able to do just that. When had the negative thoughts been allowed to creep in? When had they balanced out the positive? When had they finally begun to dominate?

He was definitely not the man he had once been. He should have given up the game playing a long time ago. Not for his own safety, but for the safety of all others involved. His attitude was no longer what it should be. His physical and mental reflexes were simply not functioning at the peak they should have.

Dialta waves bounced off the mountain ridges, sending audible pings back to the spacecraft. The Dzi Scholar could read that audio. Sounding right, it was obvious the computer was keeping the ship on course. The Dzi Scholar had nothing to do but sit and wait—for whatever might happen.

He felt the force played against him and the craft as the spacepod veered sharply to the right. Dialta pings became louder and more frequent, finally fading altogether as the spacecraft topped a high pinnacle of stone thrust up from the valley floor, and, then, shot over a wide plain pockmarked with circular craters.

He switched video to survey the upcoming ground level. The computer was still fully functional, but The Dzi Scholar wanted to reassure himself. There was the possibility he might catch something which the computer might miss.

What he saw was the floor of an approaching crater drop

away, revealing a hole of complete darkness. Nothing unusual, there. There were never any lights until after the spacecraft was landed, the docking roof reinserted.

Why were his thoughts of strangeness so persistent? Everything checked. Nothing seemed outwardly wrong. It did little good to worry. Definitely, he was committed. The computer had stopped the craft, implemented a depreciating hover sequence which was, even then, lowering the spacepod into the pit that had opened for it.

Down…down…contact made. Engines disengaged. The sideward movement of the craft caused by a shift of the landing pad beneath it, as the spacecraft was placed in a side berth.

The Dzi Scholar heard no sounds. What he had, though, was the feel of what was happening around him. Sensations vibrated through the fuselage of the ship and, then, through him in turn. He had a visual of the exterior that became clearer as he was suddenly confronted by the illumination of the docking area by flood beams.

Aside from his craft, the zone was empty of other space vehicles. Again, that was nothing unusual; there were two other available docking facilities, and, if one was occupied, it was logical for another to be provided for the landing of The Dzi Scholar's craft. The computers would have conversed and made that docking decisions based upon the premise that it was never wise to place all of one's eggs in the same basket. In case of trouble, there was always a better chance of successful retreat if there was more than one alternative exit. With two ships in one dock, one well-placed strike of a lazo or projectile cannon could have cut off all avenues of escape.

Still, logically, The Dzi Scholar might have expected someone sent to meet him. The docking space remained completely empty of personnel. However, a welcoming party or not, The Dzi Scholar had come this far, so there was little point in not going the rest of the way. Besides, once in, it was difficult to maneuver an escape, especially if there was an enemy on board the asteroid who had any intentions of keeping The Dzi Scholar

contained where he was now.

He switched into the Tilox computer, filing for an immediate exit. To his surprise he got a quick approval, so he cancelled the request. The enemy wouldn't have so easily cleared him for retreat. Or, was The Beast merely playing a waiting game, since allowing the computer to clear him for departure didn't mean he would have actually been allowed to vacate.

He requested the Tilox computer inform him regarding the present disposition of the other two docking areas. He was informed, and rightly so, that such information could be obtained only through a proper programming sequence found only in the main computer room. The Dzi Scholar didn't have the code book aboard this craft for any bypass proceeding. There had been such a code book with Murlock aboard the other spacepod, but Murlock had taken it with him.

The Dzi Scholar disembarked his craft, still finding no one there to greet him. Since there was a definite positive side to that (no enemies with weapons drawn), he didn't know why it should so worry him.

There was the possibility, not thought of until just then, that Murlock had—for whatever the reasons—been forced to take some kind of detour which hadn't yet allowed him to reach Tilox. Such a notion was conceivable. Tilox being as important as it was, Murlock would have taken evasive action had anything unordinary turned up on his ship's viewer screens to indicate he was followed.

Such a rationalization might normally have given The Dzi Scholar a certain sense of comfort. In this particular instance, it did very little to ease his growing apprehension.

There still remained no outward evidence that there was anything unusual in progress—except for the absence of the greeting party which wouldn't have been provided if Murlock hadn't arrived; the facility had been turned over to a purely computer watch force several tireum previous.

The Dzi Scholar entered decontamination, and was, then, admitted into one of the interior hallways. He headed for

the main control area which was reached via ele-tube. There continued to be no sign of anyone there, now, or of anyone having been there recently.

It had been a long time since The Dzi Scholar had been on Tilox, mainly because critical security had kept him and Murlock away. Not that they didn't have clearance, because they were the only two who did. They had just been loathe to call any potentially compromising attention to the pocket's existence, and, therefore, had always steered wide, except on necessary occasions.

Still, The Dzi Scholar had been there several times, his purpose to check the health of the equipment and of the guests. As regarded the latter, of particular interest was always the physical and mental maturation of Parker Stilter. It had been decided to save Parker's programming until certain of his dynic brain-cell development could take place to assure him a more complete assimilation of data scheduled to be fed him.

They shouldn't have waited. The Dzi Scholar felt that with certainty. For The Beast to get its hands on the young man at this stage could have potentially dire consequences for the adversaries of The Beast. Parker Stilter had Atlan blood, honed to its purest bastardized strain by Galun Rellix's gene experiments. Parker was the closest to an Atlan, besides the since-mutated Ayra Organa, which there was in the universe. Look what had happened to Ayra Organa. Wasn't it possible that, in the wrong hands, Parker might well be converted into a monster, in league with The Beast, rather than be the helpmate for The Beast's sworn enemies as intended?

By the time he reached the series of rooms housing the main computer system, The Dzi Scholar admittedly was a little less on edge. He had run across nothing unordinary en route, and— at least so far—the control area seemed in perfect running order. He re-verified all equipment functions on his way to the series of viso-panels that occupied one large section of wall in a room adjoining one of the nearest liv-cubicles.

He switched on visuals, watching nine screens light up and

flicker. The flicker dissolved to color pictures of the area located on Tilox's lowest level.

Betty Mae appeared in the middle screen on the left-hand side. She was in the kitchen of the farmhouse, making bread. Her arms were white up to her elbows with flour. An adjustment in the audio hinted her singing some kind of song about waving fields of grain.

The visual of Betty Mae, engaging in such a natural farmhouses chore, allowed even more of The Dzi Scholar's apprehension to drain from him. He checked the remaining eight screens for signs of Parker, but—surprisingly enough—wasn't immediately concerned when he didn't see him. There was a whole selection of visuals from which to choose. As The Dzi Scholar began switching through them, he was, now, quite confident that Parker would soon show up somewhere.

When he reached the end of the visual selection, however, not having located Parker in any of them, his sense of dread once again returned. He told himself that Parker *had* to be there. He began a repeat of the visual series.

PARKER WASN'T THERE!

The Dzi Scholar resisted a temptation to run through the visuals one more time. He had been right the first time, verified by the second, and he saw no reason for any additional confirmation by a third. The simple fact was that Parker wasn't there.

So, where was he? The obvious answer was that Murlock had arrived and taken him, except why would Murlock take Parker anywhere? Tilox was the safest pocket available to the enemies of The Beast. Anywhere else would have been more dangerous. Anywhere else wouldn't have had the facilities for Parker's programming process which was scheduled to begin shortly.

The Dzi Scholar glanced hurriedly around the room. Was there something he wasn't seeing? Was there some danger, here, now, or, shortly, to arrive, that Murlock had recognized before taking flight with Parker in tow, while The Dzi Scholar stood there and saw nothing out of the ordinary—except that Parker of Antheer-D was absent from his cage?

Could the young man have escaped on his own? To check on that possibility, The Dzi Scholar ran a survey on the computer-guard-relays positioned around the enclosure's canvas perimeter. All proved in perfect functioning order. Unless, they had been turned off, there would have been no way for Parker to have bypassed them without being gassed.

What exactly was it that was happening, here? Whatever it was, The Dzi Scholar definitely had to take action. The situation was precarious, no matter how The Dzi Scholar chose to look at it. If Murlock fled with Parker, then, there was possibly danger, here, now, or, certainly, on its way. If someone else had gotten to the young Antheerinean…well, The Dzi Scholar would just as soon not think of those consequences.

He ran through the computer banks, searching for some kind of message or clue to the circumstances which Murlock might have left behind as warning. He came up with a blank.

Obviously, his most readily available source of information had suddenly become Betty Mae.

He programmed the farmhouse kitchen for broadcast. He was aware that he was most likely about to scare the hell out of the woman, but it hardly seemed to matter at this stage. Betty Mae was hardly of any remaining value to the cause—except, of course, as she might possibly give some key to the unlocking of the present mystery surrounding the missing Parker. She had become expendable the minute Parker of Antheer-D was weaned.

He cross-examined her. And what did she tell him? Nothing! She had no idea, whatsoever, where Parker had gone. She had assumed that the same forces which had brought him, as a baby, had, now, taken him away as a young man.

The stupid bitch! The Dzi Scholar simply couldn't believe that Betty Mae hadn't seen or heard something which might give him the one clue he needed to unravel the mystery. He began to suspect that she possibly didn't tell him, because what he would have found most pertinent she had simply forgotten, or had never understood in the first place. The humanoid female

had never been all that bright.

He gassed her, and, then, went down to the lowest level, entering the enclosure with her. He attached the mind-leech to her and scraped her cretin brain clean, coming up with nothing except that she had gotten up the morning of Parker's disappearance, had been somehow compelled to go to the meadow behind the barn where she had fallen asleep. Gassed? By whom?

He sniffed the air, thinking that his imagination only put the sweet-sour smell of gas upon the air. Then, he saw them, already coming for him, before he lost consciousness. There were four of them, all wearing head-shield-gas-filters to protect them from the sleep-inducing fumes.

And...how...long...had...they...been...there?

CHAPTER TEN

Excerpt from THE BOOK OF RELLIX:

Now, however, The Beast was only amused. It enjoyed little games, even though there could be only one outcome to them, this latest one included.

There had been only two possible sources capable of offering a real challenge to its supreme power, one having perished in Cataclys IX. The other The Beast still truly feared—as it lurked possibly within it.

"YOU!" HE SAID, regaining consciousness. He, of course, recognized her right off, first because she was the exact image which had been registered on the mind's-eye of Drawler: The Suicide; two, because she was as different from the inferior humanoid Betty Mae as night was from day.

"Yes, I," Organa said, sitting in the chair across from his cot. Aside from lying, sitting seemed the most comfortable position for her humanoid manifestation. "I thought it was time to bring an end to this particular game before further deterioration of it should make us all forget just how many good moments it has afforded us."

She straightened the folds of her gown, rearranging its drape over her voluptuous hips and shapely legs.

"You do see the merits of ending the game, now, don't you?" Organa asked.

"Game!" he shouted at her. She *did*, then, actually take all of

his efforts, all of Murlock's efforts to stop her, as nothing more than a game.

"You, too, are glad that it is over," Organa said. "Confess it."

The Dzi Scholar was prepared to confess nothing to this bitch.

"You should be flattered that I have never sat across from such worthy opponents before," Organa said. Her breasts swelled seductively, threatening to spill over the low bodice of her gown, as she breathed. "But, it would seem, you grow too tired and too old to maintain your previous high performance of play. Your fellow players, anyway those having the most value and skill on the board, also grow old and tired. Those who have been brought in as replacements are all easily removed to the sidelines by enticements that never did persuade the likes of you, Murlock, Galun Rellix, Drawler: The Suicide, or Saintal Ann—to name but a few."

"Just because you have me doesn't mean that there won't be others who...."

"Others?" Organa interrupted in a decidedly sad voice. "Like Murlock, you mean?"

"Yes, like Murlock," The Dzi Scholar affirmed.

"Murlock of Rysox? Who is now dead?"

"I don't believe it!"

"Oh, of course you do," Organa contradicted. "Did you think he was any the less tired than you? He, too, had grown weary, or else it would have been far less easy for me to capture either of you."

"There are others besides the two of us," The Dzi Scholar insisted.

"Like Gungol Fox who offered me Murlock on a silver platter in return for a few planets and the people and buildings thereon?"

"No!" The Dzi Scholar moaned, feeling more and more as if his will was completely draining from him. The Beast was right: The Dzi Scholar was tired of the game playing.

"Of course, you're tired," Organa affirmed, having caught

traces of his thoughts. "Well you should be, for you and but a few others, like you, have been carrying on the majority of the play for your side for quite some time now. Without new replacements of similar ilk, it does seem best to end it all, now, doesn't it?"

"A game...a game," The Dzi Scholar chanted, shaking his head in disbelief. The Beast had looked upon it all as nothing...more...than...a game. *Just as The Dzi Scholar had always suspected and always feared.*

"You mustn't look down upon your achievements," Organa said. "After all, life has always been a game. It wasn't as if you were engaged in playing merely checkers, either. There are degrees of game playing, as there are degrees of everything else."

"Did we ever have a chance of winning?" The Dzi Scholar asked.

"I shall be kind and not answer that," Organa said. "See, even The Beast can be considerate. For were I to say, yes, then, you would merely be despondent because of moves missed which might have given you victory. Were I to say, no, you would be despondent because of having used up your whole life, not to mention used up the whole lives of so many others, for a cause that was lost to you from the start."

Yes, she was right. The Dzi Scholar really didn't want to know.

"In the end, you die knowing that a piece of you survives in the universe," Organa said.

He knew she referred to his and Tindala's whelp, spirited off by the Mammoosse on Siphion-6. However, he wasn't prepared to muster up any sire grief at having his seed kidnapped into the enemy camp.

"What is my fate, then?" The Dzi Scholar asked, quite prepared to face it.

"Death, of course," Organa said. She got no reaction from The Dzi Scholar, since he was well aware that death was the fate of all those captured in play. He had been merely curious as

to what manner of death would be utilized. So, Organa obliged him. "Death at the hand of Parker of Antheer-D."

"Yes, I suspected you had him, too," The Dzi Scholar said. Actually, he had more than just suspected. He had *known*.

"He was, as you might have guessed, very upset by the tele-playbacks that showed him what you did to his foster mother, Betty Mae. She was the only mother he ever knew, and you turned her into a vegetable. I must permit him his traditional right of vengeance."

"You could have taken me on Tilox, at any time, preventing the mind-leech of Betty Mae." It wasn't a question.

"Of course," Organa admitted, "but now that this game is won, it is imperative that I arrange for one to replace it. My existence, you know, could get quite unbearable if I didn't have diversions. Sadly, it is becoming more and more difficult to find challengers to take seriously. The days are quite gone when opponents raise whole armies at the mere suggestion that a woman aspires to the supreme godhead."

Organa's smile was decidedly sympathetic.

"So, Parker of Antheer-D will kill you," Organa said. "He will be raised as a friend to your whelp, only for your whelp to discover, at some future date, that Parker, with the assist of The Beast, murdered the whelp's father. Thus, I have the foundations of a new game, begun on revenge, complicated by whatever affection blossoms between your whelp and his father's killer."

The Dzi Scholar was made genuinely ill by how she had mapped out that beginning. Had she, then, sat in another room, at another time, telling someone else, who was about to die, that her next game involved The Dzi Scholar and his streak of male chauvinism that would push him to such great lengths to put a male deity back on the supreme throne?

"Oh, I never plan out every detail in advance," Organa said, "for that would surely take the fun out of the playing. There is always such enjoyment in discovering unexpected nuances and surprises as I go along."

"One day, you will arrange a game that will backfire and make you the loser," The Dzi Scholar prophesied, wishing that game would be the one in which his whelp was destined to be a key player.

"Possibly," Organa surprised by admitting. "I confess, there is a certain excitement I find in placing myself in danger, and, then, scrambling to save myself at the very last instant. As time passes, it becomes more and more difficult for me to hold back the boredom."

"Nothing lives forever," The Dzi Scholar reminded, although he certainly wasn't sure that applied to The Beast.

"Certainly *you* won't," Organa said, coming to her feet.

She went to the door, opening it to admit Parker of Antheer-D who, scima-knife in hand, had come to avenge the mind-leech of the only mother he had ever know.

ABOUT THE AUTHOR

WILLIAM MALTESE, an international best-selling author of novels, short stories, including his popular Wildside Mystery Double, *Incident at Aberlene* and *Incident at Brimzinsky* (Spies & Lies #1-2), has published (under various pseudonyms) close to 200 books in genres ranging from straight and gay erotica, mystery, romance, western, adventure, espionage, cooking, wine, young adults and children, and twenty-four science fiction/fantasy/horror novels, beginning with *Five Roads to Tlen* in 1969 (as "William J. Lambert III") through *Bond-Shattering* (2007). For a comprehensive list of his literary output, see *Draqualian Silk: A Collector's and Bibliographical Guide to The Books of William Maltese, 1969-2010* (Borgo Press, 2010). With a Business/Advertising degree, Maltese enlisted in the U.S. Army, where he achieved and was honorably discharged with the rank of Sergeant (E-5). You can find him at:

www.williammaltese.com
www.facebook.com/williammaltese
www.myspace.com/williammaltese
williammaltese@yahoo.com (e-mail)